Orion's Awakening

Reworked

Leon C.M. Joseph

Printed in the United States of America

First Printing: Aug 2017
Second Printing: February 2025

ISBN: 9798301568404

DEDICATION

This book is dedicated to my grandmother, Grace Ann Joseph, who always taught me that no matter how dark times may seem, brighter days are always ahead.
It is also dedicated to all the children in care, always hold your heads high and never let anyone bring you down. You can achieve anything you set your minds to.

Table of Contents

1 The Dream 2

2 Life as usual 8

3 new beginning's 14

4 back to school 19

5 betrayal 28

6 Camping 35

7 Choices 44

8 The Journey 49

9 The Arrival 58

10 The Palace 65

11 Echoes of the Past 71

12 Whispers of Fate 79

13 Saving Aurorina 86

14 royal duties 98

15 The First Farewell 106

16 A spark of hope 112

17 The Tale of Two Brothers 118

18 Following the pilgrimage 124

19 Entering Eymd's Dream 134

20 Rescuing Lillithan 142

21 The Bond 155

22 Preparing for War 163

23 The Eve of War 173

24 The Final Battle 181

25 Waking up 188

1 The Dream

It was close to midnight on a narrow, silent street in the village of Fittleworth. The moon hung low in the sky, casting a pale light over a row of quiet cottages. Among them stood one that seemed to crouch in shadow, as though it was too tired to face the world.

The house was old and crumbling, with bricks that looked ready to fall apart at the slightest touch. One of the front door's glass panes had been boarded over with warped wood, the guttering sagged like a tired rope, and the roof was missing enough tiles to reveal patches of sky. The garden was wild and untamed, as though it had long forgotten the touch of a gardener's hand.

Most who passed by this house assumed it was abandoned, too forlorn to have a story left to tell. But if they had looked closer, they might have noticed a flicker of light from an upstairs window and heard the faint sound of snoring from within.

Inside, three boys slept in a small, shabby room that smelled faintly of old wood and damp plaster. Two of them, twins, snored loudly from a bunk bed tucked against the wall. The third boy, Orion, lay sprawled on a mattress on the floor, tossing and turning under his thin blanket. His dark curls clung to his forehead, damp with sweat, as his face twitched with the intensity of a dream.

And oh, what a dream it was.

In his dream, Orion stood in the centre of a massive room unlike anything he had ever seen. The walls were draped with golden tapestries that shimmered as if alive, each embroidered with the initials *I.O.* Above him, a ceiling vaulted so high it seemed to fade into the heavens, its surface painted with scenes of fiery phoenixes soaring through a starry sky.

A grand throne stood at the heart of the room, carved from radiant crystal that seemed to pulse with its own light. Beside it was a polished wooden table, piled with strange and beautiful objects: golden goblets, intricate metalwork, and sparkling gems that refracted the light like tiny rainbows. The air smelled faintly of something sweet and floral, like fields of blossoms carried on a breeze.

Orion turned, taking in his surroundings, but the vast room was empty. As he moved, his bare feet whispered against the cool marble floor, echoing faintly in the stillness. A large arched window across the room drew his attention, its open frame inviting him closer.

When he stepped up to it, the view took his breath away.

Beneath him lay a sprawling city of gold, its towers and spires gleaming under the light of two suns. The streets sparkled like rivers of starlight, winding between elegant buildings that stretched into the horizon. And in the sky above, a massive planet hovered so close that its swirling clouds and shimmering rings seemed almost touchable.

"What is this place?" he whispered, his voice barely audible over the faint hum of the city below.

The air felt warm and alive, as though the entire city were breathing. Orion glanced down at his hands, noticing they were trembling,not from fear, but from a sense of overwhelming awe. Everything felt so real: the golden light on his skin, the faint breeze that tugged at his curls, the distant sounds of music floating up from the streets.

He turned back toward the throne and the mysterious table beside it. His eyes fell on a crystal goblet, its surface intricately etched with the same initials that adorned the tapestries. He reached out, curious, and picked it up. The goblet felt surprisingly heavy in his hand, its cool surface smooth as water.

"What does it mean?" he murmured, tracing the initials with his finger.

Before he could wonder further, the sound of a door slamming open shattered the silence. Orion spun around, his heart pounding. In his shock, he dropped the goblet. It struck the floor and shattered into a thousand shimmering pieces, scattering like stars across the marble.

From the doorway, a tall, plump figure appeared, sliding to a stop just before him. The man, or rather, the creature, was unlike anything Orion had ever seen. He was clad in a neatly pressed grey uniform and had skin that shone a brilliant sapphire blue. His deep-set golden eyes twinkled with both urgency and warmth as he bowed deeply.

"Cobossal Orion!" the man exclaimed in a voice so deep it seemed to rumble through the floor. "At last, I've found you! Wandering the palace alone, of all days!"

Orion blinked, too stunned to speak. "I…I don't… what's going on?" he managed to stammer. "Who are you? And where am I?"

The blue-skinned man straightened, adjusting the silver buttons on his coat. "I am Jasper, your personal butler. And you, young master, are in the Summer Palace." He looked at Orion as though expecting him to recognize the name. "Come now, we have no time to waste. The ceremony is nearly upon us."

"The what?" Orion's confusion only deepened. "I think you've got the wrong person. I'm not…."

Jasper held up a hand, cutting him off. "Not another word, sire. All will be explained soon enough. For now, you must come with me."

Before Orion could protest further, Jasper took him gently but firmly by the arm and began ushering him out of the room. The corridor beyond was unlike anything he could have imagined. Glowing orbs of light floated overhead, casting a soft, golden glow on the walls, which were lined with portraits of strange and regal-looking figures. Their faces were striking, human-like, but with features that felt impossibly refined, almost otherworldly. Orion couldn't help but feel their painted eyes following him as he passed.

"This has to be a dream," Orion muttered to himself. "I'll wake up any second now."

Jasper glanced at him but said nothing, his long strides purposeful as he guided Orion deeper into the palace. They passed an open archway where three figures in lilac robes hovered cross-legged in mid-air, their hands clutching thick tomes. One of them rotated lazily as he hummed to himself, glancing up only briefly to give Orion a knowing smile before returning to his book.

Orion barely had time to process what he had seen before Jasper stopped abruptly in front of a towering golden door. It bore the image of a phoenix rising from flames, its wings spread wide. Beneath it was a crest with the initials *I.O.* shining brightly.

"Here we are," Jasper announced, his voice filled with reverence. "Your chambers, sire."

Jasper pushed the enormous golden doors open, and Orion stepped inside. The room beyond was breathtaking, like something out of the fantasy novels he loved to read. A massive, pod-like bed stretched along one wall, its surface glowing faintly with silver light. Five towering wardrobes lined another wall, their reflective surfaces gleaming like mirrors. A glass dresser stood in the corner, laden with bottles of swirling, multi-coloured liquids that seemed to glow from within.

But Orion's gaze was drawn to something else. In one corner of the room, a portion of the stone wall slid shut with a low rumble. Standing before it were six figures, all cloaked in robes of lilac. Five of them kept their hoods tightly drawn, their faces hidden in shadow, but the sixth figure stepped forward.

She pulled back her hood, revealing a strikingly tall woman with long, flowing silver hair and eyes that flickered between gold and silver like molten metal. Her presence was commanding, her movements fluid and graceful. She bowed deeply, her voice ringing with authority as she spoke.

"Welcome home, Cobossal Orion. It is an honour to gaze upon your face once more."

Orion froze, unsure of what to say. "I think you've got the wrong person," he said, his voice shaking slightly. "I'm just Orion. I'm nobody special."

The woman straightened, her expression softening slightly. "You are far more than you realize. I am Lillithan, chief maiden of the palace, and there is no mistake. You are Cobossal Orion I, rightful heir to the throne of the Intenfli and Intenfna, the rulers of this star system."

Orion took a step back, shaking his head. "This can't be real. I'm just a kid from Earth. I live in a run-down house with my brothers. You've got the wrong person."

Lillithan's gaze was steady, unwavering. "You were sent away for your protection as a child, hidden among the humans. But now, the time has come for you to return to your rightful place." She gestured toward the glowing crest pinned to her robe, which bore the same initials and phoenix symbol Orion had seen everywhere. "You are the last of your line, the only one who can restore balance to this system."

Orion stared at her, his mind racing. He thought about the golden city, the initials, the overwhelming sense of familiarity that tugged at his heart despite the strangeness of it all. Was it possible? Could she be telling the truth?

Before he could speak, Lillithan beckoned him toward a door in the far corner of the room. "There is much to prepare, Your Highness. Come."

The next room was just as grand as the last. A large, oval-shaped stone bath filled the centre, steam rising from its surface. The air was filled with a sweet, calming aroma that made Orion's head swim. Two of the hooded figures, whom Lillithan referred to as the Kalligah, stood silently beside the tub, their shadowy forms flickering faintly beneath their robes.

"Once the bath is ready, you will enter," Lillithan instructed. "You will be cleansed and dressed for the ceremony."

Orion hesitated. "I can wash myself," he said, his cheeks reddening slightly.

Lillithan chuckled softly. "The Kalligah are not as you are, young master. They are creations of your parents, beings of pure magic and light. You have no reason to feel embarrassed."

To demonstrate, she pulled back the hood of one of the Kalligah. Beneath it was no face, no body, just a swirling mass of golden light, like stardust captured in a shadowy form.

Orion's jaw dropped. "They're... alive?"

"They are loyal servants, designed to assist you," Lillithan said simply. "Now, into the bath."

Orion reluctantly obeyed. As he stepped into the steaming water, the Kalligah moved with eerie grace, scrubbing and rinsing him with soft, glowing hands. The process was thorough, almost too thorough, and by the time Orion stepped out, his skin felt scrubbed raw. He winced as he dried off and slipped into the robe, they handed him.

But the strangest part was yet to come.

The Kalligah dressed him with precision and speed, layering garment after garment over his frame. Orion barely had time to register what was happening before a golden crest was pinned to his chest. Thin metal tendrils shot out from it, wrapping around his body and weaving themselves into a shimmering breastplate that fit him perfectly. His trousers turned to chainmail, glinting silver and gold.

When it was over, Orion caught his reflection in a mirror and froze. The boy staring back was no longer the sixteen-year-old he knew. His skin had taken on a faint silver sheen, and his eyes glowed like miniature suns. His once crinkled afro was now a crown of sharp, spiky strands, shimmering with golden light.

"What... what happened to me?" he whispered, touching his face.

Lillithan appeared behind him, smiling gently. "You are awakening, Cobossal Orion. The true you."

Before he could respond, she tugged his arm. "Come. The entire star system is waiting."

The journey to the throne room was a blur of golden halls and glowing corridors. When they reached the grand doors, Lillithan stopped and turned to Orion, her expression solemn.

"Remember: stand tall, keep your head high, and walk with purpose," she said. "You are their king, and today, you must embrace your destiny."

The massive red doors swung open, and trumpets blared. Orion stepped forward, his heart pounding, as he took in the sight before him. The golden city glittered under the light of the twin suns, and the streets below were filled with cheering crowds. Above them, a hologram of his transformed self floated in the sky, radiant and regal.

At the end of the red carpet stood the golden throne, blazing with light. The air buzzed with energy as Orion approached, his every step heavy with the weight of expectation. When he sat, golden straps emerged, holding him in place. He struggled, but Lillithan placed a steadying hand on his shoulder.

"Do not fear," she said. "The throne recognizes only those of pure heart and blood."

Orion's mind screamed for him to wake up, to return to the safety of his crumbling room in Fittleworth. But the truth was undeniable: this wasn't a dream. It was his destiny.

The golden straps tightened briefly, making Orion gasp. He fought the urge to struggle as Lillithan's calming presence steadied him. The crowd's cheers below turned to an expectant hush, the weight of thousands of eyes on him. Suddenly, a figure materialized out of thin air in a swirl of golden mist, a tall woman robed in shimmering gold, holding a blade that seemed to hum with power. Her face was serene, her gaze piercing as she approached.

"This is the test of purity," Lillithan said softly. "Do not fear, Cobossal Orion. You are ready."

The robed woman raised the blade high above her head, the strange runes on its surface shifting like liquid. Orion tensed, every instinct screaming for him to run, but he was held firm by the throne's glowing restraints. He clenched his eyes shut, bracing for the strike.

Instead, he felt a sharp prick on his fingertip.

He opened his eyes and saw the woman holding his hand delicately. A single drop of golden blood glimmered at the edge of the blade. The woman stepped back, her face expressionless, and flicked the drop of blood onto a small, ancient chest that sat on a pedestal nearby. The blood shimmered like sunlight as it touched the chest's surface, and then.

BOOM.

The chest erupted in golden flames, crackling with energy. Orion flinched, but the flames quickly subsided, leaving behind three dazzling objects: a golden crown inlaid with jewels that seemed to glow with inner light, a rainbow-colored sceptre, and an elegant sword made of gold and silver. The sword's blade shimmered, its strange, shifting script now glowing brightly.

The robed woman picked up the crown and approached Orion once more. "You have been tested and found worthy," she said, her voice carrying the weight of ancient authority. "Accept the symbols of your reign, Cobossal Orion I."

She placed the crown gently on his head, and the restraints around him vanished. As Orion rose to his feet, the sceptre and sword were presented to him. He grasped them both, feeling a surge of energy course through him, a sensation that was both foreign and familiar, as though some long-forgotten part of him had awakened.

Lillithan stepped forward, fastening the sword to his side. Her voice rang out, amplified so that it echoed across the entire city and beyond.

"Citizens of the Star System of Auryn, behold your ruler, His Royal Highness Cobossal Orion I. May his reign bring peace and prosperity to us all!"

The city erupted in celebration. Fireworks lit up the sky, casting dazzling colours over the golden towers. The streets below were filled with music, cheers, and singing. Orion turned to face the crowds, his heart racing. The weight of the crown pressed lightly on his head, a constant reminder of the responsibility he had inherited.

But as he looked out at the jubilant faces below, a strange dizziness overtook him. The world began to blur and spin, the golden city dissolving into streaks of light. He tried to steady himself, but the weight of everything, his crown, his sceptre, the sheer enormity of what had just happened, was too much.

2 Life as usual

Orion jolted awake in his bed, gasping. His heart pounded as he tried to shake the vivid memory of his dream. Why had it felt so real? He rolled over in the dim light, fumbling for his phone. The screen glowed faintly: 6:30 a.m. Sighing, he slid out of bed quietly, careful not to wake his brothers. His bare feet touched the cold wooden floor, grounding him in reality.

As he entered the bathroom, he glanced at his reflection in the mirror. Bruises darkened his cheek, and his lip was swollen and split. He frowned. How was he supposed to explain these away? He couldn't just tell people, *my dad hit me*. Shaking his head, he splashed cold water on his face and took a deep breath before heading downstairs.

The house was silent, save for the creak of the old floorboards. As Orion reached the bottom of the stairs, he nearly tripped over his father, who was sprawled on the floor. Lawrence lay surrounded by empty whiskey and beer bottles, his snoring loud and uneven. Orion bent down, picked up the bottles silently, and carried them to the recycling bin in the kitchen.

Pouring himself a glass of orange juice and a bowl of cornflakes, he sat at the table. The events of his dream replayed in his mind, the shimmering palace, the golden city, the phoenix crest. He wished it were real. Even with the danger of war, it had to be better than his current life. Here, he was just a punching bag for his drunk father. Sighing, he rinsed his bowl and glass before preparing lunches for himself and his twin brothers, Jake and Anton.

Dreading what he was about to do next, Orion returned to the hallway and crouched beside his father.

"Dad. Dad. DAD!" he shouted, shaking Lawrence's shoulder.

Lawrence stirred, muttering under his breath, then sat up abruptly, swinging a hand that Orion narrowly dodged.

"What?" Lawrence growled, his breath reeking of alcohol.

"It's almost time for you to take us to school," Orion said, instantly regretting his words as his father's glare hardened. The smell of whiskey was overpowering.

"Get me a coffee," Lawrence grumbled. "And wake your brothers."

Orion hurried to the kitchen, made a quick cup of instant coffee, and handed it to his father. Then he dashed upstairs to wake Jake and Anton. Voices drifted from their room. Expecting to find them up, Orion pushed the door open. Both twins were still sound asleep.

"Jake. Anton. Time to get up," he called, pulling their uniforms from the wardrobe.

The twins groaned but sat up reluctantly, rubbing the sleep from their eyes. Silently, they dressed and followed Orion downstairs. After making breakfast for them, Orion sat at the table, his stomach twisting with anxiety. He could hear Lawrence shuffling around, muttering to himself. When the twins finished eating, all three boys slipped out the front door and climbed into their father's beat-up car.

From the passenger seat, Orion caught sight of their neighbour, Mr. Thomas, peering through his window, his expression one of disdain. Lawrence stumbled out of the house, climbed into the driver's seat, and started the engine. The car sputtered and backfired loudly as they pulled away.

The drive to school was tense, punctuated only by Lawrence's muttered curses at other drivers. Orion sat stiffly, staring out the window, grateful when the school gates finally came into view.

"Don't forget to pick us up today," Anton said as they slowed.

"You'll have to walk. I'm busy," Lawrence snapped.

"Oh, can we have money for the bus then?" Jake asked timidly.

"WHAT DO I LOOK LIKE, A BANK?" Lawrence roared, making all three boy's flinch.

Before their father could yell more, they jumped out of the car and hurried through the gates, relieved to be away from him.

"Bro, you look rough. What are you going to tell people about the bruises?" Jake asked as they walked.

"I fell down the stairs, like always," Orion said, forcing a smile to reassure his brother.

"I don't think that'll work this time," Anton muttered.

Orion sighed. "Meet me outside after school. I'll figure out how to get us home."

Leaving the twins, Orion made his way to the assembly hall. He spotted Rachel, his best friend, waving at him from the back. As he approached, he accidentally bumped into a man sweeping the floor.

"Sorry, young man," the caretaker said. His amber eyes glinted as he studied Orion briefly.

"No problem," Orion said, hurrying away. But something about the man seemed familiar. Orion glanced back and saw the caretaker watching him. When their eyes met, the man quickly turned back to sweeping.

"What took you so long?" Rachel asked when Orion reached her.

"Oh, I bumped into the new caretaker. What happened to Jim?" he asked, sitting beside her.

"Dunno. Maybe he's sick," Rachel replied casually.

The school buzzer blared, signalling the start of assembly. As the headteacher droned on about half-term events, Rachel leaned closer.

"He hit you again, didn't he?" she whispered.

"What lesson do you have first?" Orion asked, avoiding her question.

"Maths. You?"

"Science," he replied with a grin.

"You're such a nerd, Egg," Rachel teased.

Orion scowled. "You know I hate that nickname."

Rachel laughed. "Yeah, but only you get excited about science."

Before Orion could retort, Miss Harris, their head of year, glared at them from across the hall, silencing their chatter.

When assembly ended, Orion said, "See you at break in the usual spot." He turned and headed for the science labs, but as he walked down the corridor, he felt a prickle on the back of his neck. Turning, he saw the caretaker standing at the far end of the hall, staring at him. Orion looked away, but when he glanced back, the man had vanished. Uneasy, Orion shrugged it off and entered the lab.

Orion took his usual seat by the window in the science lab. Mr. Fox began explaining chemical equations and reactions, but no matter how hard Orion tried, he couldn't concentrate. His mind kept drifting back to the dream. The golden city, the glowing throne, the strange blue-skinned man, it had all seemed so real. He shook his head, trying to focus on the textbook in front of him.

"Mr. Bailey," Mr. Fox's stern voice interrupted his thoughts. "Am I keeping you from something outside that window?"

Orion snapped back to attention. "Sorry, sir," he mumbled, his cheeks flushing.

"I would appreciate it if you left your daydreams outside of my classroom."

"Yes, sir. It won't happen again."

The rest of the class erupted into laughter, making Orion sink lower in his seat. Not only was he an outcast, but now he was the butt of their jokes too. He buried his head in his textbook, hoping the period would pass quickly.

The crackle of the school announcement system startled him. "Would Orion Bailey please report to Miss Harris's office immediately," the receptionist's voice said.

A wave of unease washed over him. Packing up his books, he could feel the stares of his classmates following him as he left the room. His steps felt heavier with each stride down the hall. When he reached Miss Harris's door, he knocked hesitantly.

"Come in," Miss Harris called.

Pushing the door open, Orion's eyes landed on Anton, who was sitting with tear-streaked cheeks. Orion's heart sank.

"Take a seat," Miss Harris said, her voice unusually gentle.

"Miss, what is this about?" Orion asked as he sat down beside his brother.

"I've just had a very interesting conversation with your brother, and I have a few questions," Miss Harris said. She handed Anton another tissue and then turned back to Orion. "Would you like a glass of orange juice?"

"No, thank you," Orion said, fidgeting with the hem of his shirt. "What do you want to know?"

Miss Harris sat down and folded her hands on the desk. "I'd like to know how you got the bruises on your face and the swollen lip."

Orion froze, his stomach twisting into knots. He gulped before answering. "I… I fell down the stairs, Miss."

Anton sniffled beside him. "Tell her the truth, Orion," he said, his voice trembling. "I won't let him hurt you anymore."

Orion looked down, unable to meet Miss Harris's steady gaze. The silence in the room was deafening.

"My dad did it, Miss," Orion finally admitted, his voice barely above a whisper. Tears welled in his eyes, and he quickly wiped them away.

"I suspected as much," Miss Harris said softly. "But I couldn't do anything without confirmation."

"It's not his fault," Orion said defensively. "He was drunk…"

"My poor child," Miss Harris said, her voice breaking. "Don't make excuses for him."

She stood and walked around the desk, crouching beside him. She reached out to touch his arm, but Orion flinched, yelping in pain when her hand brushed against a large bruise.

"I've called children's services," she said. "I'll drive you and your brothers to their offices shortly."

Before Orion could respond, there was a knock at the door. The school nurse entered, followed closely by Jake.

"What's going on, you two?" Jake asked, looking from Orion to Anton.

"I'll explain on the way," Miss Harris said.

"Miss Harris, a word, if I may," the nurse said, stepping back into the hallway. Miss Harris followed, leaving the boys alone in the office.

Orion turned to Jake, his voice low. "They know. About Dad."

Jake's eyes widened, and his lip quivered. "What's going to happen to us?"

"They're taking us to children's services. It's time this stopped," Orion said firmly. "He won't be able to hurt us anymore."

Jake nodded, his eyes filling with tears. "You're right. It's time."

The door opened again as the school bell rang, signalling the start of break. Miss Harris returned and motioned for them to follow her. The three boys walked behind her to the staff car park. As Orion climbed into the backseat, he glanced up and saw the caretaker standing at a nearby window, watching him with a soft smile. Orion frowned, uneasy but unsure why.

Just as he closed the car door, he spotted Rachel standing on the school steps, her face a mask of worry. He managed a small wave before the car pulled away.

"Seatbelts, please," Miss Harris said as she started the engine.

Once they were buckled in, she glanced at Orion in the rearview mirror. "I'm so sorry this has happened to you."

"It's not your fault. I was good at hiding it," Orion replied quietly.

Miss Harris's voice softened. "Things will get better for you three now. I'm sure of it."

The rest of the drive was silent. When they arrived at the children's services office, Orion noticed a tall, grey-haired man in a tweed suit standing outside. He checked his watch, then looked up as the car pulled in. Reaching into his briefcase, he pulled out a file and approached the car as Miss Harris parked.

"Are you Orion Bailey?" the man asked as he opened the door.

"Yes," Orion replied warily.

"I'm Mr. Fray. I work with children's services. If you'll follow me inside, we can get everything sorted out."

Orion and his brothers followed Mr. Fray into the children's services office. The lobby was dimly lit, with a security guard seated behind a desk, staring at a wall of monitors. A handful of people bustled through the room, their voices hushed. Mr. Fray led them to an elevator and pressed the button for the top floor.

"Miss Harris, I can take it from here," he said, turning to the teacher. "You should get back to school."

Miss Harris hesitated. "If you're sure…"

"Quite sure," Mr. Fray said with a polite but firm nod.

She crouched down, looking into Orion's eyes. "You're brave, Orion. Remember that."

Orion gave her a weak smile before she turned to leave. As the elevator doors closed, he caught sight of her walking away through the glass lobby doors.

The ride up was silent, save for the faint hum of the elevator. Another security guard, nearly identical to the one at the front desk, stood inside with them. His gaze lingered on Orion, making him uncomfortable. The air felt heavy, and Orion had to fight the urge to fidget under the scrutiny.

The elevator came to a halt, and Mr. Fray led them into a large, open office space filled with desks. Only a few were occupied, and the faint clatter of typing echoed in the room. Orion glanced around, puzzled by how empty the space seemed.

"Come this way," Mr. Fray said, leading them into his private office.

The room was stark, with a large desk, two chairs, and a filing cabinet. A single picture of a young girl rested on the desk, the only personal touch in an otherwise sterile environment.

"Foster homes have been found for you and your brothers," Mr. Fray said as he sat down behind the desk.

"What do you mean 'foster homes?'" Orion asked sharply, his fists clenching.

"I'm afraid I don't have a single home available that can take all three of you," Mr. Fray said, his tone calm but apologetic.

"No," Orion said firmly. "I'm not leaving my brothers."

Mr. Fray tilted his head, studying Orion for a moment. As if on cue, his desk phone rang. He answered it with a polite, "Yes?" His expression shifted to one of mild surprise as he listened. After a moment, he hung up and turned back to Orion.

"Well, it seems the foster carer who was meant to take you, Orion, has offered to take all three of you instead. It's as though they anticipated your response."

Orion exhaled, relief washing over him. "Thank you."

"It's not a problem," Mr. Fray said, standing. "Let's get going."

He led them back to the elevator, which descended silently. As they stepped out into the lobby, a short woman approached Mr. Fray, whispering something in his ear before walking away. The boys exchanged puzzled glances but said nothing.

Outside, a car was waiting. Another security guard stood by the driver's side, handing the keys to Mr. Fray. The boys climbed into the backseat, their schoolbags piled at their feet. Orion noticed Jake's nervous fidgeting and reached over to squeeze his hand.

"Are you okay?" Orion asked.

"I guess," Jake said, shrugging. "It's just… weird."

"Yeah," Anton added quietly. "But at least we're away from Dad."

Orion nodded, glancing at Mr. Fray through the rearview mirror. Their eyes met briefly, and Mr. Fray smiled. For a split second, Orion thought he saw a flicker of something in the man's eyes, a glimmer that seemed almost inhuman. He blinked, shaking off the thought.

As the car merged onto the motorway, Orion leaned back in his seat, trying to relax. Trees and road signs blurred past the windows, but he couldn't shake the strange feeling lingering in his chest.

The car turned onto a tree-lined road with mansions towering on either side, each grander than the last. Orion and his brothers, Jake and Anton, stared wide-eyed out of the windows, their schoolbags clutched tightly in their laps. These homes were the kind they'd only ever seen on TV. Surely, a foster family couldn't live in a place like this?

Before any of them could voice their disbelief, the car rolled to a stop in front of a towering wrought-iron gate. Mr. Fray leaned out of the driver's window, pressing an intercom button that buzzed sharply before crackling to life.

"How may I help you?" a calm female voice asked.

"I have Orion, Jake, and Anton here," Mr. Fray replied.

"Come on up to the main house. Someone will meet you there," the voice responded, and the gates began to slide open.

The boys exchanged bewildered glances as the car climbed a long driveway lined with ancient trees. When the mansion came into view, they gasped. It was enormous, larger than any building they'd ever been inside. Its arched windows stretched across two stories, and its sprawling grounds seemed to go on forever.

"Out of the car, boys," Mr. Fray instructed cheerfully as the vehicle came to a halt. The boys scrambled out, standing awkwardly beside their foster bags.

A tall, thin man with pale blonde hair and a stern expression stepped out of the mansion's front door. Beside him was an elegant woman with raven-black hair, a warm smile softening her otherwise regal features.

"Welcome, boys," she said, her voice as soothing as the hum of a summer breeze. "I'm Mrs. Twinkle."

The man's sharp voice cut through her warmth. "Mr. Fray, we have paperwork to handle."

Without another word, the man turned on his heel and strode back inside, leaving Mrs. Twinkle to gesture for the boys to follow.

The entrance hall was unlike anything they had ever seen. The marble floor gleamed under the light of enormous diamond chandeliers. Two grand oak staircases spiralled upward, meeting in a balcony above. Antique furniture, polished to perfection, lined the walls. Sunlight streamed through arched windows, casting rainbows across the space as it hit the chandeliers.

"Wow," Jake whispered, his voice barely audible.

They were ushered into a massive living room with a wall-sized television, a sectional sofa big enough to fit an entire classroom, and shelves stocked with every gaming console imaginable. A glass coffee table gleamed in the centre of the room.

"Make yourselves comfortable," Mrs. Twinkle said. "You can watch TV if you'd like. This is your home now."

Jake hesitated. "Can we? Really?" He flinched as if expecting a reprimand.

"Of course," she said gently.

Orion, Jake, and Anton exchanged looks before cautiously settling onto the enormous sofa. For the first time in what felt like forever, they let themselves relax. Orion pulled out his phone, the screen lighting up to reveal missed calls and messages from Rachel. He quickly hit redial, his heart warming at the sound of her frantic voice.

"Orion! What's going on? Where are you?"

"We've been placed with foster parents," he explained, glancing around the opulent room.

"How are you holding up?" Rachel asked.

"We're... good, I think." Orion's voice softened as he glanced at his brothers. "Better than we've been in a long time."

They ended the call after a promise to talk later. Orion leaned back, soaking in the unfamiliar sensation of safety and comfort.

About twenty minutes later, Mrs. Twinkle and her husband returned. Jake hastily switched off the TV, and the boys sat up, unsure of what to expect.

"I'm Mr. Twinkle, but you can call me Zanek if you prefer," the man said. "And this is Alexi. While you're here, you'll be under our protection."

Orion frowned. "What do you mean, 'protection'?"

Zanek shifted uncomfortably before Alexi stepped in. "We just mean you'll be safe with us. Now, how about we show you your rooms?"

The boys followed Alexi upstairs. She opened the door to a bright, colourful bedroom with bunk beds built into one wall. The others were covered in hand-painted murals of comic and movie scenes. A flat-screen TV hung opposite the beds, and a door led to a private bathroom.

"This is for Jake and Anton," Alexi explained. "It's not perfect, we didn't have much notice, but I hope you like it. I'll come fetch you when dinner is ready."

Orion smiled as he watched his brothers' faces light up. Alexi gestured for him to follow her further down the hall to another room.

The door opened to reveal a space that took Orion's breath away. A four-poster king-sized bed stood in the centre, draped in deep blue linens. A large oak desk and bookshelf full of books, some still wrapped in plastic, lined one wall. Another door led to a private bathroom.

"I'll leave you to settle in," Alexi said softly, closing the door behind her.

Orion sank onto the bed, looking around in disbelief. This didn't feel real.

His gaze fell on the bookshelf, and one old, worn book caught his eye. It had no title, just a leather-bound cover with a strange, intricate pattern. Curious, he pulled it free and opened it at the desk.

The words on the page seemed to shift and swirl before his eyes. He blinked and rubbed them, but when he looked again, the text settled, and he began to read.

Orion turned the delicate pages of the old book, feeling the weight of its history in his hands. The first page held a handwritten message in flowing, golden script:

My dearest Son,

I hope this book finds you when the time is right. Please know it was never our choice to send you away, but it was the only way to keep you safe. You will have much work to do in the times ahead, to fix all that has been undone in your absence. Be cautious in whom you place your trust. If the head maiden is still with you, she has watched over our family for many moons and will guide you well.

Your mother and I will always love you. Never forget that. The magic that runs through your veins is the strongest and most powerful there is.

Goodbye, my son.

Orion stared at the letter, his heart racing. He read it again, then a third time. It was impossible, yet here it was, in black and white. Who was this from? And why did it feel... familiar?

Shaking his head, he placed the book carefully on the desk, staring at the swirling pattern on its cover. A deep unease settled in his chest, mingling with a strange, inexplicable sense of belonging. He was so absorbed in his thoughts that he didn't hear the knock on his door.

"Orion!"

The door flew open, and his twin brothers barrelled into the room. Jake practically tackled him, while Anton flopped onto his bed, grinning.

"Did you see our room?" Jake asked, vibrating with excitement.

"Yeah, it's amazing," Orion replied distractedly.

"What do you think's going to happen to Dad?" Anton asked suddenly, his smile fading.

Orion hesitated. "I don't know. I hope he's okay."

Anton dropped his head into his hands, his voice barely above a whisper. "It's weird, isn't it? Missing him, even after everything."

Orion wrapped an arm around his brother's shoulders. "No, it's not weird. I miss him too. But we're safe now. That's what matters."

A sharp knock at the door interrupted them. Zanek stepped inside, his imposing figure filling the doorway. His eyes flicked to the book on Orion's desk for a brief moment before settling on him.

"Dinner is ready," he announced. "And there's someone I'd like you to meet."

The dining room was as extravagant as the rest of the mansion. A long table stretched down the centre, set with gold-rimmed plates and crystal glasses. The aroma of roasted meats, fresh bread, and rich gravy filled the air.

Orion, Jake, and Anton took their seats, their mouths watering at the sight of the feast before them. At the head of the table sat Alexi, her elegance matching the room's grandeur. Beside her was a girl who looked to be about Orion's age. Her dark hair gleamed under the chandelier, and her piercing black eyes seemed to take in everything.

"This is Emily," Zanek said, gesturing toward the girl. "She's been with us for some time."

Emily inclined her head slightly, her gaze lingering on Orion. He felt a shiver run down his spine under her scrutiny.

The boys wasted no time filling their plates, marvelling at the variety of dishes, roast beef, chicken casserole, lamb, pork chops, roasted vegetables, and more. It was more food than they'd ever seen in one place.

"Slow down, boys," Zanek said with a chuckle. "There's no rush. No one will take it from you."

"Sorry," the three muttered in unison, though they couldn't entirely hide their grins.

Emily, meanwhile, picked at her plate with a kind of detached indifference. At one point, she stabbed a pork chop, examined it like a science project, and took a cautious bite.

The mood was light until Zanek broke the silence. "Are you planning to return to school tomorrow?"

Orion looked up, startled. "I think so, yeah."

"Me too," Jake said, his mouth full of mashed potatoes.

"Good," Alexi chimed in. "Your new uniforms and supplies have been taken care of."

Emily suddenly slammed her fork onto the table. "Why are we wasting time with this nonsense?" she snapped, her voice cutting through the warmth of the room.

"Emily!" Zanek's tone was sharp, his usual composure faltering for a moment.

Her lips curled into a cold smile. "This charade isn't fooling anyone." She rose from her seat, brushing past Orion as she left the room. Her fingers brushed the back of his neck, sending another shiver down his spine.

"What did she mean?" Orion asked, his brow furrowing.

"She's... complicated," Zanek said, clearly uncomfortable. "Don't let her bother you."

Alexi stood abruptly, smoothing her dress. "It's getting late. I think we should all retire for the night."

The boys exchanged glances, the unease in the room palpable. Jake and Anton followed Alexi upstairs, leaving Orion to linger behind. His thoughts were racing.

What had Emily meant? And why had Zanek seemed so unsettled?

Later that night, Orion lay in his bed, staring at the book on his desk. He couldn't resist its pull.

He sat down, flipped it open, and began reading once more. As the words flowed across the page, his surroundings faded, and the world around him seemed to dissolve into an endless starry void.

The next thing he knew, he was standing in the dining room downstairs, listening to his new hosts' conversation.

"It's too early to tell him!" Zanek said.

"He has a right to know," Emily shot back.

"Just give him time, let him settle in first."

"Fine, I will play it your way for now, but my patience is wearing thin as I have my duties," Emily replied.

Then there was darkness.

4 back to school

Orion jolted awake, heart pounding, as someone shook him. Blinking against the early morning light, he saw Emily sitting at the edge of his bed, her expression unsettlingly calm.

"What are you doing here?" he stammered, trying to sit up.

Emily didn't answer right away. Instead, she reached out, gripping his arm tightly. Her nails dug into his skin, and he winced.

"Listen carefully," she said, her voice low but urgent. "You're in danger. Promise me, whatever happens today, you'll keep yourself safe."

"Danger?" Orion's mind raced. "What are you talking about? Is this about the conversation I overheard last night?"

Emily's dark eyes flickered. "You heard that?" She let go of his arm, her lips pressing into a thin line. "You weren't supposed to hear that."

"What's going on?" Orion demanded, rubbing his sore wrist.

Her gaze softened, just slightly. "Just... promise me."

"I promise," Orion said, though the words felt hollow without understanding.

Satisfied, Emily stood and moved toward the door, her footsteps light and deliberate. "Be careful," she said over her shoulder before disappearing into the hallway.

Orion got dressed quickly, his new school uniform feeling strange against his skin. It was pristine and perfectly tailored, a far cry from the patched and worn clothes he was used to. He slung his school bag over his shoulder, glancing once more at the mysterious book on his desk.

After a moment's hesitation, he grabbed it and tucked it into his bag.

Downstairs, the dining room buzzed with quiet tension. Alexi was serving a full English breakfast, while Zanek read the morning paper with a cool, detached air. Emily sat silently, her black eyes fixed on her untouched plate.

"Good morning, Orion. Did you sleep well?" Zanek asked without looking up.

"Uh, yeah," Orion replied, sliding into a seat. The smell of bacon and eggs made his stomach growl.

"Good. A car will take you to school shortly. Everything has been arranged."

Orion ate quickly, avoiding Emily's piercing gaze. Jake and Anton were cheerful as ever, chatting about their new rooms and the strange luxury of this new life. But the tension from the night before lingered, thick and suffocating.

As they finished breakfast, Zanek handed Orion three crisp ten-pound notes. "For your lunches," he said simply.

Orion muttered a quick "thank you" and stuffed the money into his pocket before grabbing his bag. Jake and Anton followed suit, their excitement infectious as they headed for the door.

Orion paused in the entryway, turning back to Zanek. "Why does it feel like you're not telling me something?"

Zanek's smile didn't reach his eyes. "You'll understand in time, Orion. For now, just focus on being a student."

Outside, a sleek black limo awaited them, flanked by two equally polished cars. The boys stared in awe as the driver opened the door, gesturing for them to climb inside.

"This is insane," Anton whispered as they slid onto the leather seats.

The ride to school was surreal. Orion stared out of the window, his mind swirling with questions. How had their father managed to pay for a private school all this time? And why had their foster parents gone to such lengths to keep them here?

When they arrived, the twins bounded out of the limo, their excitement masking any lingering unease. Orion lingered, his attention caught by the driver, who motioned for him to wait.

"Zanek has arranged for a security detail to accompany you today," the driver said, his tone matter-of-fact.

"What? Why?" Orion asked, his confusion mounting.

"It's for your safety, sir," the driver replied, stepping aside as a tall, blond man in a black suit approached.

The man extended a hand. "Barry, sir. I'll be with you today."

Orion hesitated but shook his hand. "Fine. Let's go."

The school buzzed with its usual energy as Orion made his way toward the cafeteria. Barry followed a few paces behind, his presence drawing curious stares from students. Orion tried to ignore them, focusing instead on finding Rachel.

He spotted her at a table, her younger sister Bell chatting animatedly beside her. Relief washed over him as he slid into the seat across from them.

"Morning, Egg," Rachel said with a grin.

"Morning, Rach. Bell."

Bell gave him a quick hug before darting off to meet a friend.

"What's with the bodyguard?" Rachel asked, raising an eyebrow.

"Long story," Orion muttered, glancing over his shoulder at Barry. "Let's go outside. I need to talk to you."

Rachel nodded, grabbing her bag as they headed toward their usual spot on the field. As they walked, Orion noticed more security guards stationed around the perimeter.

When they reached the grassy area beneath the oak tree, Rachel turned to him expectantly. "Okay, spill."

Orion hesitated, then told her everything, the new foster home, the strange book, the overheard conversation, and Emily's cryptic warnings.

Rachel listened intently, her brow furrowing. "That's... a lot," she said when he finished. "But it makes sense."

"How does any of this make sense?" Orion asked, exasperated.

"Egg, I've always said you were special. Maybe this is just... proof."

Before he could respond, a small rock hit him squarely in the back of the head.

"Hey, loser!"

Orion turned to see Michael, the school bully, swaggering toward him. His posse trailed behind, their smug expressions matching Michael's.

"What do you want, Michael?" Orion asked, his patience already thin.

"I heard you got taken away," Michael sneered. "Guess your dad finally had enough of you."

Orion's fists clenched, and he took a step forward. But before he could act, a blinding flash of light erupted between them.

When the light faded, Michael and his friends were gone.

Rachel stared at Orion, her mouth agape. "What... just happened?"

"I….I don't know," Orion stammered, his heart racing.

Barry was suddenly at his side, his expression grave. "We need to leave. Now."

Orion barely had time to grab his bag before Barry pulled him away, calling for backup into his earpiece.

"We have a code white in the field, I repeat code white," Barry was shouting into his sleeve as he ran up to Orion.

"Sir, Ma'am, we need to go, now."

"Orion what did you do?" Rachel asked.

"I… I dunno. How… did… I?" Orion replied, still in a state of shock.

The rest of Orion's security detail began to close in rapidly, all looking around to see if anyone else had seen what happened. When they reached Barry, they all stood around Orion, facing out.

"Arrange a clean-up team, get Cuckoo Two and Three, then meet us at the mansion," Barry said to the closest one.

"Barry... what happened?" Orion asked.

"Three to transport, on my mark," Barry said into his sleeve before he grabbed Orion and Rachel close to him. "Now."

When he said this, the world around them fell into darkness, and Orion felt like he was falling into nothingness below. After a few seconds in the darkness, Orion felt his feet hit something, and they stopped falling. When his vision came back, Orion noticed that they were now standing in front of the mansion.

"How did you let this happen?" Alexi shouted as she ran down the steps.

"I couldn't stop it, Ma'am. A clean-up crew has been organized and will fix the damage done," Barry replied, his tone apologetic but urgent.

Orion pushed away from Barry and looked at Alexi and Barry in disbelief. He grabbed Rachel's arm and pulled her away from them too. Who were these people? What happened in the field? And how did they get here?

Orion was finding it hard to breathe. He pulled at his tie to loosen it, but he still couldn't breathe. Then, he felt it, the world around him began to spin in and out of focus. He could feel himself swaying, and he felt Rachel's arm trying to steady him, but it was too late as he fell unconscious.

Whilst his eyes were closed, Orion could hear shouting around him. He heard Rachel shouting at someone, telling them to leave him alone, and he heard Barry's voice shouting for someone to detain her until Orion woke up. Suddenly, it all fell silent. What seemed like minutes later, Orion opened his eyes slowly, not wanting to see who was there. When the room came into view, he saw his two brothers sitting beside his bed, looking worried. At the end of his bed, he saw Alexi with her face in one of her hands, and Zanek pacing back and forth, muttering to himself.

"Where's Rachel?" Orion said as he sat up.

"She went to get a drink; she will be back any moment," Zanek said as he stopped pacing and approached Orion.

"STAY AWAY FROM ME!" Orion yelled at him.

"Calm down, I will explain everything once Rachel returns," Zanek said as he sat at the end of Orion's bed.

"Stay close to me, you two. Don't go near them; they are not normal."

The twins moved their chairs closer to Orion's bed, and everyone sat in silence. Zanek opened his mouth a few times as if he was going to say something, but he quickly closed it and looked back down at the floor. A few minutes later, Rachel walked into the room and sat down on the bed next to Orion.

"Good to see you're awake, Egg," she said, smiling at him.

"Rach, why are you so calm after everything that happened?"

"They explained everything to me. I always told you there was something odd about you."

"What do you mean?" Orion asked as he grabbed the glass out of her hand and took a sip.

"I suppose that's my cue," Zanek said as he stood up. "What's the first word you think of when you look up at the stars?"

"What... Why?" Orion began.

"Please, just answer the question," Alexi said as she came to sit beside him and his brothers.

"I... think home," Orion replied, slightly embarrassed.

"That's because you were born there a long, long time ago. That book you read, it was left for you by your father before he and your mother died."

"NO, you're lying. I'm... just... Just Orion."

"I can get your human father to come and explain," Zanek said as he stood up and began to pace once again.

"Wait, he's here?" Orion said, looking puzzled.

"Yes, we detained him, pending trial, when you came to live with us."

Before Orion could say anything else, Zanek walked over to the door, poked his head out, and spoke to someone outside. Once he was done, he came and sat back at the end of Orion's bed.

"What happened to Michael?" Orion asked as he remembered the bright flash of light.

"He and his friends have been returned," Zanek said, looking up at him. "Because you have only just come into your powers, you didn't send them too far."

"He's going to tell people what happened," Orion replied, putting his head in his hands.

"No, he doesn't remember anymore. That's what the clean-up team was for."

Orion could feel the tears streaming down his face. Everything he had known was a lie. The pain he felt was horrible as his heart felt like it was breaking into a million pieces.

Before anything could settle in, the bedroom door opened, and his father walked in, followed by one of the security guards. Orion could see cuffs biting into his dad's skin, and he was wearing the same clothes that he had worn when he dropped the boys off at school on Monday.

"Dad, what have they done to you?" Orion said as he jumped off the bed and rushed over to him.

"I'm okay," Lawrence said as he smiled slightly at Orion. "I suppose they have told you about being special?"

"Yeah, but I'm your son."

"No, you were a gift, but I lost my way and you paid for it," Lawrence said as tears began to fall from his bloodshot eyes.

"What do you mean, a gift?"

"We tried so long for a baby, but it never happened," his dad said as he stared off into the distance. "And then one night, there you were in a golden basket next to our bed, a gift from the gods."

All Orion could do was stare at his dad in disbelief and hate. All this time, he had known and said nothing to Orion. He had treated him so badly, consumed by his drink. But on the other hand, he had taken in a son and raised him as one of his own. He had always made sure that Orion and his brothers had all he could afford. So, Orion thought to himself, after all this time, can I really be angry at him? He tried his best.

"Please take the cuffs off," he said to the security guard.

The security man touched the cuffs, and they melted away into nothingness. Orion leaned in and hugged his dad tightly, while his dad began to sob into his shoulders. After a few minutes, Orion pulled away and looked at the broken man that stood before him.

"Can you ever forgive me?" Lawrence sobbed at him.

"Of course, I forgive you," Orion said, smiling at his dad.

Zanek began to explain why Orion's birth parents couldn't keep him and that, to protect him, they sent him to Earth hoping that he would learn the truth when he was old enough. His parents had fallen during the war, and Orion needed to return one day to fix it.

"How can I fix something I know nothing about?"

"You have the knowledge running through you, and we will teach you to tap into it," Alexi said.

"There are a few people you have to meet," Zanek said as he opened the bedroom door.

Everyone left Orion's bedroom and followed Zanek to the balcony by the stairs. Around thirty people had assembled in the hall below, and Zanek began to introduce them.

"These are the kitchen staff."

Ten people stepped forward, bowed at Orion, and walked off.

"These are the cleaners of the house and other things."

Ten more people walked forward, bowed, and walked off.

"These are your teachers and gardeners."

Ten more people stepped forward, bowed, and walked off, leaving behind Emily and three men. Zanek took Orion by the hand and led him down the steps, where he stopped in front of Emily and the three security guards from the social services office.

"This is Eymd," he said as he pointed at Emily. "She will be your main protector when we return, and these three are Bob, Todd, and Rod, your new security."

It was all too much for Orion to take, so he ran out of the front door and through the gardens. By the time he stopped, he was by a beautiful fountain that had three cherubs in the centre of it, spraying water into the basin below. The summer sun caught it in such a way that the water looked like liquid gold. As he sat down to catch his breath, there was a rustling in the bushes in front of him. He looked up and saw the three security men emerging, followed by his dad, who came and sat beside him.

"It's okay to be afraid; it's a lot to wrap your head around."

"I know, but I don't know if I can do it," Orion replied, staring into the sky above.

"I know, but perhaps the letter that was attached to you might help you figure it out. I think your mother still has it."

Orion smiled at his dad, as this was the dad he remembered, the one he had before he started drinking. Lawrence stood up and offered his hand to help Orion up. As they walked back toward the house, they couldn't help but admire the gardens. Birds sang in the trees, and all around them, beautiful flowers grew. As they entered the main doors, they could hear someone shouting.

"DON'T TELL ME WHAT TO DO, WHAT HAVE YOU DONE TO THEM?" yelled one of the twins.

When they walked into the front room, the twins ran at Orion with relief on their faces.

"Let's sit down and talk about all of this, you two."

As they sat and discussed everything, Orion noticed the devastation on the twins' faces as they realized that he was not their older brother.

"What will happen to us?" Jake asked as tears streamed down his face.

"You two are still my brothers, and nothing will ever change that."

"Where will we live?" Anton asked.

"Well, if you want, we can all live here."

Both boys nodded, wiped away their tears, and started jumping around the front room. Lawrence shook his head and laughed. Despite all he had put Orion through, his son had still turned out noble and kind.

"Right, Rach, I'll talk to you in a sec. Let me just call my mum."

Rachel nodded at him as he walked out into the main hall.

Orion grabbed his phone from his pocket and dialled his mum's number. The phone rang a few times, then a female voice answered.

"Orion, not now. I'm busy," she said sharply.

"Dad told me today how I became your son. If you still have the letter, could you bring it over, please?"

"Yes, I can, but I won't be able to stay long, as I have things to do. Where are you?"

Orion gave her the address and said he would see her soon. When he hung up, he saw his dad standing behind him and turned to look at him.

"She didn't seem bothered at all."

"I'm sure it's because she knew this day would come," Lawrence said reassuringly.

He shrugged and went in search of food. As he walked down the hall, he noticed a door open. When he peered inside, he saw nothing but an empty room. He closed the door and continued down the hall until he reached the kitchen. As he opened the door, everyone inside jumped to attention.

"Um, sorry, I was just looking for something to eat. No need to get up, I can do it myself," he said.

"Nonsense, sir. I can make you something," one of the cooks said.

Orion looked at her, a little surprised, since he was perfectly capable of doing it himself. But he stood his ground. "I can do it, thank you. Please carry on with what you were doing."

The cook eyed him up and down but nodded in agreement, returning to the table, as did the rest of the room. Orion began to potter around and found everything to make himself a ham and cheese sandwich. Before leaving the kitchen, he stood and watched the strange card game the kitchen staff were playing. Two of the staff laid cards down on the table, and what must have been holograms appeared in front of each card, beginning to battle with each other. He watched as a six-headed hellhound emerged and charged toward a cow-like creature. Just as the hellhound lunged in for the kill, the cow transformed into a dragon and sent a fireball at the six-headed creature. As it hit, the whole room erupted in cheers. Orion decided to leave and headed back to the front room.

As he sat back on the sofa, the door opened, and Zanek walked in, followed by Orion's mother, who entered and just stood there, looking like she wanted to leave.

"Rach, do you mind if I talk to my mum first?" Orion asked.

"Nah, go for it. I'm gonna call my mum to let her know I'm here."

Orion got up and led his mother out of the room. When they entered the main hall, Orion sat in one of the chairs and beckoned her to sit next to him. As she sat, Marie pulled a piece of silver paper from her pocket and handed it to him. He unfolded it, and written in gold lettering was:

Please look after our son. He is very important to us and many others, but he will not be safe here. You must only hand him this letter when he finds out the truth about himself, not before.
His name is Orion, and he holds hope for all of our people. Please protect him.
Thank you,
Aurorina.

Orion finished reading and realized that he had tears streaming down his face.

"Thank you for keeping this."

"It's fine. Right, I really need to go. I have tomorrow off, so I'll pop over then."

She stood up and walked out the front door, leaving Orion to think about everything. He folded the letter and put it in his pocket. Then, he opened the front room door and called Rachel out into the hallway, where they both sat down on the stairs.

"See, I told you that you were meant for better things," she said as she sat down.

"I know you've always been interested in magic and aliens, but you have to admit that this is strange."

"It is a little, but it's cool. By the way, my mum asked if you want to go camping this week."

"Yeah, that would be nice. I think I need a break."

"Cool, I'll let her know."

"What did you tell her?" Orion asked.

"Just that you went into care. I don't think she would believe the rest."

They both got up and went back into the front room, where they found Orion's brothers playing on one of the consoles. Orion sat down next to them and watched them playing until he drifted off to sleep.

He was back in the same hall from his previous dream, but this time, it lay derelict before him. The grand golden pillars had crumbled, the throne was broken into a million pieces, and the once golden floor was now bloodstained. It looked like the palace had been empty for years, judging by the amount of dust.

"Orion," said a voice from the shadows.

A figure stepped out, and he recognized it as Lillithan immediately, but she looked injured. He ran forward to help her. As he did, she collapsed and was unconscious in seconds. He leaned over, picked up one of the tapestries, bundled it up, and placed it under her head. Then, he sat down next to her and waited.

Orion sat in the derelict throne room, looking around for what felt like hours before Lillithan finally regained consciousness. She looked up, beamed at him, and then slowly sat up, wincing with each movement. The slashes across her face were deep, with green slime oozing out of them.

"Good, you're still here. We have much to discuss, but so little time," she said, her voice a mixture of pain and determination.

"This isn't a dream, is it?" Orion asked, his voice barely above a whisper.

"No, this is real. Earlier, I was trying to show you the truth."

Orion swallowed hard, his eyes filled with a mix of confusion and curiosity. "I've seen my father's letter, and he says I can trust you. Where are we, by the way?"

"We are on one of the planets in a constellation you know as Orion's Belt," Lillithan replied, crying out in pain as she tried to stand.

Orion immediately reached out, placing a gentle hand on her shoulder. "Wait, you shouldn't push yourself. Let me help."

She offered him a tired smile, her eyes softening. "Thank you, but I've endured worse, protecting the Summer Palace, my lord. Don't worry; it's only a flesh wound."

Orion looked at her in disbelief. How could this be considered just a flesh wound? Her arm hung at an odd angle, there were scorch marks above her heart, and her face was marred by deep slashes. He frowned, unsure if he should insist that she rest before they talked.

"What troubles you?" Lillithan asked, her voice cutting through his worried thoughts.

"How did you know?" Orion replied, his brow furrowed.

"You are truly your father's kin; he used to wear his worries on his face, just as you do," she said, smiling gently at him.

Orion smiled back, a sense of warmth blooming in his chest. He wondered what it would have been like to know his parents. It felt like he was slowly piecing together fragments of a life that had been hidden from him.

"I assume you know of the house and staff?" she asked. "There are three I sent to guard you. They were made a long time ago, but you can trust them."

"What do you mean, 'made'?" Orion's curiosity was piqued.

"They are made from star magic, just like the Kalligah, but with a more human-like appearance. Next time you see them, look into their eyes. If they are truly mine, they will have one gold eye and one silver."

Orion hesitated, his gaze dropping to the ground. "My father's note says I can use star magic, but I'm just a normal teenager."

Lillithan tilted her head, her eyes softening with sympathy. "I bound your magic before the sisters took you to Earth. It should have lifted the moment you held the book."

"Yeah, about that... there was an accident in the field at school," he said, his voice cracking slightly as he remembered what had happened to Michael and his friends. The fear in their eyes haunted him still.

Lillithan coughed into a handkerchief, trying to hide the purple blood that now stained it, but Orion saw and quickly grabbed her hand to stop her.

"You're hurting," Orion said, tears streaming down his face. He couldn't bear the thought of losing someone he had just begun to know, someone who was tied to his father.

"Hold out your hands and think about healing her, nothing else, just healing. Imagine her injuries disappearing," a voice said inside his head.

Orion held up his hands and did exactly as the voice instructed. He thought of nothing but warmth and healing. His hands began to glow, and a beam shot out, hitting Lillithan square in the chest. She screamed, and Orion heard a snap. He quickly closed his eyes, dropping his hands as fast as he could, too afraid to look.

I've killed her, he thought, his heart pounding in his chest. But then someone suddenly grabbed him in a tight hug. Slowly, he opened his eyes to see Lillithan. She looked so much better, her arm was back to normal, and the burnt skin above her heart was gone, though scars remained where the slashes had been.

"Thank you," she whispered, her voice filled with gratitude. "It would have taken me weeks to heal myself, but you managed it in mere seconds."

Orion hesitated, his emotions overwhelming him. "It's okay... a voice inside told me how to do it."

Lillithan smiled, stepping back and gesturing for him to follow her. "You are stronger than you think, Orion. Your father would be proud." She reached out, giving his hand a reassuring squeeze before letting go.

They walked to where the throne had once stood. Lillithan stopped and waved her hands in the air, conjuring a dark oak table and two chairs. One chair was gold with dark red velvet cushions and jewels encrusting its edges, while the other was a simple oak chair. Lillithan sat down in the plain chair and gestured for Orion to take the other. Her eyes were ablaze with swirling silver and gold, just as they had been when he first met her.

"As you can see, using star magic leaves an echo for a while," she said, gesturing to her eyes. "The more we use it, the more it shows."

"Will that happen to me?" Orion asked, concern evident in his voice.

"No. You come from pure star magic, like your ancestors. Only those outside the royal line are affected in their appearance by using it," Lillithan explained, her gaze softening as she watched him.

Orion nodded, trying to process everything. He was getting thirsty and wished he had something to drink. A moment later, a jug appeared in front of him with two glasses. He poured a drink and noticed the deep blue syrup-like liquid smelled sweet. He took a sip and was surprised that it was warm and tasted mildly like cream soda. He poured Lillithan a glass and passed it to her.

"This drink is called Jadican. How did you know about it?" she asked, her eyes twinkling with curiosity.

"I didn't. I was thirsty, and it appeared."

Lillithan chuckled, and they both drank in silence for a while, looking around the throne room. Eventually, Lillithan broke the silence.

"So, my dear, to the matter at hand, could you tell me who gave you the book?" she asked.

"A man called Zanek put it in my room at the manor."

Lillithan jumped up at the mention of Zanek's name.

"HIM!" she shouted, making Orion jump. "What's he doing there? Orion, you cannot trust him. I'm sure he has a hidden agenda."

"Who is he?" Orion asked, his heart pounding with unease.

Lillithan took a deep breath, trying to calm herself. "Sorry for the outburst. He was once your father's best friend, but he disappeared when the war started. Now I know where he went."

She began pacing back and forth, leaving footprints of fire in her wake. Orion watched her, a lump forming in his throat. He had trusted Zanek. The thought of betrayal cut deep.

"Okay, when you go back, do not tell him of our meetings. There's a safe full of money beneath the stairs, just press your hand on the picture there to access it."

Before Orion could respond, he heard his name faintly in the background.

"It looks like our time is up, young master. Just think of me when you sleep, and you will appear wherever I am. Until then, I bid you farewell."

As her last words were spoken, the floor beneath him disappeared. A gust of wind hit his face, and he instinctively closed his eyes. When he opened them again, he was in his bed, with all but one curtain drawn.

"Sorry to wake you, Master Orion. It's 10 a.m., and I have your breakfast," said Alexi from beside him.

Orion smiled at her, his heart heavy from everything that had happened. "Um, thank you. Why are you bringing me breakfast?"

"Well, now that you know about your powers, I have returned to my original role as your personal maid."

"Oh, there's no need to change what you were doing," Orion said, looking sad.

Alexi knelt by his side, her voice soft. "As you wish, young master. But please know I would do anything for you."

Orion's eyes welled up, and he placed a hand on her shoulder. "I know, Alexi. And I'm grateful."

She bowed, opened the rest of the curtains, and left the room, leaving Orion to eat his breakfast. As he cracked the top of his boiled egg, there was a knock at the door.

"C...ome," he said through a mouthful of toast.

The door opened, and his brothers ran in, jumping onto his bed and helping themselves to his breakfast. Orion just laughed and looked at his dad as he walked in.

"Morning," Orion said, still smiling.

"Morning," his dad replied as he sat at the desk, looking happy. Orion was glad that everyone seemed relaxed.

"We need to talk," said Lawrence, his eyes meeting Orion's.

"Um, is that a good talk or a bad talk?" Orion asked, looking worried.

Lawrence's expression softened. "It's a good one. I just wanted to know if you've thought about camping."

Orion looked at his brothers, who were now having an egg-eating contest. He laughed. "I would like to go, if you guys want to too."

"YEAH!" the twins shouted together, their excitement contagious.

"That's settled then, but we need to get some camping supplies. Let me get dressed, and I'll meet you downstairs."

Lawrence and the twins left him to get dressed. As Orion got out of bed, he realized he was now wearing pyjamas and wondered who had undressed him.

He showered, brushed his teeth, and started putting on the clothes Alexi had laid out for him. As he put on the shirt, he noticed it had the same crest as the door from his dream. He brushed his fingers over it, and it glowed softly. Once dressed, he made his way downstairs, where Rachel and his mother, Marie, were waiting for him along with everyone else.

"Morning, Egg. You passed out last night, so Zanek said I could stay in one of the guest rooms," Rachel said, nudging him playfully.

Orion smiled, glad to see her. "Morning."

His mother, Marie, gave him a cold nod. "Morning."

"Morning, guys. So, is everyone ready for shopping?" Orion asked, trying to sound cheerful.

The door to his left opened, and Zanek emerged, walking over to Orion.

"What would you like to do today, sir?"

"Please call me Orion. I'd like to go shopping for camping supplies."

"We've only just got you back, young master. Can you not postpone the camping trip?" Zanek asked, his expression serious.

"No, I need to clear my head, and I've already told Rachel I'm going."

"Of course, si... Orion. I will have the cars brought around and tell Alexi that she needs to prepare."

"Why does Alexi need to come?" Orion asked.

Zanek frowned before answering, "She will accompany us to pay for items." Without further explanation, Zanek walked off in search of Alexi.

Rachel gave Orion a look, her eyebrows raised. "How could he say that, like Alexi is nothing?"

"Maybe it's just the way things are done here," Anton replied, trying to diffuse the tension.

Orion's face darkened. "I DON'T CARE. SHE'S A PERSON TOO!" He shouted, his voice cracking.

Jake stepped forward, putting a reassuring hand on Orion's shoulder. "You can change that. This is your house, Orion. You have the power to make things right."

Orion nodded, the fire in his eyes simmering down. He made his way out the front door, where Alexi was already waiting outside with two standard black cars and a limo in the centre. The limo driver opened the door as Orion approached. He got in, followed by Rachel and his family. He watched out the window as Alexi and the security team climbed into the first car. As soon as her door closed, the cars started down the driveway.

Orion stared out of the window, only half-listening to the conversation. He was thinking about the conversation with Lillithan about Zanek, wondering if he should tell his family. He looked over at them, laughing and joking, and decided they didn't need to know just yet. The limo slowed, and Orion realized they had arrived at the huge shopping complex. The limo door opened, and the driver stepped back to let them out.

"Thank you," Orion said as he climbed out.

"It's not a problem, young master," the driver said with a huge grin.

They made their way into the camping shop, joined by Alexi and the security team, which now included Barry.

"Do they have to follow us?" Rachel asked, her eyes narrowing.

"Apparently so," Orion shrugged, giving her a sheepish smile.

Jake walked over to Orion, holding a huge package. "What are we allowed to get?"

"You can get anything you want," Orion replied, trying to keep his spirits up.

"Would you like me to pick some things out for you, Master Orion?" asked Alexi from beside him, her eyes wide with excitement.

Orion was about to say he could do it himself, but seeing her enthusiasm, he decided against it. "Yeah, sure. Knock yourself out."

Alexi smiled broadly and walked off, pulling a clipboard from her handbag. Orion watched her stop at items and jot down notes. He could also hear the twins messing around somewhere in the shop, but his mom, dad, and Rachel stayed close to him.

"You guys can pick anything you want, you know," Orion said, trying to lighten the mood.

"Why would I want anything?" Marie spat at him. "I don't want to go."

Orion looked at his mom, shocked. She didn't have to work now, he would take care of her. He noticed she kept shuffling from one foot to another, glancing at her watch as if she couldn't wait to leave. His dad must have noticed too, as he asked Rachel if she would help him find a tent.

"Mum, what's wrong?" Orion asked as they walked away.

She looked at him for a moment before replying, "I don't like this, not one bit. Look at you; you can't even go anywhere without these goons hanging around."

"Mum, I..."

"No, Orion. I'm not your mother. This is why I left, I never wanted any of you," she snapped.

With that, she turned and walked away without looking back.

"MUM, WAIT!" Orion shouted, but it was too late. She was already gone.

He felt his heart shatter, how could she say such hurtful things? Tears streamed down his face. He ran out of the store and into the limo, climbing inside and sobbing into his knees. He pulled out his phone and dialled his mom's number. It rang twice and cut off, which only made him cry harder. Why had she waited until now to say this?

He wanted nothing more than for the ground to swallow him whole, just to escape the pain. The car door opened, and Orion looked up to see his dad climbing in.

"Orion..."

"Don't, Dad. I just want to be alone right now," Orion sobbed.

Lawrence leaned forward and kissed his son's forehead. Before climbing out, he said, "Okay. Just know I'm here if you need to talk."

After what felt like ten minutes, the car door opened again, and everyone piled in.

"Alexi said someone will come to collect the stuff later," Jake said.

"Oh. Okay," Orion replied, his voice hollow.

The journey home was quiet, with no one wanting to talk about what had happened. When they pulled up to the house, Orion didn't wait for the driver to open the door. He jumped out, ran inside, and went straight up to his room. He began throwing things across the room, trying to vent his anger.

He thought to himself, *Maybe I'd be better off alone.*

"WHAT?" he yelled when there was a knock at the door.

The door opened slightly, and Emily's face appeared.

"What's wrong with you?" she asked as she walked in.

"Family problems. Sorry for yelling at you," he replied sheepishly.

"Family problems, that's all?" she laughed. "Try going through the transformation into this. I can't use my powers, and I look ridiculous."

"What do you mean, transformation?" Orion asked as he started picking things up.

"In my natural form, I'm a warrior, not some puny little girl. I'll tell you what, I'll swap moms with you. At least yours didn't try to kill you as an infant," Emily replied, helping him tidy up.

"She tried to kill you? Emily, I'm so sorry."

"I'd appreciate it if you called me Eymd. And don't be sorry, it's a rite of passage where I'm from."

"Oh," was all Orion could manage, suddenly feeling like his own problems weren't as significant.

Eymd gave him a small smile, her expression softening. "Look, Orion. I get that it hurts. But you can't let it break you. You're stronger than you think."

Orion wiped his tears, a spark of determination lighting in his eyes. "Thanks, Eymd. I'll try."

"Your father sent Rachel home. She'll meet us here tomorrow."

"Okay... I'm not sure I still want to go," Orion admitted.

Eymd rolled her eyes. "Stop being a baby about it. Don't let it change your plans, before you know it, everything will be gone."

She gave him a pat on the back and walked out, leaving him alone with his thoughts

6 Camping

Orion didn't join everyone downstairs for dinner that evening; he just sat in his room, thinking about everything that had happened over the last few days. Finally, he drifted off into a restless sleep and dreamt about losing everyone he cared about. He jumped awake when someone knocked at his door. As he opened his eyes, he saw Alexi walking in holding a tray.

"Good morning, sir. I hope you are feeling better today."

"Yes, thank you."

"Good. Are you still going camping?"

Orion thought for a moment as he speared a bit of bacon and nodded at her.

"I have laid out clothes for you, and everything has been packed into the RV. I've also called Miss Rachel and informed her to arrive by 11 a.m."

"RV? Where did that come from?" Orion asked, puzzled.

"Master Zanek had one delivered last night. I caught him mumbling about it being safer than a tent."

They both laughed at the thought of Zanek roaming around mumbling to himself.

"Right, sir, I will leave you to dress."

"One thing before you leave."

"Yes, sir?"

"Please call me Orion, not sir or master."

Alexi smiled and nodded in agreement as she left. Orion jumped out of bed and rushed to get ready. As he walked down the stairs, he looked out the window facing the gates to see if he could spot Rachel's family coming up the drive, as it was nearly 11. Instead, what he saw turned him pale and made him take the rest of the stairs three at a time.

"ZANEK, ZANEK!" he yelled at the top of his voice.

Zanek came crashing out of a door close to where Orion stood, with shaving foam still on his face, a towel wrapped around his waist, and a blazing golden sword in his hand.

"What is it?" Zanek asked, slightly out of breath.

The front room door burst open, and Orion's family rushed into the hall, looking frightened when they saw Zanek holding the sword.

"The caretaker from the school is standing outside watching the house."

"Who?"

"He started the same day I came here, and I thought he was following me. Now I'm sure of it."

Zanek put his fingers in his mouth and let out a shrill whistle. Orion's security team appeared and surrounded him. Moments later, more people arrived and swarmed out of the front door, heading toward the gate.

"Orion," he heard one of his brothers say.

He pushed one of his guards out of the way so he could see his family. All three of them stood there shaking, and both his brothers had tears streaming down their faces. He rushed forward and grabbed his brothers tightly.

"Don't cry, you two. It will be okay. Zanek will sort it out."

His words crackled from his mouth and had an instant calming effect on everyone. Orion knew it wasn't just the words but the power he had put behind them that calmed everyone. One of the people who had run outside now returned and spoke in hushed tones to Zanek. Once he finished talking, Zanek walked over to Orion, and his blazing sword melted into nothing.

"He was gone by the time they got there. I'm sorry, sir," Zanek sighed.

"It's not your fault," Orion replied reassuringly.

"In light of this event, I would like to bring along a full security detail with us."

Orion knew there was no point in arguing with him about it, but he also knew that when he next saw Lillithan, he would tell her that he thought Zanek could be trusted. The fear that had shown in his face could not have come from someone who meant him harm.

"Very well."

The door opened, and Rachel and her family walked in, followed by the rest of the security team.

"What's going on?" asked Sharon.

"Nothing to worry about, ma'am, just security training," Zanek replied.

"Right, are we ready to go then?" asked Orion.

He walked out the front door and was instantly cast into a shadow from the huge RV that was parked on the driveway. It was as long as a lorry and looked like it would fit ten families into it comfortably.

"Whoa, dude, you don't do things by halves, do you?" said Rachel's little sister Bella.

"If you would all please get on, everything is getting loaded underneath, and once it is done, we will depart," Alexi said.

Everyone piled into the RV. It seemed bigger on the inside, and Alexi started showing everyone to their rooms. When she arrived at Orion's room, she curtsied and beckoned him to follow her. They arrived at a door that looked remarkably like the one from his dream, except it had a plaque that said "Orion" in gold letters.

"We tried to make it as close to the original as we could, but because we had to shrink it, we had to get rid of the wardrobes," she said with a big grin.

She pushed the door open and stepped in with Orion close behind. He gasped as he entered; the room was a replica of the one from his dream, minus the wardrobes.

"But how can this be in the RV?" asked Orion.

"The RV is the same size, but all the doors are portals leading to rooms in the Summer Palace. They were frozen in time before the war. If you look in the top corner of the door, you will see the shimmer of the portal."

Orion looked where Alexi had pointed and saw what she was talking about. In the top corner, there was a blurry patch that constantly changed colour.

"I have one more surprise for you, sir. Master Zanek saved him and has kept him safe until he could be returned to you."

She walked over to a wall and pressed one of the stones. The wall slid up to reveal a secret room. Alexi grabbed what looked like a lead and started walking backward, followed by a creature that resembled a lion but had golden wings attached to it. When it spotted Orion, it ran towards him, and as it did, it changed into a Labrador and licked his face, then ran around in circles around him.

"He is called Pragor and was a gift for you on the day of your birth from your great uncle."

"What is it?" Orion asked.

"He is a Yondelot. He was bound to you and was close to death, yearning to be once again reunited with his partner. Zanek's magic is the only thing that has kept him alive," Alexi explained.

Orion looked at the creature that was now sitting in front of him, wagging its tail. When he stroked Pragor, he was surprised that its fur felt like cool liquid under his fingertips. There was a knock at the door, which made Orion jump. As he did, Pragor turned into a lion and roared at the door. Zanek walked into the room, chuckling.

"What, old friend, don't you remember me?"

Pragor turned back into a Labrador and licked Zanek's face.

"Alexi, would you mind giving us a minute, please?"

"Of course, sir," she said as she bowed and left the room.

Orion was a little nervous, as he had not been alone with Zanek since the first time they had met. Zanek sat down and played with Pragor, rubbing his belly.

"I am not sure if you know, but I was very close to your family," he said, looking up at Orion. "It was due to my own guilt that I was so hard on your human family."

Orion nodded at him but said nothing.

Zanek stood up and started pacing around the room. "When the war started, I ran because I was afraid. When I returned, the war was lost, and you had been sent away," Zanek's voice cracked, and Orion could see the tears in his eyes. "I found out Lillithan had set up a house for you, so I made my way here."

"Where does the book come into it?" asked Orion.

"When I arrived, the book and the three that were here to protect you stood and watched as your life fell apart around you. So, I took it upon myself to get it to you as soon as possible."

Zanek hugged Orion and went back to playing with Pragor. Orion watched the two of them playing and noticed that Pragor could change shapes as he pleased.

"If it's okay, I would like to start your training while we are away."

"What kind of training?" Orion asked.

"Combat training and how to channel your star magic. I see you already have some control over it. You did well calming down your family," remarked Zanek.

Just as Orion was about to reply, they heard a bell chime in the background, and Zanek told him they had arrived at their destination. Before they left the room, Zanek gave Orion two rings and told him to tell Rachel they were for her mother and sister, so they would be okay with star magic and not ask questions.

They walked out of the room and made their way to the entrance of the RV. Outside, they walked into a small valley with a crystal-clear river running through it. Orion noticed that around thirty security guards had already surrounded the camp.

"Egg, can we talk?" Rachel asked from behind him.

"Sure, let's go down by the river."

"So, what's up with all the security?" she asked, looking around.

Orion told her what had happened at the mansion and shared his dilemma with Zanek.

"Wow, Egg, talk about messed up. But he seemed worried about you. My mum and sister keep asking a lot of questions, and I'm running out of excuses."

Orion remembered the rings Zanek had given him. He reached into his pocket and handed them to Rachel. "Give them these. They will rose-tint everything so you can tell them the truth."

"Thanks. So, what are you going to do?"

"I don't know. It's a lot of responsibility," he sighed.

Rachel laughed and hugged him. "You'll be okay. You've always been strong at heart, and look at how many people will be around."

Orion stood up and started skipping stones across the water, thinking about how much danger everyone would be in if they stayed around.

"I don't want people to be in danger, though."

"That's going to happen no matter what. Surely, it's better to have them close so you can protect them."

"True. I'll figure it out. Thanks, hun. You always know what to say."

He hugged Rachel as she got up, and they made their way back to the camp.

"Right, I've got to go and give these to my mum and sister, then explain all of this," Rachel said as she headed off toward her mum.

A table had been set up outside the RV. Orion sat down and looked at the river beyond, wondering what was to come, whether he could deal with it, and what he should do about his family and friends. He was so lost in his thoughts that he didn't notice an eagle soar down and land beside him, where it turned into a cat. It nuzzled him, trying to get his attention.

"Hey, Pragor," Orion said absentmindedly.

The cat nuzzled into Orion's face, purring loudly.

"I don't know what to do. I wish I knew."

Pragor stopped nuzzling and looked at Orion quizzically. Orion laughed and continued stroking him.

"Master Orion, sorry to disturb you. Lunch is ready," Alexi said from behind him. "Where would you like to take it?"

"I'll take it down by the river, please. I need time to think."

He got up and walked toward the river, followed by Alexi. When he reached the spot, he had been at earlier, he stopped and went to sit down, but Alexi stopped him. Her eyes glowed silver, and a table with one chair appeared in front of her. Orion gasped; he had not realized she had powers.

"For you, sir," she said as she pulled the chair out for him.

He took his seat, and as he did, food and drink materialized on the table before him.

"Enjoy," she said as she bowed and walked off.

The smell of the food hit his nose, and he realized how hungry he was. Reaching forward, he picked up a pasty and bit into it. Pragor had turned back into the Labrador and was now sitting under the table, with his head resting on Orion's lap and puppy dog eyes looking up. Orion reached forward, put some food onto an extra plate, and placed it down for Pragor, who rushed forward and started to eat.

"It's so beautiful and peaceful here, isn't it, Pragor."

As he ate, he looked over at his family and friends in the distance and decided he must do everything he could to protect them all. If that meant having such a huge burden on his shoulders, then so be it. He saw Zanek approaching him, so he finished his mouthful of food and stood up to greet him.

"I trust lunch was good," Zanek said, looking at the empty plates.

"Yeah, I think Pragor enjoyed it too."

Zanek conjured himself a chair and sat next to Orion, looking out at the river.

"Such a lovely view. Back home, we had a valley like this, it had the darkest blue river running right through it."

"It's only just occurred to me, where is home?"

"I was wondering when you would ask," Zanek chuckled. "It's a planet on what humans call Orion's Belt. That's why you were named as such, and because the seers said that's how it should be."

"A seer?" Orion asked, confused.

"Yes, it was foretold that your parents would bear only one child, and he alone would lead the system back into the light from the darkest of times that lay ahead."

"How big is this system?" Orion asked.

"Let's see... Before the war, five hundred planets. Then the war happened, and only five planets have remained loyal."

"Five hundred planets?" Orion choked. "How is anyone supposed to manage all of them?"

"They don't. A council is selected by you, and each council member holds fifty planets each."

"But I'm only sixteen, and I don't have a clue about any of this."

Zanek grinned at him and then handed Orion the book he had given him originally.

"That's why you have this and your teachers," he explained.

"Okay, when do I start?" asked Orion nervously.

"Tomorrow, but for tonight, your family needs you."

They both got up and made their way back to the camp, accompanied by Orion's three security guards and Pragor. When they reached the camp, Jake ran up to Orion and hugged him tightly.

"What's wrong?" Orion asked.

"Just thought I'd let you know I love you, big bro."

The rest of the night passed with everyone playing games and telling ghost stories around the fire. Zanek even relaxed a little and joined in. It got to about eleven o'clock, and Orion felt tired, so he went to bed happy in the knowledge that his family was safe.

The next morning, Zanek woke Orion early. He opened the door to find Zanek standing there, holding a staff. "Time to start your training, Orion," he said, his voice firm but kind.

Orion yawned and rubbed his eyes. "Already? I thought we'd have more time to settle in."

Zanek shook his head, smiling. "The sooner you start, the sooner you'll understand the strength within you. Let's go."

Orion dressed quickly and followed Zanek outside to a secluded part of the valley. The air was crisp, and the first rays of sunlight were filtering through the trees. They stopped in a small clearing, and Zanek handed Orion the staff.

"This is a focus for your magic," Zanek explained. "It will help you channel your power until you can do it on your own."

Orion took the staff and felt an immediate warmth spread through his hands. The wood seemed to hum in his grip. "What do I do?"

"Close your eyes and focus. Feel the energy within you, the same energy that helped calm your family yesterday. It's there, deep inside you, waiting to be unleashed."

Orion closed his eyes, taking a deep breath. He tried to remember the feeling from before, the warmth, the power that had flowed through him. Slowly, he felt it again, a spark igniting in his chest.

"Good," Zanek said. "Now, I want you to direct that energy into the staff. Picture it flowing from your body, through your hands, and into the staff."

Orion did as he was told. He imagined the warmth traveling from his chest, down his arms, and into the staff. Suddenly, the staff began to glow, a soft golden light emanating from its tip.

Orion opened his eyes in awe. "I did it."

Zanek nodded, a proud smile on his face. "That's just the beginning, Orion. Your power is immense, but it's also unpredictable. You need to learn control."

They spent the next few hours practicing. Zanek showed Orion how to direct his energy to perform simple tasks, lighting a fire, moving small rocks, even creating a barrier around himself. Each time Orion succeeded, he felt a little more confident, a little more in control.

But it wasn't all easy. There were moments when Orion's frustration got the better of him. When he tried to move a larger rock and failed, the energy backfired, knocking him off his feet.

"It's okay," Zanek said, helping him up. "Magic isn't about force. It's about balance. You have to let it flow naturally."

Orion took a deep breath, nodding. He tried again, this time focusing on the flow of energy rather than the outcome. Slowly, the rock lifted off the ground, hovering in the air before settling back down gently.

Zanek clapped him on the back. "Well done. You're getting it."

As the day went on, Orion began to feel a connection to his magic that he hadn't felt before. It was no longer something foreign and frightening; it was a part of him, something he could wield and control.

After a long day of training, Orion felt both exhausted and invigorated. He returned to the camp to find everyone enjoying a lazy afternoon by the river. Rachel was skipping stones with her little sister Bella, while their mother sat under a tree, reading. Orion smiled at the peaceful scene and let himself relax, sitting on a rock near the riverbank with Pragor curled up beside him.

But the peace didn't last.

A sharp, guttural growl echoed through the valley. Everyone froze. The sound came again, closer this time, and Orion's heart began to race. From the shadowed edge of the forest, a massive wild cat emerged. Its sleek, golden fur shimmered in the sunlight, and its eyes glowed with a fierce intensity. It was larger than any predator Orion had ever seen, easily twice the size of Pragor in his lion form.

The cat locked its gaze on Rachel and Bella by the water. Its low growl reverberated through the air as it crouched, ready to pounce.

"Rachel, get Bella and move back!" Orion shouted, leaping to his feet.

Rachel grabbed her sister and tried to retreat, but the wild cat snarled and lunged forward. Without thinking, Orion stepped between them and raised his hands, instinctively calling on the energy he had practiced with earlier.

The staff Zanek had given him wasn't nearby, but Orion didn't need it now. He felt the familiar warmth ignite in his chest and flow outward. A golden barrier shimmered into existence between him and the charging beast. The wild cat collided with the barrier, snarling and clawing at it. Sparks flew with every strike, but the barrier held.

Rachel and Bella scrambled back toward their mother, who was now clutching them protectively. Zanek and the guards rushed toward the commotion, but they were too far away to intervene.

Orion's heart pounded as he stared into the wild cat's glowing eyes. It wasn't just an animal, there was something unnatural about it. He could feel a dark, malevolent energy radiating from the creature, as if it were being controlled by someone or something.

The cat roared and leaped back, preparing for another attack. This time, it pounced higher, aiming to clear the barrier and land directly on Orion. Without hesitation, Orion focused his energy again. He raised his hands and sent a blast of golden light toward the creature.

The light struck the cat mid-air, knocking it to the ground. It rolled and sprang to its feet, snarling, but now it hesitated. The glow in its eyes flickered, and for a moment, it seemed confused.

Pragor, who had been standing protectively at Orion's side, let out a deafening roar of his own. In an instant, the Labrador transformed into his lion form, his golden wings flaring wide. He leaped at the wild cat, tackling it to the ground. The two creatures wrestled, Pragor's strength and agility matching the wild cat's ferocity.

"Orion, focus!" Zanek's voice rang out as he reached the scene. "It's under a spell. You need to break it!"

Orion closed his eyes, reaching out with his magic. He could feel the dark energy surrounding the cat, a tangled web of malice and control. Concentrating, he channelled his golden light into the creature, pushing against the darkness.

The wild cat roared again, thrashing under Pragor's weight. But as Orion's magic flowed into it, the glow in its eyes began to fade. The snarls turned into whimpers, and the creature's massive body relaxed. Finally, the cat lay still, its breathing heavy but calm.

Pragor stepped back, his lion form towering over the subdued animal. He looked at Orion, his golden eyes full of pride.

Orion knelt beside the wild cat, placing a hand on its side. He could feel its heartbeat, strong but steady. The dark energy was gone.

"What... what was that?" Rachel asked, her voice trembling as she approached with Bella and their mother.

Orion stood, still catching his breath. "I don't know, but it wasn't just a normal animal. Someone, or something, sent it here."

Zanek stepped forward, his blazing sword in hand. "It was likely a test. Whoever is behind this wanted to see how you would handle a threat." He knelt beside the wild cat, examining it closely. "It's a messenger, not a killer. Its purpose was intimidation."

Orion looked at the creature, now curled up as if in a deep sleep. "What do we do with it?"

Zanek's expression softened. "We let it go. It's not evil, it was being controlled. Your magic freed it."

Orion nodded and stepped back. Pragor nudged the wild cat with his nose, then let out a soft growl. The cat stirred, opened its eyes, and looked at Orion. For a moment, they locked gazes, and Orion felt a strange understanding pass between them.

The wild cat rose to its feet, gave a low rumble of gratitude, and turned to disappear into the forest.

As the camp returned to a cautious calm, Rachel hugged Orion tightly. "Thank you," she whispered. "You saved us."

Orion hugged her back, his heart still racing. He had protected the people he cared about, but the encounter left him with more questions. Who had sent the cat? And how many more challenges would he face in the days to come?

One thing was certain, he couldn't do this alone. As he looked at his friends, his family, and Zanek, he knew he had to rely on them as much as they relied on him. Together, they would face whatever lay ahead. Rising from his spot, he made his way back to the R.V., ready to call it a night. The day had been long, and he was utterly exhausted.

Orion found himself back in the main hall of the palace. He recognized it instantly, the crumbling walls and eerie emptiness were unmistakable. The air smelled of dust and magic, a lingering reminder of battles fought and lost. Scanning the room, his eyes settled on Lillithan. She stood by the throne, her back to him, leaning over a table littered with maps and strange artifacts. She flinched at his approach, letting out a startled gasp.

"Orion!" she exclaimed, her voice a mix of surprise and relief. "I wasn't expecting you so soon."

"Neither was I," Orion admitted, his voice heavy with exhaustion. "It's like every time I fall asleep, I end up here."

Lillithan nodded solemnly and gestured to the chair beside her. "Come, sit. We have much to discuss."

Orion sank into the chair, recounting everything that had happened on Earth. He told her about Zanek, his cryptic warnings, and the fear he'd seen in the man's eyes when mentioning the caretaker. As he spoke, Lillithan listened intently, her expression growing darker with each word.

"I know of no others being sent to Earth," she said, her voice low and serious. "You must tread carefully, Orion."

"But what of Zanek?" he asked, his brow furrowed. "Can we trust him?"

Lillithan hesitated, her gaze fixed on the table. "He was a coward when we needed him most, but... I see no reason to doubt his sincerity now."

She reached for a thin sheet of metal in the centre of the table and tapped it. A shimmering projection of a star system sprang to life, its glowing planets orbiting a central star. She pointed to a large blue planet near the heart of the system.

"This was Auratium," she said, her voice tinged with sorrow. "The palace once stood here, before Rohanas destroyed it. He is the Intenfli of the neighbouring star system."

At her words, the star map dissolved, replaced by the image of a man. His shoulder-length hair glowed a sickly green, and his eyes, dark as the ocean's depths, seemed to devour the light around them. A jagged scar marred his face, a testament to his violence.

"He is the reason we went to war," Lillithan said, her voice breaking. "The reason your parents fell."

Orion's throat tightened as he fought back tears. "Why? Why would anyone do something so terrible?"

"Jealousy," she replied bitterly. "He craved power and envied your father for ruling a stronger system."

The revelation hit Orion like a blow. His tears spilled freely as the weight of her words sank in. Lillithan reached across the table and pulled him into a comforting embrace.

"I'm sorry, Orion," she murmured. "I didn't mean to hurt you."

Straightening, he wiped his face and nodded. "Please, go on."

Lillithan hesitated, her fingers sparking with nervous energy as she paced. Finally, she stopped, her expression pained.

"What makes it worse," she said, "is that Rohanas... was your father's brother."

Orion's blood ran cold. "My uncle?" he whispered, his voice trembling.

She nodded gravely. "He has taken over this system, spreading lies that you perished along with your family."

Orion's fists clenched. "What do I do?"

"You must return," Lillithan said firmly. "Claim your inheritance. Take your place as ruler."

"But what about my family?" he asked, desperation creeping into his voice.

Lillithan hesitated again, sparks swirling from her fingertips. "There is a way they could come with you," she said finally. "But..."

"But what?" Orion pressed.

"They could never return to Earth," she admitted. "And it must be their choice."

Before he could respond, an ear-splitting bang shattered the air. Lillithan spun around, her face pale with fear.

"WAKE UP, ORION! THEY'RE COMING!" she screamed, her voice laced with urgent magic.

The words hit him like a tidal wave as a massive fireball hurtled toward them.

Orion bolted upright in his bed, his heart pounding like a war drum. Without hesitation, he sprang up and ran for the door, flinging it open only to collide with a guard. The impact sent him sprawling to the floor.

"Sir, are you all right?" the guard asked, helping him to his feet.

"I need Zanek," Orion said breathlessly.

The guard radioed for Zanek, who arrived moments later, struggling to pull on his robe. His hair was dishevelled, and his face was drawn with worry.

"Orion, what's happened?" Zanek asked, his voice steady but concerned.

Orion told him everything, the dreams, Lillithan's warnings, and the impending danger. Zanek listened, his expression grim.

"It's true," he said finally. "Only you have the power to bring your family with you. But once they leave, there's no going back. It must be their choice, and there is great risk."

As dawn broke, Orion sat with his family at the breakfast table, the weight of his decision pressing down on him. When the meal was finished, he stood and addressed them all.

"I have to go back," he said, his voice steady but filled with emotion. "To my home. To my planet. It needs me."

The room erupted into chaos, voices overlapping in protest. Orion slammed his fist on the table, silencing them.

"This doesn't just affect me," he said firmly. "You can come with me, but if you do, you can never return here."

The gravity of his words settled over the room. After a long silence, his father, Lawrence, spoke.

"I'll go with you," he said. "We're family. We stick together."

His brothers echoed their agreement, but Rachel's mother, Sharon, was less willing. The argument that followed was heated, and Rachel stormed out, leaving Sharon to chase after her.

Hours later, as Orion stood outside with Zanek, where the night sky shimmered with stars, an eerie contrast to the heaviness in Orion's chest. A circular platform appeared in the clearing, glowing faintly. Zanek gestured for Orion's family to stand upon it.

"This will be the last time you see this world as you know it," Zanek said solemnly. He turned to Orion. "Are you ready?"

Orion nodded, though his trembling hands betrayed his nerves. Zanek handed him the ancient spell book, the pages glowing faintly with golden script. The words seemed alive, writhing and shifting as if they were aware of their importance.

"This spell is unlike anything you've attempted before," Zanek warned. "It will transform them down to their very essence, rewriting their molecular structure. They will become like us, star-born, bound to the magic of our kind. But it is not without cost."

"What cost?" Orion asked, his voice faltering.

Zanek's expression darkened. "You must give a part of yourself to each of them, your star magic. This bond will connect you to them, but it will also weaken you temporarily. And remember, once the transformation is complete, they can never return to Earth as they are now."

Orion turned to his family, their faces a mixture of fear and resolve. His father, Lawrence, stepped forward. "We're ready, son. Do what you have to do."

Taking a deep breath, Orion opened the book, its pages glowing brighter as he began to chant. The language was ancient and melodic, each word resonating with power. His hands moved through the air, tracing intricate patterns of light that seemed to ripple and dance. Streams of golden energy erupted from his fingertips, weaving around his family like ribbons of fire and starlight.

"Shanna, Helfana, Zamo, Teagro," he intoned, his voice deepening as the magic surged.

The streams of light thickened, encasing his father and brothers in shimmering cocoons. The air crackled with energy as the spell grew more intense, the colours of the cocoons shifting from gold to silver, then to a kaleidoscope of hues. Orion's eyes began to glow, a brilliant gold light pouring from them as he continued the incantation.

The energy in the air became almost unbearable, a mix of heat and cold that pressed against everyone present. Orion felt his strength waning, his limbs trembling as the spell demanded more from him. Sweat poured down his face, and his breath came in short gasps, but he pressed on.

Finally, the last word escaped his lips, his voice a thunderous roar that echoed through the clearing.

"ROMANGASS!"

A blinding flash of light erupted, forcing everyone to shield their eyes. When the light faded, three glowing pods stood where his family had been. The pods pulsed with life, their surfaces swirling with shifting colours like an aurora. Within, Orion could barely make out the forms of his father and brothers, their faces peaceful as they slept in suspended animation.

Exhausted, Orion stumbled back, nearly collapsing. Zanek caught him, steadying him.

"You've done it," Zanek said, his tone a mixture of pride and caution. "But you're not finished yet."

Orion nodded weakly, straightening himself. He turned back to the platform and began weaving the spell again, this time for himself. The movements came slower now, his energy nearly depleted, but he pushed through. As the cocoon of light began to form around him, he glanced at Rachel one last time.

"I'll miss you," he said, his voice barely a whisper.

"I'll miss you too, Egg," she replied, tears streaming down her face.

The cocoon sealed around him, glowing brighter than the others, a brilliant gold that outshone the stars above. The ground trembled slightly as the pods pulsed in unison, their light casting eerie shadows on the surrounding trees.

Zanek turned to Rachel and her family, handing her a small crystal disc. "This will allow you to contact him. Think of him, and you will appear wherever he is."

Rachel clutched the disc tightly, her tears falling freely. "Thank you," she whispered.

Zanek nodded, then gestured to the rings he held. "Put these on. They will protect your memories of Orion. Without them, you will forget him entirely."

Rachel and her family slipped the rings on, watching as they dissolved into their skin, leaving faint, glowing scripts on their wrists. The glow faded, but the bond remained.

"Goodbye," Zanek said, bowing deeply. With a final wave of his hand, the pods, and Orion, vanished in another flash of light.

The clearing was silent. Where the RV had once stood, only a 4x4 remained. Rachel collapsed to her knees, overwhelmed by grief and the enormity of what had just transpired. Tears streamed down her face as she clutched the crystal disc, the last connection she had to her best friend.

The night sky stretched above, vast and unchanging, as if mocking the irrevocable change that had just occurred below.

Orion awoke feeling slightly refreshed. He reached out and touched the cocoon, which crumbled around him. As the room came into view, he gasped. He was in a room surrounded by beeping machines. In the centre, there was a white table with various instruments laid upon it.

"Attention on deck!" a guard said as Orion walked out of the alcove that had housed his pod.

"No need for that," Orion replied, his voice oddly commanding.

Orion felt an overwhelming sense of familiarity with his surroundings, and to his surprise, he seemed to know everything about the war and the ship he was traveling on. Zanek entered the room, walking straight toward Orion. When he stopped, Orion noticed that he was now at least two feet taller than Zanek and was wearing a simple cotton robe.

"Your Highness, I took the liberty of downloading some vital information into your pod while you slept," Zanek said, bowing slightly.

"What's happened to me?" Orion asked, his voice laced with confusion.

"You have undergone the transformation into your true self," Zanek explained. "There's a mirror over there if you wish to see."

Orion walked over to the mirror and gasped. He was now at least eight feet tall. His skin had taken on a shimmering silver hue, his hair was spiked, and his eyes, just as they were in his dream, were gold. He turned to look at the three remaining pods where his father and brothers still slept.

"When will they wake?" Orion asked. "And where is Eymd?"

"They'll wake in about two days," Zanek replied, studying Orion closely. "Eymd is attending to her duties. There's much to do while they sleep."

"Okay."

Zanek began pacing around the room, picking up bits of equipment and then placing them back down neatly.

"You have much to learn about what's happened since you've been gone," Zanek continued, "and how you are connected to all the planets within your system through your heritage."

"That's a lot to learn in such a short space of time," Orion replied, looking concerned. "By the way, how is it that everyone speaks English?"

"Well, just like I downloaded information into your pod, the same was done to everyone here," Zanek explained. "As you can guess, I don't usually look like this, but I haven't gone into my pod yet because I wanted to be here when you awoke."

Orion was now pacing around the room, panicking about all of his new responsibilities. How could he stop a war that had been going on for 300 years?

"How will I be able to communicate and understand everyone?" Orion asked.

"What language are you speaking now?" Zanek asked.

"English," Orion answered, puzzled.

"Wrong. You started speaking Mankassan as soon as you began to panic," Zanek said with a slight smile.

Orion gasped. He hadn't even noticed that he had changed languages. It frightened him a little. Zanek beckoned a man over who was the same height as Orion, with emerald green eyes and skin a dark shade of purple. His face looked as though it had been slashed open many times.

"This is Vando, my second-in-command. He will take care of you while I'm in my pod," Zanek introduced.

Vando stepped forward and bowed deeply to Orion.

"My Lord," he said softly.

"I must retire to my pod now," Zanek said, bowing, before walking over to the empty alcove Orion had left. A silver cocoon formed around him as he stepped in.

"If you would please follow me, I'll lead you to your chambers," Vando requested.

"Yeah, lead the way. How long have you been in the army?" Orion asked.

"Two hundred years, sir. I wished to follow in my father's footsteps," Vando replied.

"But you look as young as me."

"My father, Zanek, is over five hundred years old, sir."

"Zanek is your dad? He never said," Orion replied, looking at Vando. There was no resemblance between them at all.

Vando made his way toward the door, followed by Orion. When the door opened, they stepped into a long white corridor. As they walked, Orion kept seeing tiny people moving around in the corner of his eye, but when he turned to look, no one was there. Vando laughed when he saw Orion turning his head rapidly, trying to catch sight of the tiny people.

"You're not going mad," Vando said, laughing softly. "They're called Danans. Your new eyes will get used to them soon. It took me almost a week when I first came aboard."

"What are they?" Orion asked.

"They are the inhabitants of a small moon in the system. They keep the ship's systems running smoothly," Vando explained.

Orion nodded and continued walking. As they moved through the ship, Orion noticed parts of it appeared to be breathing, pulsing gently with life. They turned a corner and entered a golden corridor lined with suits of stone armour. At the end of the corridor, two suits of armour stood in front of a door, standing to attention. This was echoed all along the hall.

"These are the Stone Guard," Vando explained. "They were crafted by the best star smiths there were."

Orion stared, wide-eyed, at the suits. They were truly remarkable, and if you squinted, you could make out the sparkling stardust within them.

"They have always guarded your family," Vando continued, "because they can't be bought, they can't betray, and they only answer to you. Watch this."

Vando stepped forward and pressed his hand against the door. Red sparks erupted from it, and the Stone Guards stepped forward with their swords drawn at his throat.

"Quick! Tell them to stand down, before they chop off my head!" Vando exclaimed.

"At ease!" Orion commanded hastily.

The guards lowered their swords and stepped back into position.

"Thanks," Vando said with a grin. "I couldn't deal with getting my head reattached. Go ahead and put your hand on the door to open it."

Orion stepped forward, hesitant. What if there had been some horrible mistake and he wasn't really who everyone thought he was? He gulped and slowly pressed his hand against the door. It glowed green, and the door melted away, allowing them entry. Vando went inside first, followed by Orion.

The room before them was beautifully decorated. A wooden table sat in the centre, with a massive throne at one end and six high-backed chairs along each side. The walls looked like mirrors, and the floor seemed to stretch infinitely, showing the stars zooming past.

"This is the council chamber," Vando said. "To the left are your quarters. I'll show you to the bridge and send the cleaners in here. As you can see, this room has been sealed for three hundred years."

"Three hundred years?" Orion asked. "I've only been on Earth for sixteen."

Vando chuckled. "Ah, I see my father neglected to tell you how time passes differently. Please, take a seat, and I will do my best to explain."

He studied Orion briefly, wondering if the boy could take much more after all that had happened to him in just a week.

"First of all, I must ask how you are holding up with everything that has happened."

"Well, I've always known that I didn't quite fit in, so it's good to know I wasn't going crazy," Orion replied. "I feel slightly lost about who I should trust," he said, feeling the tears start to stream down his face. "Finding out my mom never wanted any of us, and the loss of my best friend are the things I'm finding hardest right now."

As he turned his head to try to hide his tears, Vando smiled softly at him.

"There is no shame in your tears, sir," Vando said gently. "Most people would have fallen apart by now. But I suspect you'll make a great leader."

Orion smiled back at Vando, appreciating the man's comforting words.

"Well, time passes differently where we are from. For every year that passes on Earth, eighteen years and nine months pass for us. Although you are sixteen in Earth years, you are three hundred in ours."

"That kinda sucks," Orion chuckled, trying to lighten the mood. "Means I'm older than my dad."

Vando laughed and jumped up from his seat. "Right, let's get on with the tour."

As they left the room, the door re-materialized behind them, and the Stone Guard returned to attention. They turned down another corridor and walked for what seemed like an eternity. Finally, Vando stopped in front of an open door and walked inside. Inside were four people who turned and bowed as Orion entered.

"This is Sanjen. He will teach you about star magic and its origins," Vando said.

A tall man with purple-tinted skin, red eyes, and tattoos of constellations across his face and arms stepped forward and shook Orion's hand vigorously.

"This is Laurena. She will teach you combat magic," Vando continued. As Laurena stepped forward, Orion noticed she looked remarkably like Lillithan.

"Finally, you have Garent and Rishga. They will teach you the history of our people and etiquette," Vando finished. The last two men stepped forward and bowed. Orion was sure they were twins.

"Nice to meet you all," Orion said as he bowed back.

"Your classes will start this evening with Master Sanjen and Laurena," Vando added.

As they left the room, Vando turned to Orion. "Laurena looks very much like Lillithan. Is she Lillithan's daughter?"

"No, she's Lillithan's sister. And she is also the best combat star mage around."

"How long will it take for us to arrive at our destination?" Orion asked.

"We will arrive in two days, sir."

They stepped into what Orion could only describe as a glass lift. As the doors closed, he saw the vast universe beyond. The lift detached itself from the hull of the ship and made its way slowly upward.

"It's beautiful," Orion gasped.

"Yes, it is," Vando replied, reaching forward and pulling a microphone out of nowhere. "Take us above the ship."

The lift lurched and shot upward until they hovered about ten feet above the ship. Orion gasped as the ship looked alive, there were no engines in sight, and it moved like a manta ray swimming through space.

"What is it?" Orion asked.

"It's a ship, but at the same time, it's more than just a ship," Vando explained.

"Is it alive?" Orion asked, his curiosity piqued.

"In a way, yes. It's like the Stone Guard, but it changes its shape and interior depending on what it's needed for," Vando said.

"Remarkable," Orion whispered in awe.

"Take us to the bridge," Vando said into the microphone.

The lift rocketed toward the top of the ship, where a massive dome awaited them. Orion ducked as they approached, only to realize they had passed through the dome as if it were water. Inside, trees and plants grew, some purple, others shifting colours. Birds chirped, and Orion wondered if there were any other animals below.

"Why is this here?" Orion asked.

"This place provides the atmosphere for the whole ship," Vando explained.

The lift halted and hovered briefly before descending to the grass below. It stopped with a hiss, and the doors opened to reveal the bridge.

"Attention on deck!" a voice called out.

Everyone in the room jumped up from their stations and saluted as Orion entered.

"At ease," Vando commanded.

The six people in the room returned to their seats, tapping at unseen items. Three chairs faced the stars beyond.

"This is the bridge," Vando explained. "From here, you can control the fleet once they arrive."

"How do you control the ship?" Orion asked, noticing the lack of wheels or computers.

"When you sit in the command chair, the ship integrates with you," Vando explained. "All you have to do is think, and the ship will do it."

Orion looked around the bridge in awe. Before he could ask more questions, a young man accidentally dropped a tray of tools onto the floor.

Without thinking, Orion stooped down to help him pick up the items.

"Sire, you must not," the young man said, his voice nervous.

"Nonsense, I want to help," Orion said.

Vando stood behind Orion, a smile tugging at his lips. He had heard his father speak of their new ruler's kindness, but seeing it firsthand was another matter entirely.

"Thank you, sir," the young man said, his voice filled with gratitude as Orion picked up the last item.

"It's no problem. What's your name?" Orion asked.

The young man bowed deeply. "Maximus, sire."

"Please, call me Orion," he said, feeling uncomfortable with the formalities. "What do you do here?"

"I help where I'm needed, picking things up and cleaning up after the troops."

"Stay there for a moment," Orion ordered.

Orion walked over to Vando and asked him to follow. He glanced back at Maximus, wondering why he looked so different from the others. He was six feet tall, skinny, with long mousey brown hair, and normal-looking skin, except for his eyes. One was yellow, the other pink.

"What's Maximus's story?" Orion asked once they were out of earshot.

"He was born on the ship when we were orbiting Earth. That's why he doesn't look like a normal soldier. But he wanted to help, so my father gave him the job he currently holds," Vando explained.

"What is he good at?"

"He's good at paperwork, with his words, and making people listen when needed. But, as you've already seen, he's a little clumsy."

Orion nodded, mulling it over. "Is there another job for him?"

"You are still yet to appoint a royal advisor, sir," Vando pointed out.

Orion thought for a moment, then made up his mind. He walked back toward Maximus, who was now bowing deeply, trying to hide his nervousness.

"Please kneel," Orion said, his voice firm.

Maximus kneeled, his face pale with fear.

"Vando, your sword," Orion ordered.

Tears streamed down Maximus's face, his bottom lip quivering.

"S... sire, I'm s... sorry if I offended you," Maximus stammered.

"Silence," Orion commanded.

Everyone on the bridge stopped working and stared at them. Vando unsheathed his sword and handed it to Orion. Orion tapped the sword on Maximus's shoulders.

"I, Orion, hereby promote Maximus to the role of royal advisor," Orion declared.

Everyone gasped. They had expected Orion to behead Maximus, not promote him.

"Rise, please," Orion said.

Maximus stood up, wiping away his tears, and bowed deeply. "Thank you, sire," he said with a big grin on his face.

Vando stepped forward and waved his hand, and Maximus's coveralls disappeared, replaced by golden armour and a surcoat bearing two trumpets beside the royal crest. The room erupted into applause.

"Right, sir, you have your first lesson now," Vando whispered to him.

Orion nodded, and the trio entered the lift again. This time, the journey felt much faster, with blurs of colour zipping past them as the lift moved. When it stopped, there was no hissing sound, and the doors opened to reveal a corridor with two doors along it. Vando stopped at the closest one and opened it for Orion.

"Just in here, sir. We will wait for you outside."

The office inside was simple yet spacious, with a large wooden desk at the far corner, a wide open space in the centre, and bookshelves lining the walls.

"Orion," a voice called out from nowhere, making him jump.

Suddenly, Master Sanjen appeared, stepping out of a wall and floating across the room.

"Evening, Orion," Sanjen said, his voice calm but with an edge of urgency. "Let's just jump right in, shall we?"

"Evening, Master Sanjen."

"Please, take a seat, and we'll begin."

He beckoned Orion to sit down in an empty chair, then sat opposite him.

"As you've been told, the star magic that runs through you is the most ancient kind, and it's far stronger than any I've seen," he paused for a moment. "Your uncle's powers are almost as strong as yours, but he's had three hundred years to perfect his own."

Orion nodded.

"But the stars in this system will always answer to you more, as you are the rightful heir. That being said, it comes with a terrible burden you must bear."

"What kind of burden?" Orion asked, his curiosity growing.

"You are connected to every planet you rule. If a planet is in pain or suffering, you will feel it. You will hear it."

"But I haven't felt anything."

"Since we found you, I've been blocking those signals so they wouldn't overwhelm you," Sanjen explained. "But once we reach any planet within Orion's belt, I won't be able to block them anymore. Prepare yourself. You'll have to find out why they are in pain and then fix it."

"I understand... I think," Orion said, nervous yet determined.

Sanjen clapped his hands and stood up. "On a brighter note, once we arrive at the planet, you'll be crowned and given your sceptre."

"Sceptre?" Orion asked, confused.

"Yes, it helps you channel your magic."

Sanjen reached behind him and pulled a book from the shelf, handing it to Orion. "I'd like you to read this before our next meeting."

"Okay."

"That's all for today. I know you have much more to do," Sanjen said with a smile.

Orion stood up and bowed, then left the room. Maximus and Vando were still waiting outside.

"All done, sir?" Vando asked.

"Yes, what's next?" Orion replied.

"Your combat class with Lady Laurena, sir," Maximus answered, stepping up behind them.

Orion nodded, and they made their way to the next lesson.

They made their way down the corridor, the sound of their footsteps echoing in the vast, pristine ship. Vando opened the door to the training room, and Orion stepped inside. The room was spacious, with a combat dummy set up in the centre, a training mat on the floor, and a strange-looking mirror that seemed to glow softly along one wall. The air was heavy with anticipation.

"Sire, I am going to send a low-level volt ball at you," Laurena's voice called from across the room. She stepped out of the glowing mirror, her presence commanding. "Let's see how much of your ancestor's knowledge flows through you."

Orion stood tall, ready, though he wasn't entirely sure what to expect. "What do you want me to do?" he asked, his voice steady.

"Whatever feels natural," Laurena replied, her eyes twinkling.

Orion took a deep breath, clearing his mind. His eyes locked onto the small orb of energy Laurena had summoned with a flick of her wrist. The ball crackled with electricity as it hurtled toward him, but before it could reach him, Orion's eyes began to glow a brilliant gold. The world around him seemed to slow, the volt ball freezing in mid-air, and even Laurena stood frozen, caught in the same suspended time.

He stepped to his left, the ball now hanging motionless before him. As soon as he moved, time resumed, and the lightning ball shot across the room, crashing into the combat dummy with a resounding explosion. The force sent bits of the dummy flying in all directions, the energy of the impact vibrating through the room.

"Well done, sir, well done!" Laurena exclaimed, clapping in approval.

But her eyes darkened as she narrowed her gaze at Orion. "Let's see what else you can do."

Without warning, Laurena lunged at him with a knife drawn, her movements swift and fluid. Her expression was determined, but Orion was ready. His eyes glowed once again, and with a wave of his hand, Laurena was thrown backward with a force that made her skid across the room, crashing into the far wall.

She stood up quickly, dusting herself off, her face a mix of surprise and admiration. "I don't think I have much to teach you, sire. Your ancestor's magic protects you and assists you without even thinking. You have a power far greater than I anticipated."

"Thank you," Orion said, feeling a sense of relief wash over him.

Laurena gave him a respectful bow. "Goodbye, sire," she said as she turned to leave.

Orion exited the room, his mind racing with what had just happened. He had never felt such power before, and yet it felt so... natural. It was as if it had always been a part of him, waiting to be unlocked. He almost bumped into Vando, who was standing outside the door.

"Done already?" Vando asked with a raised eyebrow.

"Yeah, I think I'm starting to understand," Orion replied, still processing the experience. "I would like to go to my chambers now."

Vando nodded and led him back through the corridors to his quarters. When they arrived, Orion noticed that his room had been cleaned, and Pragor had been let in. The creature bounded up to him, its tail wagging happily. Pragor licked his face in greeting, and Orion chuckled, kneeling down to give the creature a scratch behind the ears.

"If you need anything, sir, just ring the bell," Vando said, bowing as he stepped out of the room.

Orion was left alone in his quarters. He sank onto the edge of the bed, still feeling overwhelmed. Pragor settled next to him, curling up contentedly. Orion absentmindedly stroked the creature's fur, his mind racing with all the new knowledge he had gained in such a short time. But something else lingered in his thoughts, something he couldn't shake.

A sudden bang from inside the wardrobe broke his concentration. He jumped up, his heart racing. Slowly, he approached the wardrobe, his hand reaching for the handle. The door creaked open, and as it did, a figure stepped out.

Orion froze, his breath caught in his throat. There, standing before him, was the caretaker from his school, the man he had seen only in brief glimpses throughout his life. The one who had always seemed too ordinary yet too watchful, always just out of reach.

Orion tried to shout, but his voice failed him. His mouth opened, but no sound came out. Panic surged through him. How had this man gotten here? What was he doing in this place, on this ship?

The caretaker smiled faintly, a cold, unsettling smile. "Hello, Orion," he said, his voice calm and unnervingly familiar. "We need to talk."

Pragor roared as he changed into a bear, placing himself between Orion and the man, barring his teeth. Orion's body tensed as he prepared to defend himself, every instinct telling him to fight. The man stepped forward, unfazed by the massive creature standing between them. Pragor swiped at the air, his claws grazing the space before the man's face, but the man didn't flinch. He simply stood still, unyielding.

"Please, do not press it," the man murmured softly, his voice calm and measured. "I mean you no harm."

"Who are you?" Orion demanded, his voice sharp with suspicion.

"I was made by your father before he died, to pass on his last words to you," the man replied solemnly, as if the weight of the words had carried them through time to this very moment.

Pragor walked cautiously toward the man and sniffed him. After a few moments, he turned into a kitten and began to purr, curling up at the man's feet. Orion watched the transformation in stunned silence, unsure whether this was a good sign. He took it as such and relaxed, sitting back down.

"You look so much like them," the man said, smiling gently, his expression filled with an emotion Orion couldn't quite place. "Your parents loved you dearly."

"What should I call you?" Orion asked, his voice softer now that the danger had passed.

"Call me Ed," the man replied. "But it's not important. The message I carry is."

Orion nodded, the curiosity burning inside him. "I'm ready. Please, tell me."

The room fell silent, and Ed's face went blank. Suddenly, a loud explosion echoed from his mouth, followed by a male voice, deep and filled with sorrow.

"Orion, if you are hearing this, your mother and I have ceased to exist. There will be difficult times ahead, and I hope you will be strong. A part of us will always be with you. Be everything I know you can be, and make me proud." The voice cut off with a harsh cough, before continuing in a female voice.

"My darling son, we love you. Follow your heart, make the right choices, and don't stray from the honourable path. I…" Another explosion of sound interrupted, and then, there was silence.

Ed closed his mouth, his gaze softening as he looked at Orion, who was frozen in place, golden tears streaming down his face. He knelt down beside Orion, his hand gently resting on his shoulder. This was the first and last time Orion would ever hear his parents' voices, and the pain surged through him like a tidal wave.

"They loved you so very much," Ed said quietly. "And it hurt them terribly to send you away."

Orion sobbed harder, clutching Ed in a desperate embrace. The ache in his chest felt as though it would tear him apart. He didn't even know them, yet the loss felt as if it were his own.

"I have to give you the knowledge your parents imprinted into me," Ed said, pulling away from the embrace. "I will share it with you now."

Orion wiped his tears away, nodding, trying to steady his breath. "Okay," he whispered.

Ed stood up and placed his hands gently on Orion's temples. The warmth from Ed's touch was all-encompassing, and as it spread through Orion, a blinding light exploded in the room. The force of the light almost knocked Orion unconscious, and he felt the knowledge of countless generations flood his mind, his ancestors' history, their wisdom, their magic, all rushing through him in an overwhelming torrent.

As the light dimmed, Orion fell to the ground, his mind reeling from the onslaught of information. When he opened his eyes again, Ed was gone. In his place, there was only a pile of ash on the floor, a symbol of the sacrifice Ed had made in passing on the legacy.

Orion could feel the magic of his ancestors now, flowing through him, alive in every cell of his body. He felt their strength, their wisdom, and their sadness.

A knock at the door broke Orion's focus. He looked up, still trembling from the experience, his senses still heavy with the new knowledge.

"Come," he called just before the knock echoed through the chamber.

"Are you okay, sir?" Maximus asked as he entered the room, his eyes scanning Orion for any signs of distress.

"Yeah," Orion replied, trying to smile. He wiped the remaining tears from his face and forced himself to look more composed.

"Why is there ash on the floor, sir?" Maximus asked, his gaze flicking to the pile where Ed had stood.

"It's not important," Orion muttered, still feeling the weight of his parents' final words pressing on his chest. He took a deep breath, focusing on the present.

"Are you sure you are feeling okay, sire?" Maximus pressed again, noticing the fatigue in Orion's eyes.

"I will be," Orion assured him, his voice steady now, though the sorrow still lingered beneath the surface.

Maximus nodded but looked concerned. "Master Vando wanted me to inform you that we will be arriving at the planet soon."

"I thought it was going to take two days," Orion said, confused.

"It has indeed been two days, sir. We thought it best to leave you to think," Maximus explained.

"But I've only just come in here," Orion said, bewildered.

"No sir, as you can see, there is still food from last night on your desk," Maximus said, eyeing Orion up and down.

"Oh, okay," Orion replied absentmindedly, realizing how much time had slipped by.

"If you could get ready, your family is eager to see you," Maximus added.

Orion jumped up from the bed, surprised at how he'd lost track of time. He quickly donned the armour laid out for him. Maximus helped fasten the clasps, and once the surcoat was on, the royal crest appeared, glowing in the light. The armour adjusted to fit him perfectly, moulding itself to his form.

"Right, let's go and see my family," Orion said, his voice determined now.

"Your gauntlets, sir," Maximus said, handing him a pair of remarkable silver gauntlets. The crests upon them seemed to flicker with fire.

Orion slid them on, feeling the magic of his ancestors flowing through them, and followed Maximus out of his room into the council chamber.

"Evening, sir," Vando greeted as Orion entered.

"Evening," Orion replied, feeling the weight of the day bearing down on him.

"I'll go inform your family that you're awake," Vando said before turning and leaving the room.

"I'll get you some food, sire," Maximus offered, his voice calm and professional.

Orion took a seat at the head of the table. Moments later, Alexi walked in, carrying a tray. She placed it before him and removed the lid.

"What is it?" Orion asked, eyeing the exotic green meat on his plate with curiosity.

"It's Mankeit, sir. Tastes a little like beef," Alexi explained.

Orion speared a piece and popped it into his mouth. As he chewed, he realized it did indeed taste like beef, savoury and rich. Alexi bowed and left, leaving Orion alone to eat.

There was a knock at the door, and in walked Orion's family. They had undergone a smaller transformation than Orion, but they were still changed. They were now taller, their eyes glowing silver, their once curly hair now spiked, and their brown skin was speckled with silver and gold. Their faces were more defined, more chiselled.

Orion's brothers were the first to reach him. They gave him a warm hug, their smiles full of relief and happiness, before sitting beside him. His father smiled as well, sitting next to Orion and resting a hand on his shoulder.

The chamber door opened, and Zanek walked in, followed by six others. They all took seats around the table, studying Orion with curiosity. Zanek stood at eight feet tall, his skin a moving flame, his hair now short and blue.

"Evening, Your Highness," they all greeted as they sat.

Orion inclined his head in acknowledgment. Zanek stood up and began speaking, his voice commanding.

"Your Highness, these are the remaining lords and ladies of the council. Introductions, if you please."

Sanjen, the tall man Orion had met earlier, stood up.

"We have already met, my lord. I am Lord Sanjen, and I control the Pinaxir system on your behalf," he said, sitting back down.

The woman next to him stood. She had long auburn hair, a pale blue tiara atop her head, and white eyes.

"I am Lady Valoria, and I control the Lignorium system on your behalf," she said, sitting back down.

The next person, a younger woman, stood. She wore a pink tiara and a red and gold flowing dress.

"I am Lady Untria, and I control the Comparni system," she introduced herself.

"I am Lord Noxium, and I control the Xanruir system," a man next to her said, glaring at Orion with cold grey eyes.

"You will address His Highness with the respect he deserves," Zanek roared.

"Why should I?" Noxium sneered. "He is but a child and has no claim to the throne. His uncle has claimed it and has done a good job for the last three hundred years, he should be put down like his parents."

The tension in the room was palpable. The Stone Guard entered, weapons drawn.

"HOW DARE YOU? SEIZE HIM!" Zanek shouted.

The Stone Guard moved swiftly, grabbing Noxium's wrists, and their hands turned into shackles, restraining him.

"What would you like done with him, sir?" Zanek asked.

"Place him in a cell. He will stand trial once we arrive," Orion said, his voice firm.

The Stone Guard marched out of the room, dragging a screaming Noxium behind them. The room resumed its calm as everyone took their seats.

"Right, now for the last two introductions," Zanek said.

A tall purple man with a turban and the royal crest stood up.

"I am Lord Jandavinr, and I control the Quirtiam system for you," he announced, then sat down.

The final person stood. She had pale blonde hair, a golden tiara, and a gold-and-silver dress.

"Cousin, so nice to finally meet you. I am Lady Kirand, and I control the Fortanda system for you," she said with a smile.

"Nice to meet you all," Orion said, smiling warmly.

"We will arrive at the planet in five minutes," Zanek said. "When we do, a procession of cars will be waiting for us. Then preparations for your crowning ceremony will begin. Any questions?"

"I have one," Orion asked. "What planet are we going to?"

"We are going to Yimmana, sire," Zanek replied. "You will meet the last remaining council members, Lord Rafna and his wife, Lady Tanzia."

Just then, a speaker crackled to life behind Zanek, and a female voice boomed out.

"Prepare to disembark. We will be landing momentarily."

Orion stood up and dismissed the council.

"Orion, what should we do?" Anton asked.

"Come with me and stay close," Orion instructed.

They left the council chamber, following Zanek and Vando to the exit ramp. Behind them, the Stone Guard moved into formation, flanking Orion protectively. When they reached the large door, Zanek stopped and pressed a button. There was a loud hissing noise, and the door opened. Trumpets blasted as Orion stepped out, but the sound of the trumpets was quickly drowned out by an excruciating scream that made Orion double over in pain.

"What is it, sire?" Maximus asked, rushing to his side.

"Can you not hear it?" Orion gasped, his breath ragged.

"Hear what?" Maximus asked, confused.

"The screaming. The pain and the anguish," Orion murmured.

"It's the planet, sire. It's in a lot of pain," Sanjen's voice echoed in Orion's mind. "Remember what I told you to do. Use your magic to reach out."

Orion took a deep breath, his connection to Yimmana already growing stronger. He reached out with all the magic inside him, feeling his body lift off the ground. As his feet left the surface, a surge of power filled him. His body shone with every colour of the rainbow, tendrils of light shot toward the planet's surface, and everything around him went silent.

The tendrils of light reached deep into the planet's core, and Orion could feel the heartbeat of Yimmana, faint but persistent, struggling to survive. The softest voice he had ever heard spoke in his mind, neither male nor female, but soothing.

"I have waited many moons for you, Intenfli. I never thought I would feel the warmth of your magic again."

"Who are you?" Orion asked, his voice filled with awe.

"You already know the answer to that."

"You're the planet's consciousness."

"Indeed, I am. It has been too long. What am I to call you?" the voice gasped. "As I know the ancient magic that runs through you, but the face is new."

"I am Orion, son of Auren and Aurorina. Tell me, why are you screaming?" Orion asked, his heart heavy with the planet's pain.

"The people above have forgotten the old ways," the voice said, full of sorrow. "They dig where they should not. Their suffering I cannot bear. I feel them starving and dying, only to be replaced by more. We are all connected."

"What has made them forget?" Orion asked.

"The one that leads them only cares about his gold and riches, not the people or the planet."

Orion's connection to the planet deepened, and he could feel the heartbeat of Yimmana fading. The planet was dying, but its last bit of energy was being used to speak to him, to plead for help.

"You are dying," Orion cried, his voice full of anguish.

"Yes, I have held on all these years in the hope of your return, but I fear it is too late to do anything."

"NOOO!" Orion shouted, his body glowing brighter than ever before.

He felt his power surge. The magic inside him, inherited from his ancestors, became an unstoppable force. The scream that erupted from him was louder than anything the world had ever heard, a wave of energy that rattled the very core of Yimmana. The sky above cleared, the rivers purified, and the earth healed. Yimmana's heartbeat quickened.

Orion's magic connected every living being on the planet, their hearts beating as one. He didn't take their magic gently. He ripped it from them, taking all the Star magic, they could give, and poured it into the planet. The connection between them all became so deep, so tangible, that the planet's wounds began to heal. The land revitalized, the skies cleared, and the oceans turned crystal blue again. New life sprang from the earth.

"I thank you, Orion," the planet's voice whispered.

"There is no need to thank me," Orion said, his voice soft. "I do this for you, Yimmana."

With his final burst of energy, Orion descended to the planet's core. He embraced it with all his strength, breathing new life into its heart. The planet, once on the brink of death, now pulsed with vitality.

As he returned to the surface, the world around him had transformed. The factories and machines that ravaged Yimmana's surface were gone, floating in mid-air, disassembled by the magic he had summoned. The people of the planet, once bound by suffering, now stood united in their gratitude and awe.

"Remarkable," Sanjen said as Orion descended, the glowing aura around him fading as he landed.

"No one has ever brought a planet back from the brink of death before," Sanjen added in awe.

"We have to go to the palace now," Orion said, his voice steady but tinged with exhaustion. He leaned on his two brothers for support.

They made their way down the ramp, and Zanek opened the door to the middle car for Orion to get in. As the car doors closed, the procession began, winding through the streets of Yimmana. Orion looked out the window, taking in the poverty of the people. A child sat on the sidewalk, begging for food. The fields lay barren, and the houses, once homes, now stood in ruins.

"Are you okay, big bro?" Jake asked, concern in his voice.

"Yeah, just a bit tired," Orion replied with a faint smile.

The cars slowed as they approached the palace gates. The grandeur of the palace stood in stark contrast to the city outside, but it wasn't just the palace Orion saw. He felt the weight of his responsibility, the planet's healing had only just begun, and there was still much work to do

10 The Palace

The procession of cars came to a sudden stop outside the grand marble steps of the palace, the sound of the engines echoing off the ancient stone. Orion's heart beat faster as the magnitude of the moment hit him. The palace, once an oppressive symbol of corruption, now felt like a place of destiny,his destiny. To his surprise, the Stone Guard had already arrived, their towering, statuesque forms lining the steps, their armour glinting under the pale sunlight. Behind them, palace guards peered curiously, their gazes tracking his every movement.

Zanek opened the car door and, noticing Orion's weakened state, offered his support.

"Sir, we can do this later," he said gently, offering Orion his hand.

But Orion's resolve was unwavering. "No, we do this now," he replied firmly, his voice filled with authority that surprised even himself.

Zanek nodded, understanding the weight of the moment, and helped Orion out of the car. They both turned to face the grand staircase leading up to the palace doors. The air was heavy with anticipation, but it was also charged with something more, an electric undercurrent of change.

As they began their ascent, the palace doors burst open with a loud, metallic clang. A plump man, his robes of pure silver flowing like an overripe fruit in the breeze, came running down the marble steps, his gait unsteady and frantic. His head seemed too small for his body, as though he were a caricature of himself, and when he reached Zanek, he halted, glaring at the two men with an arrogant sneer.

"Why are you here, peasants?" he bellowed. "I bet it's to steal my gold!"

Zanek didn't flinch, his voice calm and measured. "This is Intenfli Orion, and he is here for his coronation. You can't have missed the commotion when we arrived."

The man looked perplexed for a moment before bursting into laughter. "No, the palace is soundproof and magic-proof, so I heard nothing," he admitted nervously, catching the disgusted look on Orion's face.

"Then perhaps you should pay closer attention," Orion muttered under his breath, his patience wearing thin.

Behind them, Alexi pushed through the crowd, her movements graceful yet determined. "If you would like to follow me, sire, I will show you to the main bedchamber," she said, guiding them past the flustered lord.

As they ascended the stairs, the Stone Guard moved forward with a tremendous crash, the sound reverberating throughout the grand courtyard. Two of the guards pushed open the massive palace doors with ease, and the rest followed, forming a line inside the grand hall. The entrance was marked by towering columns and intricate carvings of past rulers, their faces frozen in stone, witnessing the arrival of the new ruler.

Orion paused for a moment, feeling the weight of the history around him. But there was no time to linger. "Right, let's go," he said firmly, ready to face what awaited him.

The vastness of the main hall was staggering. As they entered, Orion immediately understood where the wealth of the planet had been spent. The walls were covered in towering piles of diamonds, shimmering jewels, and gold bars, glittering in the sunlight that filtered in through the high, arched windows. The sheer extravagance of it was overwhelming, and for a moment, Orion's anger flared. This wealth had been taken from the people, hoarded by those who had no respect for the land or its people.

"I want to go to the throne room first," Orion said, his voice cold.

Alexi, who had been walking beside him, nodded and led the way. "It's up ahead, sir."

When they entered the throne room, the sight before them took Orion by surprise. The room was opulent beyond belief, golden chandeliers hung from the high ceiling, their light cascading down onto a vast marble floor. But amidst the grandeur, something far more disturbing caught his eye. A large woman, sprawled across two massive sofas, was being hand-fed by servants. Her attendants, both dressed in rags, stood by, fanning her lazily.

"What do you want?" she hissed, barely acknowledging their presence.

Before Orion could react, Zanek's hand shot out, and a whip of lightning appeared in his palm. With a swift flick, he struck the woman's ankle, pulling her harshly from her lounging position. She slid across the floor, her body thumping against the cold stone.

"You will address His Highness Intenfli Orion I, accordingly," Zanek roared, his voice filled with righteous fury.

The woman gasped in shock and immediately scrambled to her knees. "Forgive me, Your Highness," she muttered, her voice a mixture of fear and disdain.

Orion, however, did not acknowledge her. He walked past her, the grandeur of the thrones at the far end of the room drawing his attention. Two magnificent thrones, each grander than his own, sat side by side. He stopped in front of them, his gaze falling upon the intricate carvings that adorned the seats, each one more elaborate than the last.

Without hesitation, he sat in one of the thrones, his posture straight and commanding. As he settled into the seat, he beckoned Maximus forward and whispered to him.

Maximus nodded and stood at attention, his face impassive. "Lord Rafna and Lady Tanzia approach, His Royal Highness wishes to speak with you."

Lady Tanzia scrambled on her knees across the floor and bowed in front of the throne while lord Rafna walked over slowly and merely bowed his head towards Orion.

"You have both disrespected my parents' honour," Orion began, his voice clear and resonant.

"Your Highness, you do not understand," Lady Tanzia said, her voice trembling.

"SILENCE!" Orion shouted, his voice booming through the hall, causing everyone to stop in their tracks. His power, his authority, was undeniable. "I am speaking!" he continued, his eyes blazing with intensity. "You are a disgrace. Your people live in squalor while you lived in luxury. Children beg for food while you were hand-fed…"

"But it's ours! They live to serve us!" Lord Rafna sniffed, his voice dripping with arrogance.

"I SAID SILENCE!" Orion's fury was palpable now. He pointed at both of them, and light shot from the tip, striking their mouths and sealing their lips.

The room was silent as Orion stood, his gaze never leaving the two humbled nobles. "You will live as your people have lived. You will do the work you've forced others to do for you. And as for your powers… they will be bound."

He waved his hand, unsealing their mouths.

"Please, Your Highness, not that. I can't do manual labour. It's beneath me," Lord Rafna pleaded.

"You will," Orion replied coldly. "You will clean the streets, live as you've made others live, and feel the suffering you've caused."

Orion stepped forward, and with both of his hands raised over their hearts, he pulled. Thin threads of starry light appeared and coiled themselves in his palm. There was a blinding flash of light, and as Orion stepped back, the threads absorbed into his skin. Their powers and their connection to the stars, was severed.

"Take them away and put them to work," Orion ordered.

The guards moved forward, attempting to drag Lady Tanzia out of the room. She was too large, so more guards had to come to her aid. As they struggled to remove her, their cries of anger and defiance echoed through the hall.

Orion stood still, watching them, his resolve unshaken. "Right, now time for their replacements," he said with quiet determination.

Orion returned to the throne and took a deep breath. There was much to be done. After a moment of thought, he stood once more.

"Zanek and Alexi, please step forward."

They both moved forward and bowed deeply before him.

"Vando, your sword please," Orion commanded.

Vando stepped forward, unsheathing his sword, and handed it to Orion.

"It seems like having a couple running this system has led to its fall, so instead, I appoint two of my trusted aides to run it as I would," Orion said, his voice steady with authority.

With a swift, decisive motion, Orion tapped the blade to each of Zanek and Alexi's shoulders.

"I declare thee Lord Zanek and Lady Alexi, rulers of the Onartian system," he announced, his words echoing in the throne room.

Both Zanek and Alexi rose. A wave of magic flowed from Orion's hands, and Alexi's maid outfit dissolved into a flowing silver dress, a tiara appearing atop her head. Zanek's armour turned silver, and a small crown appeared on his head. As he continued his work, Vando's armour shifted into gold, and a dark red surcoat with the royal crest appeared on him.

"Vando, I hereby promote you to Vice Admiral," Orion said, nodding to his loyal servant.

"Sir, I… thank you so much," Vando replied, his voice filled with gratitude.

Orion turned to Zanek and Alexi. "Right, what's the first thing you two wish to do?"

Zanek and Alexi exchanged a brief conversation before Alexi stepped forward.

"We will provide gold and food to the people. We will also begin restoring the city," she said, her voice firm and filled with purpose.

"That is acceptable," Orion nodded. "But do not fall into the same trap that Rafna and Tanzia did. Treat my people well."

"Yes, sire," they both replied in unison.

"Right," Orion said, his eyes scanning the room. "I believe it is time for the coronation to proceed."

As Orion stood from the throne, Pragor bounded over to his side, his massive paws thundering on the floor. Together, they walked to the royal chambers. The room was as grand as the rest of the palace: gold-framed windows, diamond-encrusted mirrors on the walls, a ruby dresser that stretched across an entire wall. Orion gazed at his reflection in a nearby mirror, his face looking weary yet resolute.

He caught the eyes of his brothers, who were watching him with a mixture of concern and awe.

"You guys adjusting, okay?" he asked, breaking the silence.

"It's a little weird," Jake admitted, his voice filled with both excitement and uncertainty.

"I think it's cool," Anton said, a grin spreading across his face.

"It's a little strange, but I'll get used to it," Lawrence added.

Orion smiled, nodding in agreement. "I'm happy to have you all by my side."

Alexi entered, carrying four parcels. She handed one to each of Orion's family and then gave him the largest one.

"You will need these, sire," she said with a knowing look.

They dressed in silence. Orion's family donned robes of gold and silver, while his own was pure gold, with a high-backed cloak to match. Just as Orion fastened the last clasp on his cloak, there was a knock at the door.

"It is time, sire," Vando's voice came from behind.

Orion stood and followed Vando out of the room. The moment he stepped into the grand hall, the sound of trumpets filled the air. Palace guards and council members bowed low as he passed, their respect for him evident. He made his way to the throne, the weight of the world settling on his shoulders. He took a seat, his brothers stood on one side and his father and Vando on the other. A man in a golden robe covered in stardust then moved behind Orion and placed the crown upon his head.

"By the power of the ancestors and the royal bloodline, I crown thee Intenfli Orion I. May your rule be long and honourable."

As the crown touched his head, the sceptre turned to liquid and flowed into Orion's arm, settling into a phoenix-shaped tattoo on his forearm. The entire hall erupted in cheers and applause, the sound deafening in its intensity.

"My gift to you," he heard the planet's voice say inside his mind: *"Thank you!"*

The planet itself erupted in song, a melody of happiness, hope, and renewal.

"Right, for my first act," Orion began, his voice ringing out over the crowd. "Can Jake, Anton, and Lawrence step forward, please?"

The three of them bowed in front of the throne. With a wave of his hand, smaller versions of his own crown appeared on each of their heads.

"You will now be known as Prince Anton, Prince Jake, and Prince Lawrence. This is in title only, and you will have no claim to the throne."

Maximus approached Orion and whispered in his ear. Orion stood, his voice booming across the planet.

"Ladies and gentlemen of Yimmana, your time of suffering has come to an end. It would be my great honour if you would attend the feast that has been prepared for this gracious occasion."

Maximus whispered again. "Emergency teleport system."

Orion nodded, smiling. "If you would like to attend, please step onto any emergency teleport system, and I will transport you to the palace in five minutes."

Orion turned to see his brothers shooting sparks at each other with their newfound powers, Lawrence looked at him and they both laughed.

"You two, do you want to help me set up the hall?"

The twins jumped not realizing their brother was watching them and came to stand beside him.

"Everyone, step aside please," bellowed Vando.

"Dad, do you want to help?"

"Yes, but I don't know what I'm doing," Lawrence replied.

"Hold out your hands and think of long tables with chairs along them, I think maybe a hundred tables with twenty chairs each should do."

They held out their hands and tables began to appear, they were very mismatched, one of them had conjured a bright pink table and chairs, at the sight of it the whole hall erupted in laughter. When they finished, there were tables and chairs of all sizes and colors.

"Right, now to bring people here," said Orion rubbing his hands together.

He cleared his mind and though one-word *'Teleport.'*

The hall buzzed with energy as people began to teleport in, filling the room in moments. The feast was set, the tables filled, and laughter echoed throughout the hall.

A child approached Orion's table and smiled at him, she reached into her pocket and drew out a red flower, as she held it out towards him, he stood up and walked around the table towards her and sat down on the step beside her.

"Is that for me?" he asked.

The girl nodded, and Orion held out his hand to take the flower.

"Thank you very much, what's your name?"

"Andrea," she whispered back.

"Well, that's a lovely name, would you like to come and sit at the table with me?" he asked.

Again, the girl nodded, so Orion got up and swooped her up into his arms, when he sat down Andrea tucked straight into a plate of food, while Orion looked around the hall at all the happy people.

11 Echoes of the Past

Everyone was laughing and eating to their heart's content. Orion didn't think he had ever seen such grateful people. He watched as some of the children loaded up their fourth plate of food, while others began hiding bits in their pockets. These people had been through so much, and he was happy he could make their lives a little easier. Their faces, once hollow with fear and hunger, now beamed with a glimmer of hope.

But the warmth of the moment was suddenly shattered. The hall fell silent. The planet spoke.

"He is approaching."

"Who is?" Orion asked, his heart beginning to race.

"The one who has destroyed many of my kin."

The doors of the hall suddenly burst open with a deafening crash, shaking the very stone walls. The stone guard surged forward, their armoured footsteps like thunder as they surrounded Orion's table. People screamed in terror, the air thick with panic as they rushed toward the exit in a chaotic frenzy.

Orion's eyes narrowed, his pulse quickening. He stood, the power that surged within him ready to erupt. The people's fear, his people, gnawed at his soul. This wasn't just a threat to him, it was a threat to them.

"STOP AND SIT BACK DOWN!" Orion bellowed, his voice cutting through the panic like a whip.

A stillness fell over the room. The people, trembling but resolute, slowly returned to their seats, their eyes fixed on him, some with hope, others with uncertainty. But they stayed. They trusted him.

"You are in no danger," Orion said, his voice cold and commanding, though his heart was burning with fury. "I will protect you all."

A see-through figure materialized before him, flickering in the air like a ghost. His presence sent a chill down Orion's spine. He immediately knew who it was. The same man who had ruined his family, the same man who had torn his world apart. The man who now stood between him and his future.

"Uncle," Orion said, his voice low, controlled, but full of malice. "To what do I owe this pleasure?"

Rohanas, the embodiment of cold power, looked down at Orion with disdain, his holographic form standing tall and imposing. A smirk twisted his lips as he spoke.

"Orion, I see you have returned to defy me by helping these people," Rohanas sneered, his words dripping with venom.

"Defy you?" Orion repeated, his tone sharp as a knife. "You have no claim to any of this. These people are not yours to rule, and neither am I."

"You dare speak to me like this? The one true Intenfli? The one who has built this empire? You are nothing but a child pretending to wear his father's crown," Rohanas growled, his voice becoming a weapon in itself. "Your defiance will be your downfall."

Orion's blood boiled. He took a step forward, his every muscle tense, his gaze never leaving his uncle's form. He placed Andrea, his closest confidante, on his chair before he strode toward the hologram of his uncle, the weight of his fury nearly overwhelming.

"Enough!" Orion snapped, his voice a thunderclap, vibrating through the hall. "What have you come here for? To threaten me? To threaten them? You'll find that I do not care for your games."

Rohanas' eyes burned with cruel amusement. "I will let you have this day, Orion. I will let you play hero. But make no mistake. You will surrender your claim. Or..." Rohanas' voice dropped to a deadly whisper. "...you will die. Just like your pathetic father and mother."

The words hit Orion like a physical blow. His heart thudded painfully in his chest as loss for the parents he never got to know. His eyes darkened with rage, and the room seemed to grow warmer, the air thickening as his emotions roiled inside of him.

"Then prepare for a battle, Uncle," Orion said, his voice seething with a fury that could not be contained. "Because you've destroyed everything my parents worked so hard to build. And I will not stand idly by and watch you destroy everything else I love."

Rohanas' smile twisted into something far more dangerous, like a predator circling its prey. "Survival of the fittest, my boy," he said with a cold chuckle. "I'll give you a week. One week to surrender. If you do not, I will crush you and all your pitiful followers beneath my heel."

The hologram of Rohanas flickered and disappeared, his words lingering in the air like poison. The room was still, but the silence was deafening. A low murmur started to ripple through the hall as people looked to Orion, their faces a mix of fear and hope. They had seen the anger in his eyes, the very anger that would either save them or destroy them.

Orion stood frozen for a moment, his hands clenched into fists at his sides. The weight of the threat, the burden of his responsibility, all crashed into him at once. The fear in the room, the fear in their eyes, it gnawed at him. He wasn't ready. He wasn't strong enough. But he had no choice.

With a strangled gasp, Orion collapsed. His body gave out under the pressure, his vision swimming as darkness crept in. His knees buckled, and the floor rushed up to meet him.

Orion awoke and looked around the room. He was no longer in the hall but in a bedchamber, with Vando, Zanek, and Alexi standing around his bed looking worried.

"How are you feeling?" Vando asked.

"I'm fine. What happened?"

"You used a lot of your star magic, and your body's not used to it yet," Zanek answered.

Orion sat up and looked around the room he was in. It was different from the one he had been in earlier, but just as magnificent, covered in gold, gems were strewn everywhere, and he could swear the furniture was made of platinum.

"I'll go and inform everyone that you're awake," Alexi said from beside him.

"Who's still here?" Orion asked, curious.

"Everyone from the feast, sire. No one wanted to leave you."

"We must prepare for my uncle's arrival."

Orion got out of bed and headed toward the bathroom. After changing back into his armour, he grabbed his crown but decided he didn't need it right now and placed it back down.

"Let's go," he said as he walked toward the door.

Everyone followed him as Alexi led them down a network of corridors until they reached the main hall. When they entered, everyone within fell silent and bowed to him as he walked toward the main table.

"Thank you all for remaining here. Please, do not bow, as there is no need to. It is I who should bow to all of you for staying and believing in me."

He waved Maximus over and asked where the safest place was for people when the war started.

"I'll find out for you, sir."

Maximus bowed and walked off toward a door on Orion's left. He returned moments later with a flustered-looking woman who wore a purple tunic with a crest of keys and a set of orange gates. She approached Orion and curtsied.

"Your Highness, I am Tameretta, the prison mistress."

"Why has Maximus brought you to me?" Orion asked.

"He said you wished to know where the safest place was for all of these people, and I know of such a place."

"And… where is it?"

"It's below the palace. The previous Lord had it installed so he could hide his treasures, but it's more than large enough to hold everyone on the planet inside comfortably," she replied.

"Thank you."

She bowed and went to leave but turned back to face him.

"Begging your pardon, sir, a lady is waiting to be sentenced. Shall I bring her up?"

"Take her to the council chamber," Orion said.

She bowed once again and made her way toward the door she had entered from. Orion got up and made his way toward the door marked "Council Chamber." He pushed the door open and was surprised to see the room looked exactly like the council room on the ship. The stone guard lined the walls, and the council members were in their seats waiting for him. Orion took his seat and looked around at the stars beyond. It was truly beautiful, and he felt like he could just get lost in them for hours.

The door opened, and Tameretta walked in, followed by a person who had a black sack over their face. Whoever it was had shackles of shining silver. Orion could see the magic that infused them and wondered why they would need such strong magic to bind them.

"What is this person accused of?" he asked.

"High treason, sire. This will be the first time I've seen her. I was told to lock her up with her sack on by Intenfli Rohanas's second in command," replied Tameretta.

She pushed the woman forward and removed the sack. Everyone in the room gasped and bowed deeply at the woman who stood before them. Orion had seen her face somewhere before, but he couldn't quite place it.

"Your Highness," Lady Kirand said.

It then dawned on Orion who this woman was and where he had seen her before. She was the woman from the painting in his study, but she looked different. Her clothes were in tatters, her once bright face now looked sunken, her eyes and skin had lost their shine, and her once brilliant golden hair now sat matted against her head, with tears of red running from her eyes.

"Mum," Orion gasped, his voice cracking as he stepped forward.

The moment he spoke, the woman's eyes, which had been clouded with confusion, flickered with recognition. She looked at him, her expression blank, before her lips trembled.

"Orion…?" she whispered, her voice raw, like it had been broken by years of pain.

Tears welled up in Orion's eyes, but he forced them back. He could hardly breathe, his heart pounding in his chest. "Mum, it's really you. You're alive. You…."

She winced at his touch as he reached out to her. She recoiled slightly, her body tense with fear, but he gently placed his cloak around her trembling shoulders. The roughness of her skin, the scars from the torture, sent a wave of agony through him. He tried to comfort her, but she pulled away.

"I've been waiting so long, Orion," she whispered, her voice breaking, "So long…"

Orion gently lifted her chin, his fingers shaking as he touched her scarred face. "You're safe now. They won't hurt you anymore."

But the woman's eyes were still lost, and her voice was hoarse. "You're not my son. He's dead. He can't be alive."

Orion's heart shattered as he knelt before her, holding her hands, feeling the coldness in her touch. "Mum, it's me. Orion. Your son."

The confusion in her eyes deepened, and she seemed to be fighting something inside her, as if a dark veil was clouding her memories. "You look like him… but they said he was gone…" she muttered.

A strangled cry escaped Orion's throat. "I'm here, Mum. Please, don't you remember me?"

Before she could respond, Lord Sanjen stepped forward and examined her head. His eyes glowed faintly, and his face tightened with concern.

"Orion, she's been tortured. Her memories… they've been altered," he said softly.

Orion's blood ran cold. "Can you help her?"

Sanjen nodded slowly. "It will take time, but we'll try. She's been through horrors I cannot begin to imagine."

Orion felt a surge of rage, but he clenched his fists to keep it in check. The thought of his mother being tortured this way, broken by the very people he had sworn to destroy, filled him with an unrelenting fury.

"Please," he whispered, his voice strained, "fix her. Do whatever it takes."

Sanjen placed a hand on Orion's shoulder. "We will. We will, Orion."

Orion stood, but his heart was heavy with guilt and grief. The warmth of his mother's presence should have felt like a reunion, but instead it was like a fragile dream, something on the verge of slipping away.

He could feel the anger burning inside of him. His uncle thought she was dead, so why had someone hidden her away all this time? Orion could feel his humanity slipping away. He wanted to hurt someone for this, and he would let a whole planet burn just to find out who was responsible.

"Calm yourself, Orion. We will find who is responsible for this," Sanjen said.

Orion opened his eyes; his whole body was engulfed with fire, and the gold door behind him began to buckle from the heat he was producing. Sanjen was holding Orion's arm, wincing in pain as the flames hit him. When Orion looked down, he was horrified to see that Sanjen's hand was burned to a crisp from where he had touched Orion.

"I am so sorry," Orion said, his voice filled with regret as the flames extinguished.

"It's okay. I probably should have mentioned that your powers are tied to your emotions, so try not to let them get the better of you," Sanjen said with a slight wince, though his voice remained calm.

Orion nodded, his gaze falling to the remnants of his friend's hand. He took Sanjen's hand within his own, and sparks shot into Sanjen's palm, healing it immediately.

"Thank you," Sanjen murmured. "Now, let's get back in there, and remember to take it slow with your mother."

They both entered the room to find everyone bustling around, trying to make Aurorina comfortable. Sanjen walked over to her, and she smiled at him.

"Sanjen, you look old," she said softly.

"Yes, Your Majesty. Many years have passed since we last saw each other," Sanjen replied, a faint trace of nostalgia in his voice.

She eyed him suspiciously before suddenly bursting into laughter, the sound manic and hollow. "You'll have to do better than that, Rohanas, making me think I've missed so many years of my son's life," she shouted at the wall.

Sanjen stepped forward, placing a gentle hand on her head. She immediately fell into a deep slumber, and Lady Kirand, Lady Valoria, and Lady Untria rushed forward.

"If it's okay with you, sire, we will take her to your chambers, bathe her, and let her rest," Lady Valoria said, her voice soft and respectful.

"That's fine," Orion said, though his tone was laced with concern, "but I would like my cousin to remain, please."

Lady Untria murmured a few words, and Aurorina's body was gently hoisted into the air, drifting out of the room behind the two ladies.

Orion took a seat on his throne, his mind heavy with the gravity of everything that had just unfolded. He looked at Lady Kirand, his gaze intense.

"Cousin, I'm sorry to keep you here, but I have a few questions," he said, his voice strained.

"It is understandable," she replied, her posture respectful but her eyes cautious.

"To which side of my family are you related?" Orion asked, his curiosity rising.

She chuckled softly, finding the question slightly amusing. "I am related to your mother, sire. She is my father's sister."

Orion nodded, understanding the family connection more clearly. "I have always remained loyal to her, unlike my father, who joined Rohanas."

Orion met her eyes. "I will give you, my trust. Do not make me regret it."

"I won't, sire. Now, may I please go and tend to my aunt?" she asked, her patience wearing thin.

"Of course."

As she rushed out of the room, the remaining council members took their seats and looked at Orion, waiting for him to speak.

"Right, there are two people I wish to talk to: one being Noxium, and the other being Rafna," he said, trying to remain calm despite the chaos weighing heavily on his shoulders.

There was a knock at the door, and Jake walked in, hurrying over to his brother and sitting beside him.

"What's wrong?" Orion asked, noticing the concerned look on Jake's face.

"Nothing. I just got told you were awake. We didn't get to see you after you collapsed," Jake said, his voice carrying a mixture of worry and relief.

"Oh, okay. Where's Dad and Anton?" Orion asked, feeling a flicker of hope.

"They're helping people in the hall. I said I would come and check on you," Jake replied, trying to offer a reassuring smile.

"Okay, I have a few things to take care of before I can see them," Orion said, his focus drifting back to the business at hand.

The chamber door opened once more, and in walked the palace guards, followed by Rafna. They stopped in the centre of the room, saluted Orion, and pushed Rafna forward. He looked rough. In the few hours he had been put to work, his robes were now black, and he appeared exhausted.

"Why did you have my mother locked up in the dungeon?" Orion asked, his voice low and dangerous.

"Y... y... o... u... rr mother, sire, she's dead," Rafna stammered, clearly shaken by the intensity of the confrontation.

Orion stood up, his fists clenched. He slammed his fist down on the table, and it shattered under the force.

"Enough! I have no time for your games!" he yelled, his voice laced with fury.

Rafna dropped to his knees, tears streaming down his face. He slowly began to edge his way toward Orion, his voice desperate.

"Sire, I swear I had no idea who she was. I got orders saying I was getting a war criminal and that no one was to set eyes on her, including me."

Orion's eyes narrowed. "Who gave the orders?"

"The insignia on the letter... was that of one of the generals. When orders come from that high up, you do not question them."

Orion slumped onto his throne, his mind racing. "Great. Another person I now have to deal with."

"Go back to work," Orion said coldly, dismissing Rafna with a flick of his hand.

The guards stepped forward and escorted Rafna back out of the room. The chamber fell into an uncomfortable silence, with everyone looking at Orion, unsure of what to say.

"Who knows of my uncle's generals?" Orion asked, his voice calm but with an undercurrent of tension.

Lord Jandavinr spoke up. "I know of two, sir."

The others all shook their heads to show they knew nothing about the generals.

"One is called Pyannaf. He is violent and bloodthirsty. The second is Mirriana. She is cruel and would poke your eyes out just for looking at her the wrong way."

"Would any of them do this without my uncle's knowledge?" Orion asked, his voice sharp.

Jandavinr shook his head. "No, both are very loyal to your uncle."

The door burst open, and Vando came running in.

"He's escaped, sire. Noxium is gone," Vando said, his voice breathless.

"How?" Orion asked, his stomach sinking.

Vando stopped to catch his breath, and Orion saw the huge lump on his head.

"We got ambushed, sire. An assassin group jumped us as we were transferring him from the ship. Some of my team are dead."

Orion stood up and approached Vando, waving his hand. The lump on Vando's head disappeared.

"It's okay, we'll find him," Orion said, his voice determined.

Orion began to pace around the room, his thoughts racing. His mother, who he had thought dead, was now alive. And yet, the planet he was standing on was now in danger from his tyrant uncle. The weight of it all pressed down on him like a collapsing star. He had to find answers, and he would not stop until he did, no matter what the cost.

12 Whispers of Fate

The rest of the day passed without incident. The vault beneath the palace, once brimming with secrets, was being emptied. Orion oversaw the operation with meticulous care, but most of the items, vases, gold, diamonds, old documents, failed to capture his interest. His thoughts kept drifting back to his mother and the strange revelations surrounding her return. Each item moved from the vault felt like another piece of a puzzle, but the pieces were too small to tell the full story.

When the workers brought out a massive chest, however, something about it caught Orion's eye. The royal crest was stamped on it, and the craftsmanship was unlike anything he had seen before. It looked ancient, worn by time but meticulously cared for.

"Stop, please," he commanded, his voice firm.

The men paused, confusion flickering across their faces. With a bow, they carefully set the chest down in front of him. Orion circled it, inspecting it for any clues. The chest had no keyholes, no visible means of opening. Only a sense of mystery lingered around it, as if it were waiting for him.

"Can you take it to the second bedroom?" Orion asked, his curiosity piqued.

The men bowed again, hoisting the chest and moving down the hall. Orion watched them disappear around the corner before turning back to his task. His thoughts, however, remained anchored to the chest. There was something important about it, he could feel it in his bones.

The next few hours passed in a blur. Orion directed the removal of more items from the vault, the rhythmic motion of the workers and the clang of metal against stone nearly lulling him into a trance. Yet his mind kept racing. How had his mother survived? What had they done to her? And now, with his uncle's treachery looming, what would his role be in all of this?

Eventually, Alexi found him and led him to the main hall for dinner. He followed her, the faint scent of roasted meat and bread filling the air. As he entered the hall, he was greeted by a dozen faces, some familiar, others not. The room was full of chatter and laughter, a small comfort in such turbulent times. His brothers were already seated, and he slid into place between them.

"I hear your mother is alive," Lawrence said from beside him, his voice quiet but full of concern. "How is she?"

Orion's heart tightened at the mention of her. "She's okay. Sanjen is taking care of her, but he's not sure if she'll ever be the same. There's... there's a lot of healing left to do. Not just physically, but mentally."

Lawrence nodded, his expression sombre. "Hopefully, he'll find a way to help her."

Orion took a deep breath, the weight of his words pressing down on him. "Hopefully," he repeated. But deep down, he wasn't sure. The bond between him and his mother was undeniable, and to see her broken, her memories fractured, was something he couldn't yet fully process.

"Well, I don't mean to be insensitive," Lawrence continued, glancing around the table at the others, "but what happens to us now that she's returned?"

Orion chuckled, though it held little humour. "Nothing's changed, Lawrence. We've got a war to fight, and we're going to fight it. Now let's eat. I'm starving."

His appetite was hollow, but the motion of eating, a mindless, mechanical act, was comforting in its own way. It allowed him to push thoughts of war and destruction aside, if only for a moment.

As he scanned the room, his eyes settled on the little girl he'd seen the day before. She was sitting alone, her tiny hands clutching a spoon, her expression blank. Her family, wherever they were, seemed absent. Something about her troubled him, but he couldn't place why. Her presence felt... wrong, out of place in a room that, for the most part, buzzed with optimism.

Dinner passed uneventfully, and afterward, the work of clearing out the vault resumed. The sound of footsteps echoed through the corridors, accompanied by the occasional clink of metal. They were converting the vault into apartments for those fleeing the conflict above, a necessary but grim task. Orion had already decided that he would stay in the council chamber above, where he could oversee the coordination of the armada.

When preparations were nearly complete, he returned to the main hall. A sombre mood had descended over the room as people gathered to hear what he had to say.

"Ladies and gentlemen," Orion began, his voice steady despite the turmoil he felt. "There are tough times ahead, but I ask you to bear with us. We've come together, and we need to stay united. Anyone who wishes to join the fight against my uncle is welcome to join the palace forces. The rest will follow Lord Zanek and Lady Alexi into the vault, where you will be safe."

A tall, scarred man stood up from the back of the room. Half of his face was badly burned, and he was missing an arm. He looked like a man who had seen the worst the world had to offer.

"What about our houses?" he asked, his voice rough but steady.

Orion paused. It was a valid question. "They will be rebuilt. And if you wish to stay on the surface above, you are more than welcome to," he replied. His words were intended to comfort, though he wasn't sure they would.

The man nodded and sat down. Orion stepped away from the table, his gaze lingering on the faces in the crowd. Some looked relieved, others uncertain, but all of them seemed to carry the same weight he did, the weight of knowing their world had been upended, their futures uncertain.

He made his way to the second bedroom, eager to investigate the chest further. When he entered the room, a soft, pulsing glow illuminated the space, drawing him toward it. The chest sat there, as if waiting for him.

As his fingers brushed against the lid, the entire chest vibrated, and tendrils shot out, latching onto his wrists. For a moment, Orion froze, his heart pounding in his chest. He felt a sharp prick on his wrist, and then, just as quickly, the tendrils retracted. The chest flashed with his name, and he stepped back, startled.

"What the hell was that?" Orion muttered, forgetting for a moment that he was alone. His voice echoed in the empty room.

He heard a soft click. The lid of the chest sprang open, and Orion hesitated before leaning forward, gently touching it again. This time, nothing happened. He peered inside and found a collection of strange and powerful objects: a book, gauntlets, a matching crown, a jar filled with yellow liquid, a sword hilt, a silver-and-gold bow, and a small, rainbow-colored sceptre. His eyes lingered on each item, a sense of awe creeping over him. Each of them felt... important, as if they belonged to someone destined for greatness.

Orion reached for the book first. He opened it, but the pages were blank. No writing. No instructions. Just an empty vessel, like so many of the mysteries he had encountered in his life. He closed the book and turned his attention to the sceptre. When his fingers brushed it, the sceptre transformed into liquid, seeping into his skin. It spread up his arm, merging with the symbol that already adorned it. As it travelled, a sharp, searing pain bloomed within him, and suddenly, the room around him vanished.

"YOU ARE THE CHOSEN," a deep, resonating voice boomed from the darkness.

"Who's there?" Orion demanded, his voice trembling with a mix of fear and defiance.

"We are not important, yet we have been waiting for you," another voice replied, softer but just as powerful.

The ground beneath him gave way, and he began to fall. The sensation was disorienting, like the very fabric of reality had unravelled.

"You are the one they call Orion?" a third voice asked, laced with curiosity.

"Of course, he is," a fourth voice retorted, sharp and commanding. "He opened the chest, didn't he?"

"Why am I here?" Orion called out, his voice desperate.

Suddenly, his feet hit something solid. The darkness evaporated in an instant, replaced by an endless expanse of white. It was as if he were standing in the middle of nowhere, surrounded by floating spheres of various colours. The sensation was disorienting. The world seemed both infinite and contained, an unanswerable paradox.

"He looks a bit scrawny," one of the balls commented, its voice filled with judgment.

"I thought he'd be taller," another ball added.

Orion frowned. "Excuse me, what are you?" he demanded.

The balls zipped around him, changing colour as they moved. One hovered in front of him and spoke again.

"We are all. We are nothing. We were here before, but we cannot be here after."

Orion shook his head, trying to make sense of the cryptic words. "That doesn't make sense. Why am I here?"

"You are here to learn what must be done, what should be done, and what cannot be undone," the ball answered in riddles.

Orion was getting frustrated. "Why won't you just tell me what I need to know?"

The ball spun away, replaced by a smaller blue one.

Sorry, we are a little jumbled, the blue ball said. *We will answer your questions, but you must wait a little longer.*

The balls suddenly stopped moving, huddling together. There was a flash of red light, and then they disappeared. In their place, two figures materialized.

The first was a woman whose hair flowed like a river of light. It trailed behind her, glowing with an ethereal radiance. She wore a dress that shimmered, blending seamlessly with the surrounding white, and a crown of flowers sat atop her head. The second figure was a man, around Orion's age, dressed in black robes, his crown of fire flickering like a live flame.

The woman and the man approached Orion, bowing before him in unison.

"Come, child," the woman said, her voice soft and melodic. "Let us sit and discuss matters of great importance."

A stone table appeared, with three chairs. Orion took a seat opposite them, his mind swirling with questions.

"We are the beginning," the man said.

"The beginning of what?" Orion asked, feeling a knot form in his stomach.

"We are the creators of everything," the woman answered, her eyes filled with ancient wisdom.

Orion's confusion deepened. "What do you mean?"

"We saw what needed to be done," the man continued, his voice low and hoarse. "We gave of ourselves to create life. To create you."

The table before them morphed into a screen, showing images of worlds forming, planets materializing from nothing. Orion watched in awe as the two figures breathed life into the planets.

"Your mother... was chosen," the woman said, her voice tender. "You were created from us and from the royal line. You are the only one of your kind."

Orion's breath caught in his throat. He felt the ground shift beneath him, as if the very fabric of his existence was unravelling. He had always known he was different, but this was beyond anything he could have imagined.

"Don't cry, child," the woman said, her voice softening. "You are more important than you know."

Orion looked up at her, tears stinging his eyes. "I don't understand. Why me?"

"Because you must evolve," she whispered. "And when you do, everything will change."

Orion trembled, torn between fear and something else, something that felt like destiny.

"Do not fear what is to come," the man said, his voice steady and calm. "We will speak again, child. But for now, you must go."

Before Orion could respond, the world around him fractured, and he found himself back in the room with the chest. Time had passed, but it felt as though no time had passed at all. The symbols on his arm now pulsed with energy, entwined in a pattern of two dragons.

Orion looked down at the book in his hands and closed the chest, his mind reeling with the enormity of what had just happened.

As he walked back to the main hall, the weight of the moment pressed down on him. When he returned to the dining table, Maximus was the first to notice the change.

"Sire," Maximus said, his voice quiet but filled with concern. "What happened to your eyes?"

Orion didn't understand what he meant. Confused, he summoned a mirror. When he saw his reflection, a chill ran down his spine. His eyes were now completely black, yet within them, tiny galaxies spun, planets, stars, nebulae.

"What's happening to me?" he muttered, barely recognizing the man staring back at him.

Maximus hesitated, but then nodded, as though understanding that words could not explain what had transpired.

"Your apartments are ready," he said softly.

Orion nodded absently, his mind still spinning. The book in his hands seemed to pulse, the words on the cover shifting like living things. He had no idea what any of it meant, or what role he was meant to play in the events unfolding around him.

"I'm going to bed," he said abruptly, his voice heavy with exhaustion.

As he walked down the hall, a faint sound behind him made him turn. There, in the shadows, stood Andrea. Her face was as unreadable as ever, but her presence now felt darker, more unnerving.

"Are you lost?" Orion asked, his voice thick with unease.

She shook her head, taking a step toward him. "No," she replied, her voice cold and empty. "But you are."

Orion froze, his breath catching in his throat. "Where are your parents?"

"Dead," she said, the words slipping out like ice.

"How did they die?" Orion asked, his voice barely above a whisper.

"I killed them," she said, a wicked grin twisting her lips. "Just like I'm going to kill you."

Before Orion could react, a stone guard materialized between them. But Andrea didn't hesitate. With a wild, unearthly scream, she tore through the guard like it was made of paper, her eyes glowing with a malevolent energy.

Orion bolted, his heart hammering in his chest. He ran toward the nearest door, slamming into it with all his strength. He struggled to find the handle, panic rising within him.

Finally, he found it and rushed inside, slamming the door shut behind him. Sirens rang out in the distance, and Andrea's scream echoed in the hallway.

Orion's hands trembled as he turned, relieved to see Pragor lounging on the bed. The familiar sight was a small comfort, but his mind was far from settled.

He wasn't alone.

Vando appeared, his figure a steady presence in the chaos.

"Sire," Vando said, his eyes scanning the room. "Who attacked you?"

"The girl," Orion whispered, his voice low. "She wasn't really a girl. She's something else."

Vando nodded, his face grim. "I'll make sure you're never alone. Nowhere seems safe anymore."

Another figure materialized beside him. Vando smiled.

"There you are, Eymd," he said, his tone filled with approval.

Eymd stepped forward, her midnight-black skin gleaming in the dim light. Her glowing green eyes locked onto Orion as she bowed.

"Sire," Vando said, "this is Eymd. She's the head of our elite shadow warriors, and she will protect you at all costs."

Orion nodded, still trying to process everything. But when Eymd's voice rang out in his mind, he understood more than words could convey.

I will guard you, Sire. You are not alone.

"Right, I will leave you to sleep Sire, the stone guard will remain here while you sleep and Eymd will be posted outside," Vando said sensing Orion's tiredness.

Orion flopped back on his bed, started to stroke Pragor and was asleep instantly.

13 Saving Aurorina

Orion sat at the table once more with Grannie and Grandpa, but this time, it was suspended in mid-air, floating just above the roaring cascade of a waterfall. The world around him seemed both distant and familiar, trees stretching for miles, their branches heavy with fruit, and birds soaring overhead in graceful arcs. Below, the water churned, its current powerful and unyielding, just like the emotions that swelled inside him.

"Evening, child," Grannie's voice broke through the reverie, carrying with it a sense of warmth, yet also an underlying sadness.

"Evening," Orion answered, trying to steady his racing heart, still shaken by the magnitude of the visions he had seen.

The table in front of him flickered to life, a glowing hologram materializing from the ether. It was an image of his parents, Auren and Aurorina, standing together in a dim chamber, surrounded by cloaked figures whose faces were hidden in shadows. The air seemed to vibrate with tension, each breath heavy with the weight of an unspoken destiny.

A woman in a gold robe stepped forward. Her voice was calm but resolute, filling the air with a quiet urgency. "You must send him away. He is our only hope for what is to come."

"What do you mean?" Auren's voice trembled slightly, a flicker of fear that Orion had never noticed before.

The golden-robed woman's gaze hardened. "You may have forgotten when you met the Old Ones, when your child was created. But we have not."

Her words sent a shiver through Orion's spine. His mind reeled, trying to comprehend the depths of this secret, of what had been done to him. As the woman spoke, two more figures stepped forward and took him from his mother's arms. The look on Aurorina's face was one of pure desperation. She fell to her knees, pleading with them, her voice broken with the agony of a mother torn from her child.

"Sister, please do not cry," the golden-robed woman said softly, her voice almost tender. She lowered her hood, revealing a face that mirrored Aurorina's, same sharp features, same stormy eyes, but with an air of ancient wisdom that contrasted sharply with the young mother's sorrow. "You have my word. He will be safe. And you will see him again one day."

Orion's chest tightened. The words were like a vow, a promise that reverberated through his very soul. But what had they done to his mother? What had been taken from her that she could never get back? A sense of dread settled over him.

The scene dissolved into mist, and Grannie's voice cut through the silence. "Our existence in this dimension is almost at an end." Her words held an ominous finality. "This is why we made you, Orion. You are like us from the very beginning."

Orion's breath caught in his throat. "What do you mean, 'like you'?"

Grannie's eyes softened, and for a moment, she seemed to look past him, as if seeing the full weight of what was about to unfold. "When we first came here, we were young. We had solid forms, like you. But we are not of this world. We created it. We shaped it. And now, it is your turn to continue our work."

Grandpa's voice rumbled, deep and resonant. "You will have all the knowledge we hold, but it will not come easily. The power you inherit is as much a burden as it is a gift."

Orion looked at the sphere in front of him, glowing softly. His pulse quickened. The words echoed in his mind: *creator and destroyer in the same breath*. What did it mean for him, for his future? Could he even control such power?

The table before him vanished, and he found himself falling. The ground disappeared beneath him, and he plunged toward the water below. But it wasn't water he fell into. It was an endless chasm of darkness, pulling him deeper, farther from everything he knew.

Then, nothing.

When Orion finally opened his eyes, he found himself in a cocoon of light, suspended in a peaceful stillness. His breath came slow and steady, but his heart felt as though it was in turmoil. The presence of someone else beside him brought his focus back, and he saw Jake, his brother, sitting quietly in a chair nearby.

"You're awake," Jake said, relief evident in his voice.

Orion's body trembled as he rose to his feet. He had no idea how long he had been unconscious, but the change inside him was undeniable. His thoughts were swirling, clouded by the weight of everything he had just learned. His transformation wasn't just physical, it was soul-deep. He didn't feel like himself anymore.

He rushed to the door and threw it open. Lawrence and Anton entered, their faces pale with worry.

"I'm fine," Orion said, trying to sound more confident than he felt. "I just need a shower."

As he stepped into the bathroom, the sensation of his body changing again was overwhelming. His skin began to peel away, revealing dark blue flesh, stars twinkling beneath it like constellations in the night sky. His body grew taller, stretching unnaturally, his form becoming something *other*. When he looked into the mirror, he was no longer the boy he had been, he was something more. But something was wrong.

"This won't do," he muttered to himself.

With concentration, he willed himself smaller. His skin reverted to the glowing brown hue it had once been, his hair sprouted flames, and his eyes returned to the deep black that had always marked his humanity. He knew that these changes were only a fraction of the power that now resided within him, but how long could he keep it under control? How long before he lost himself completely?

His armour materialized around him, white and gleaming with the emblem of his royal bloodline. The cloak fluttered behind him like a river of water, its fabric flowing with an elegance that seemed almost otherworldly.

Just as he was about to step out, a sudden *crash* echoed through the room. A sword hit him square in the chest, sending sparks flying as it melted in Vando's hands. The force of the blow didn't harm him, but it was enough to send a jolt through his body.

"What was that for?" Orion yelled.

Vando's eyes narrowed, his suspicion thick in the air. "Who are you?"

"I am Intenfli Orion," he said, though the words felt foreign to his mouth. He wasn't sure who he was anymore, this person with the power of creation and destruction, this being caught between two worlds.

Vando raised an eyebrow, unsatisfied with the answer. "Prove it."

Orion raised a hand. "Stone guard, to me."

The command was instant. Stone statues of towering warriors appeared, drawn swords gleaming with an ethereal light. The stone guard saluted and stood ready.

Vando's eyes widened as he dropped to his knees. "It is truly you," he whispered. "But how?"

Orion didn't know the answer himself. The world around him felt like it was slipping through his fingers, each moment unravelling faster than he could grasp. He had been made for something far greater than he could ever have imagined.

Stand down, Eymd. It is indeed Intenfli Orion."

The shadow woman stepped out of the darkness and sheathed her swords, looking slightly disappointed. "When your brothers told me your eyes had changed, I thought that you had been replaced."

Orion waved his hand, and the stone guard saluted and disappeared. When the room settled down, Orion explained to everyone what had happened and how he had become something different. When he finished, Vando got up and excused himself, returning moments later with Lord Sanjen, who walked over to Orion and began inspecting him closely.

"Remarkable," Sanjen said. "There were legends written in ancient times about an Intenfli such as you coming to be."

He stood back up and looked at Vando, shocked. In all the commotion, Orion had forgotten that Vando had stabbed him. He looked down and saw that there was no wound at all. Sanjen began to study Orion's gauntlets, mumbling to himself, his face lighting up in excitement.

"Sire, if I may be so bold, could I ask you to remove one of your gauntlets so I could take a closer look?"

Orion nodded, took off one gauntlet, and handed it to Sanjen. Sanjen turned it over in his hands, examining the white metal closely. He then went to put the gauntlet on, and it disappeared from his hand, only to reappear on Orion's arm moments later.

"Just as I thought," Sanjen said, nodding. "They are bio-engineered to you, so no one can take them away from you. I have one more test, if it's okay with you, I need to prick you with a knife."

Vando stepped forward, his face showing concern at what Sanjen was suggesting.

"It's okay, Vando," Orion said. "Go ahead, Sanjen."

Sanjen pulled a dagger out of thin air. Orion could make out the magic contained within the blade. He held out his arm, and Sanjen stabbed down. As the blade hit Orion's skin, it burst into flames and then melted. Sanjen nodded, pulled a book from the air, and opened it to a page. He began to read, muttering to himself. After a while, he looked back up at Orion, his smile widening.

"Remarkable," Sanjen said. "You cannot die anymore. All you have to do is think of any planet in the system, and you can communicate with it. The two you met. One is known as the Creator, and the other is the Destroyer, but now you..." He smiled so widely it almost seemed as though his face couldn't stretch further. "You are their replacement, Creator and Destroyer in the same breath."

He turned the book around and handed it to Orion, who began to read:

A child will come, born of royal blood, but with older blood than theirs. He will walk amongst us. He will bring unity and peace to a galaxy that has been in disarray for so long, but he will struggle to balance the power he holds and his humanity. He must keep hold of his compassion, his love, and his heart, or all will be lost.

Orion continued reading for a while and came across a bit of writing that would help him. He looked up and realized that everyone was still standing there with their mouths wide open.

"I need to see my mother. I know how to fix what has been done to her," he said.

He got up and followed Sanjen and Eymd out of the room, down the corridor, and up to a large silver door. Orion knocked and waited. Lady Kirand opened it and stepped back to allow Orion inside.

"Your Highness," she said as he walked past her.

The room looked very much like his own, except everything inside was silver. He saw his mother lying on a four-poster bed, fast asleep. He approached her and concentrated, thinking about what he needed to fix. A small bag materialized on the bedside table beside him.

"I will be gone for a little while, as I need to enter her mind and repair what has been damaged," Orion said.

"I would like to accompany you, if that's okay?" asked Sanjen.

Orion nodded and conjured two chairs beside his mother's bed. He sat in one, and gestured for Sanjen to sit in the other. He picked up the bag and pulled out three pieces of fabric. When he unfolded them, they revealed three nightcaps. He gave one to Sanjen, placed one on his mother's head, and finally put one on his own.

"You ready?" Orion asked.

Sanjen nodded.

Three balls of light shot out of Orion's eyes, glowing like miniature stars, and hovered in front of them for a moment before zooming off in different directions. One darted into Aurorina's head, one into Sanjen's, and the last into Orion's. As soon as the lights made contact, both Orion and Sanjen fell into a deep, dreamless slumber.

When Orion opened his eyes again, he found himself standing in a lush clearing surrounded by tall, ancient trees. The air smelled sweet, thick with the fragrance of wildflowers. He glanced over at Sanjen, who stood beside him, his eyes wide with awe as he took in the surreal landscape.

"Where… where are we?" Sanjen asked, his voice a mix of wonder and confusion.

"We're inside my mother's mind," Orion said softly, his voice tinged with both concern and curiosity. "Be careful what you touch."

The words barely left his mouth before they began walking toward a gap in the hedge before them. Through the opening, they saw Aurorina standing in the centre of a sunlit courtyard, her back to them. But as they stepped forward, the gap in the hedge closed with a soft rustling sound. A moment later, more hedges erupted from the ground, forming an intricate maze around them.

Orion paused, his hand instinctively reaching out to touch one of the thorn-covered branches. His fingers brushed against the rough surface, sending a strange ripple through the air.

"This… this is her mind, protecting itself," Orion murmured. "She's built these defences around her memories."

Sanjen nodded thoughtfully. "I see. So, this maze is a barrier to keep us from reaching her?"

"Exactly. We need to be careful, or we could get lost in here for hours, days even. Her mind is fractured right now. We're dealing with more than just the physical damage."

They both stared at the paths ahead, Orion's mind racing with the possible dangers. To the left, the path seemed quiet but shadowed, while to the right, there was a faint light at the end. Orion studied the paths for a moment before deciding on the right.

They began walking down the brighter path, but as they reached the end, a sharp turn appeared ahead, and Orion chose it without hesitation. They moved quickly, but when they rounded the corner, a sudden jolt of energy coursed through the air. A stretch of broken path lay before them, and lightning arced across the sky, crackling ominously in the charged atmosphere.

Orion stopped in his tracks, the hairs on the back of his neck standing on end. He knew instantly what this was.

"This is… this is a memory of trauma," he said, voice low. "A broken part of her mind."

Without warning, a sceptre appeared in his hand, an ancient, ornate tool that seemed to hum with latent power. He swung it downward, and the ground trembled as a surge of energy spread out from the sceptre's tip. Lightning crackled, but instead of shattering, it surged along the floor, stitching the fractured ground back together. The lightning slowly faded, leaving the path whole once more. The sceptre vanished as quickly as it had come.

Sanjen looked at Orion, impressed. "That's incredible, Orion. You're tapping into her mind in ways I didn't think possible."

"We're just getting started," Orion said, his tone distant. "We have to keep going."

They continued through the maze, navigating the twisting paths with growing trepidation. Time seemed to stretch and bend within the confines of her mind. No matter which direction they turned, they always found themselves back at the same spot, the patched-up, scorched path. Orion's breath quickened as frustration built within him.

He sat down on the ground, his head dropping into his hands. "How can I save her?" he sobbed, his voice muffled by his palms. "When I can't even save myself?"

Sanjen sat beside him without hesitation, his presence steady and calming. "What's the real problem here, Orion? What's really weighing on you?"

Orion looked up, eyes filled with sorrow. "I feel like I'm losing myself. I'm not the person I was before all of this. I've lost my friends, I've lost my adopted mother… and now I have all this power, but I don't know how to control it. How am I supposed to save her when I'm losing grip on who I am?"

Sanjen exhaled, a low chuckle escaping his lips. It was a sound that felt like relief, a release of something unspoken. He waved his hand, and suddenly two old bone China cups appeared, along with a teapot and a plate of biscuits.

He poured the tea slowly, the rhythmic clink of porcelain calming the air between them.

"In my time on Earth," Sanjen said, handing Orion a cup, "I learned that a good cup of tea can help one clear their mind. It's a small thing, but sometimes the simplest gestures are what we need."

Orion stared at the tea, the warmth of the cup grounding him in the moment. He took a sip, finding it surprisingly soothing despite the chaos swirling in his mind.

"Can I be honest with you, Orion?" Sanjen asked, his gaze turning more serious, but still filled with kindness.

"Always," Orion replied, his voice tinged with a sense of trust he hadn't realized he'd built with this man.

Sanjen's eyes softened as he stared out at the sky, his voice quieter now. "You should have had more time to prepare for all of this. But the truth is, the power within you doesn't define who you are. What defines you, what will always define you, is the love and compassion you learned on Earth. You were never just a product of power. You are a product of your experiences. Of love. Of the lessons you learned. That's what makes you stronger than what the creators ever could have imagined."

Orion looked down at his hands, suddenly feeling the weight of everything he had gained, and everything he had lost. "But I'm afraid of hurting the people I care about. What if I lose control?"

Sanjen placed his hand gently on Orion's shoulder. "As long as you stay true to yourself, and remember the love and compassion that you've always carried, you will never lose your way. Power can only control you if you let it. You are more than just what's inside you, what's inside your heart is the key."

Sanjen raised his hand, and a set of golden scales appeared in front of them. The scales gleamed in the light, perfectly balanced. One side held a glowing red heart, the other a glowing gold one.

"See this?" Sanjen said, pointing to the scales. "These are your moral scales. The red heart represents your raw, unrefined power, the force inside you that could destroy everything. The gold heart represents your compassion, your hope, your humanity. As long as they remain in balance, you will be fine."

Orion stared at the scales, watching as the two hearts shifted ever so slightly, but never falling out of perfect harmony. He felt something within him settle, a small reassurance. "As long as they're balanced… I can do this."

Sanjen nodded, his eyes meeting Orion's with unwavering confidence. "Exactly. As long as you stay true to your heart, you'll never truly lose yourself."

Orion stood up slowly, feeling a renewed sense of purpose. He wasn't alone in this. Not anymore. Not while he had his mother, Sanjen, and his own heart to guide him.

"Thank you, Sanjen," Orion said, his voice steady with newfound resolve. "Let's finish this."

Sanjen stood up and offered his hand to Orion, who took it and stood to his feet. With a fluid motion, Sanjen reached into his robes and pulled out a glowing metal disc.

"Miss Rachel will be happy to hear from you," he said, a knowing smile on his face as he handed Orion the disc.

Orion took the disc and, with a focused thought, imagined Rachel. A bright flash of light engulfed him, and when it faded, he found himself standing in the grand hall of the mansion. The familiar surroundings felt like a strange comfort after the surreal journey through his mother's mind. Walking into the front room, he found Rachel curled up on the sofa, reading a book.

"Rach," he called softly.

Rachel startled, dropping the book as she looked up at him. Her eyes were puffy, and a faint tremble ran through her hands, but the moment she saw him, she rushed toward him without hesitation. She wrapped her arms around him in a tight, desperate hug, as if afraid he might vanish again.

"Orion, why are you back so soon?" she asked, pulling away just enough to look at him, worry etched in her voice.

Orion blinked, confused for a moment. "I'm not back. I'm using the disc to communicate. I've been gone a week, at least."

Rachel shook her head, her expression puzzled. "No, you've been gone twenty-four hours. Time moves slower here." She wiped her eyes quickly, as if trying to hide the lingering sadness.

"Oh," Orion said, suddenly remembering how time passed differently between realms. "I should've remembered that."

"Can we sit and talk?" Rachel asked, her voice softer now, her concern for him unmistakable.

Orion nodded, and they both sank back onto the sofa. He began to explain what had happened since his departure, the struggles, the weight of the powers within him, and his fear of losing control. His voice wavered slightly, but he spoke honestly, his emotions raw.

Rachel listened intently, her face softening with every word. When he finished, she placed her hand gently over his chest, her touch warm and reassuring.

"Sanjen's right," she said, her voice steady and full of compassion. "This is where your true self lies. Always remember that. You've always had these powers, and they're a part of who you are. They don't define you, but they're a part of your journey. You can control them."

Orion felt a lump form in his throat as he looked into her eyes. But then, something caught his attention, tears streaked down her cheeks. She quickly wiped them away, but the pain in her eyes was undeniable. Why was she trying to hide it from him?

He leaned forward, gently cupping her face with his hand. "Don't cry," he whispered. "I'll always be here for you. I can take the pain away, if you want."

Rachel smiled softly, but it was a bittersweet expression. "It's okay," she said, her voice breaking slightly. "It's... it will make me stronger. I promise."

Orion nodded, though the sadness in his heart deepened. She was so strong, but it hurt him to see her carry such pain. He got up, needing to leave, but as he passed the mirror on the wall, he paused. He caught a glimpse of himself, his old, human form. The way Rachel had greeted him suddenly made sense. She hadn't commented on his appearance because he looked like the person he used to be, the boy she remembered.

"I have to go now," he said, his voice heavy with the weight of their parting.

"I know," Rachel replied softly, her voice filled with understanding. She reached out, giving him a warm hug. "Take care, egg," she whispered into his ear, her affectionate nickname for him.

Orion hugged her back tightly before disappearing in a flash of light.

Back in the maze, he found Sanjen floating nearby, his feet lightly touching the ground as he read from a book. When he noticed Orion's return, he closed the book and tucked it into his robes with a smile.

"I trust everything went well?" Sanjen asked, his tone casual but with a glimmer of curiosity.

"Yes, thank you," Orion replied, feeling a sense of clarity after the conversation with Rachel. He reached out in front of him, and a piece of paper appeared, materializing from thin air. As he held it up, a map began to etch itself onto the page, showing the layout of the maze.

"Now to navigate this…" Orion murmured, studying the map closely. He started down the path, following the route, but soon he found himself stopped by something unexpected. He looked up from the map, and there, standing in front of him, was a slim woman with fiery red hair, her body draped in a dress of shifting purple flames.

"You are the one that is hers?" she asked in a voice that echoed with power, the words resonating in the air, causing Orion's ears to ring.

"She is my mother," Orion replied firmly, his chest tightening as he faced this strange figure.

The woman stepped forward, her fiery hair and dress shifting to a deep blue as she approached him. She stopped just in front of him and studied him with a piercing gaze. Then, without warning, she leaned forward and licked his cheek, her tongue cold as ice. Her voice, when she spoke again, held a strange, melodic quality.

"Why do you look so different?" she asked, her head tilting to the side. "You are not how she remembers you."

Orion swallowed, his heart pounding. "It's been many, many moons since she last saw me. But something has been done to her mind, something that altered everything."

The woman slumped back, her posture suddenly heavy with sorrow. She fixed Orion with a long, intense stare, as if weighing his very soul.

"You... you are the life force of a planet," Orion gasped, his eyes wide as the realization hit him.

"Yes," the woman replied, her voice softer now, filled with sadness. "I was dying. She was dying. So, I came to her... and we merged."

In a flash, a vision exploded in Orion's mind, Aurorina, laying broken in a crater, her life fading away. As her breath slowed to a whisper, a faint light erupted from the planet below. It wrapped itself around her like a ribbon of energy, entering her mouth and vanishing. Her body hung suspended for a moment before she screamed as the light healed her, mending her broken form.

The vision faded as quickly as it had come, and the woman stood before him once more, her expression softening.

"Now do you, see?" she asked gently.

"I do," Orion said, his voice heavy with understanding.

"I will mend the remaining broken parts of her mind," the woman continued, her tone now filled with resolve. "Now that I know she is safe, I can restore her. She will be whole again. But when she wakes, I will have to separate myself from her. I cannot remain once she is healed."

Orion nodded, his heart swelling with gratitude. "Thank you," he said sincerely, offering her a smile. "You've given her a second chance."

The woman smiled back, a glimmer of warmth in her eyes. Orion turned to Sanjen, grabbing his arm. With a flash of light, they were back in the room with Aurorina.

The moment they appeared, the group surrounding her stood motionless, waiting, their gazes fixed on her. The air was thick with anticipation.

Aurorina sat bolt upright, her breath coming in shallow gasps as she inhaled deeply, her eyes wide with confusion. She looked around the room, and when her gaze finally settled on Orion, golden tears began to stream down her face. Her voice was soft, trembling, but filled with a depth of emotion.

"You look so much like your father," she said, her words carrying both warmth and sorrow.

Orion smiled gently, a rush of relief washing over him. It was the first real acknowledgment of her, of their connection, since her return.

But then, her face shifted to one of concern. "She is dying," Aurorina pleaded, her voice full of urgency. "You need to help her."

Orion's heart tightened at the weight of her words. He nodded, steeling himself for what lay ahead. Without hesitation, he walked to the centre of the room, clearing his mind of the swirling thoughts and emotions. As he focused, the liquid within his arms separated, flowing gracefully towards his hands. In an instant, the liquid solidified into two shimmering sceptres, their rainbow-colored light glowing vibrantly.

"Everyone, stand clear," he said, his voice steady despite the mounting pressure.

The room fell silent as everyone instinctively moved to the edges of the space, their eyes fixed on him, waiting for the spectacle to unfold. Taking a deep breath, Orion raised the first sceptre high. He spun it in one hand, a graceful motion that seemed to defy the laws of physics. The room hummed with energy as he began to move, his body in perfect sync with the sceptres in his hands. He danced, two steps forward, an arched leap, landing with elegant precision. His form collapsed to his knees with fluidity, his body moving like water.

He laid both sceptres on the floor in front of him and, with a final roll to the left, he sprang back up. He held his hands just above the sceptres, a surge of power building as the sceptres began to rise. The air shimmered with energy, the ball of light that grew between them pulsating in sync with Orion's heartbeat.

He grabbed the sceptres as they reached his outstretched hands, and with a sudden, forceful motion, slammed them into the glowing sphere. There was a deafening bang, followed by a blinding flash of light that momentarily stole all sense of space and time.

When the light subsided, the room fell into an eerie silence. Hanging in mid-air was a sparkling crystal form, suspended by some unseen force, glowing faintly with the light of a thousand stars. The sceptres had melted away, their essence returned to the liquid that now flowed back into Orion's arm.

He took a deep breath and extended one hand toward the floating body. Gently, he blew into his palm, and a cloud of shimmering dust spiralled from his hand, catching the light as it drifted toward the crystalline form. As the dust settled, it seeped into the body, disappearing completely. Orion then pressed his hand softly against the figure's chest, and slowly, the skin began to change turning from translucent crystal to a rich, warm brown, the colour of fertile earth. Blue hair sprouted from its head, a reflection of the sky above the lands Aurorina once governed. The figure's form began to take shape, solidifying into something distinctly human.

With a subtle wave of his hand, a simple white robe materialized around the body, covering it gently. The figure slowly lowered itself to the ground, now whole but still lifeless.

"That will do," Orion said quietly, stepping back and walking over to his mother.

He whispered something softly into his palm, too quiet for anyone to hear, and then placed his hand just below her eye. A tiny wisp of light drifted from her closed eyelid, floating into his cupped hand. With that wisp held safely, he moved to the lifeless body on the floor and placed his hand just next to its mouth. The wisp entered the figure's mouth, and Orion stepped back, watching intently.

For a moment, everything was still. Then, the body jolted, the chest rising and falling with a sudden breath. A sharp cough tore from her throat, and her eyes fluttered open, glowing for an instant with a strange, ethereal light. They fixed on Orion, but something was different, one eye was dark blue, like the oceans that once ran across the land, and the other was a vibrant green, a reflection of the trees and the forests she had nurtured.

Orion watched as the figure stirred, her hair shifting from blue to a deep, mud-brown colour, the colour of the soil that had once been her domain. It was as if the earth itself was returning to her.

"Auratium," Orion spoke softly, his voice filled with tenderness and understanding. "I know it's not a planet, but it's the best I could do on such short notice."

Auratium stood up and took a few unsteady steps forward. Her movements were shaky, like a newborn learning to walk, though with a speed that was almost unnerving. She stopped just in front of Orion, gazing into his eyes with a deep intensity. She reached forward and gently cupped his chin, her touch surprisingly soft and warm.

Her lips parted, and she smiled an expression filled with gratitude and something else, something that Orion couldn't quite place. "I couldn't have asked for more," she said, her voice hoarse but filled with a genuine tenderness. "I appreciate this more than you will ever know."

Orion, exhausted beyond measure, struggled to stay awake. He was barely holding on, his body aching and drained from the immense strain of the task. He gave a weary smile and nodded, his vision blurring.

"I'll… I'll go get some rest," he murmured, his words slurring slightly from exhaustion. "Goodnight, everyone." He turned and left the room, his legs heavy as he made his way to his chamber.

As he closed the door behind him, the weight of everything that had happened the journey, the struggle, the power he wielded, and the uncertainty of what would come next finally caught up with him. He collapsed onto his bed, eyes slipping closed, the exhaustion dragging him into a deep sleep.

14 royal duties

The next day, Orion awoke in his chambers, the weight of sleep still clinging to his body. Pragor, the creature that had grown fond of him, was lying at the foot of the bed. Orion moved down the mattress slowly, absently stroking Pragor's fur as his mind wandered.

Something caught the corner of his eye, movement from the shadowed corner of the room. He barely had time to react before Eymd stepped into the light. Startled, Orion instinctively raised his hand to shield himself, and the next thing he knew, a blast of energy shot from his palm, obliterating a hole through the bathroom door. Eymd had sidestepped just in time, though the door behind her was now little more than splinters.

Orion blinked in confusion. "You really need to be careful where you aim that arm," Eymd said, her voice full of amusement as she casually took a seat on one of the nearby chairs.

"Well, maybe if you didn't sneak up on me, it wouldn't have happened," Orion shot back, his words sharp despite the residual surprise.

Eymd chuckled, her voice ringing in his mind like an echo. *What part of 'shadow warrior' didn't you get?"*

Orion frowned, rubbing his forehead. "You're not like the others. They're all polite to me."

"Please," she teased, *"why be polite when I can be honest?"*

Before Orion could respond, there was a knock at the door. Maximus entered, carrying a slate with Orion's schedule for the day. He spotted Eymd sitting in the shadows and, with a wary glance, moved toward Orion, bowing respectfully.

"Sire, here is today's schedule, and the local Mayor seeks an audience with you at your earliest convenience," Maximus announced, his voice formal.

Orion took the schedule from Maximus, his brow furrowing as he scanned the list. *So much to do,* he thought. *So much still undone.*

"Have my breakfast brought here, and tell the mayor that he may join me," Orion replied, his tone firm, though there was a trace of weariness in his voice.

Maximus bowed once more before exiting. Eymd rose as well, slipping silently back into the shadows, her presence disappearing as quickly as it had arrived. Orion sighed, glad to be momentarily alone. He slid out of bed, donning his robe, and settled into one of the chairs across from where Eymd had been sitting, trying to relax while waiting for his food to arrive.

Minutes passed before another knock came at the door.

"Enter," Orion called.

A small boy, no older than ten, stepped inside. His clothes were ragged and covered in dirt, and his face was streaked with grime. Without a word, the boy hurriedly placed a tray on the table and rushed back out, disappearing before Orion could even offer a greeting.

Orion lifted the lid of the tray, expecting a simple meal. Instead, he found an electronic tablet, a bowl filled with something that looked like jelly, a cup of what he assumed was coffee, and a couple slices of toast. He picked up the tablet, watching as it crackled to life the moment his fingers brushed the screen. An article popped up, and he began reading:

Intenfli Orion appears to have saved the day, but what will he do next, readers ask. Sources inside the palace say this ruler is back to avenge all the wrongs that have been done in this system, starting with the restoration of our beloved planet, as you saw several days ago, and the community service he offered to our previous rulers.

One palace guard says: "You should have seen him. So young, but never ceases to amaze with his kindness."

Where has he been?

Is he planning to take on his uncle?

Will we be safe?

When will our new homes be built?

These are just a few of the questions readers are asking, but we are yet to hear anything from him.

A woman claims she saw the Ancient Rahfor fly through the skies on the day Intenfli Orion arrived. Turn to page six for the full story.

Orion's eyes narrowed as he read, frustration rising in his chest. The questions in the article were valid, but he had only been back a few days. He put the tablet down, turning his attention back to his food, when Maximus walked in, followed by an elderly man.

The man wore a tattered green silk robe, and his long, grey hair hung in matted strands. His feet, visible beneath his robes, were cracked, swollen, and dry. As the man stepped into the room, Orion realized he was blind.

"May I introduce Mayor Timwanto," Maximus said, helping the elderly man to a chair opposite Orion. Once the Mayor was seated, Maximus left the room quietly, closing the door behind him.

Orion rose to greet the mayor. "Can I get you something to drink?"

"Whatever you have available will be more than enough, Sire," Timwanto replied in a raspy voice that seemed to carry the weight of years of hardship.

Orion handed the mayor the untouched cup from the tray. The man took it gratefully, gulping it down in one go. Afterward, he felt around for the table and placed the empty cup gently back onto it.

"Thank you for granting me an audience, Sire. There are a few things I wish to discuss," Timwanto said, his voice full of resolve despite his weariness.

"It's not a problem," Orion replied, settling back into his chair. "Please, go ahead."

Timwanto leaned forward slightly. "As you know, we are down in the vault in temporary accommodations while the war continues. But we are running out of clothes, food, and water, and people are beginning to get restless. Is there anything you can do to help?"

Orion's heart tightened at the plea in the mayor's voice. Without thinking, he sprang to his feet, startling the old man. He quickly picked up the bowl of jelly-like food and placed it gently in Timwanto's hands.

"Please, eat," Orion said softly, his voice filled with concern.

The mayor's eyes softened, tears streaming down his cheeks as he took the food. "Thank you, Sire."

Orion nodded and, without waiting for the man to finish, spoke. "I'll see to it that new clothes, food, and water are brought to your people. As for their restlessness... perhaps they can help around the palace. Allow them to roam freely within reason, and let them contribute where they can. It might help lift their spirits."

Timwanto's face brightened, and he bowed his head in gratitude. "Thank you, my Lord. That was everything I had to ask."

Orion hesitated before continuing. "Before you go... let me help with your clothes and feet."

With a wave of his hand, the mayor's tattered robe shimmered and restored itself to its former grandeur. A bowl of warm water appeared in front of him. Orion placed the mayors' swollen feet into the water, he then whispered a quiet incantation, sending a healing spell through the water that would ease the old man's pain.

"Thank you," Timwanto sighed deeply. "They feel better already."

Orion smiled faintly, watching the mayor relax for the first time since he had entered. He stood and walked to the door, speaking briefly with the guard outside before returning to his seat. Moments later, Maximus entered again, looking slightly out of breath.

"Sire, the guard said you needed me," Maximus said, stepping forward.

Orion gestured to the empty seat next to Timwanto. "Yes, please, take a seat."

Maximus hesitated, then sat down, his gaze flicking nervously between Orion and the Mayor.

"I would like to see as many clothes as possible brought to every man, woman, and child in the vault, along with enough food and water to sustain them. Also, allow the people to roam the palace as they wish."

Maximus scribbled furiously on his tablet, his pen moving quickly.

"Jobs should be assigned to those who wish to help, and one of the palace rooms should be cleared and repurposed into a classroom for the children."

"Classroom, Sire?" Maximus asked, raising an eyebrow in mild confusion.

"A place for children to learn new skills and socialize with each other," Orion replied firmly, his gaze steady.

Maximus hesitated for a moment, then spoke cautiously. "But we have the download process for that, Sire."

"Yes, but it's so impersonal," Orion said, his voice softening. "The children need to interact, to play, to learn from one another, not just from a machine. They need to grow emotionally, not just intellectually."

Maximus paused, absorbing Orion's words. He gave a respectful nod, his expression thoughtful. "Right you are, Sire."

With that, Maximus exited the room, leaving Orion alone with the elderly Mayor. Orion stood for a moment, his mind occupied with the weight of the decisions he was making, but he quickly turned his attention to the mayor.

He walked over to where Timwanto's feet were resting in the warm water, inspecting the healing process. The mayor's swollen, cracked feet had now fully healed, the redness and discomfort replaced by the normal colour of healthy skin.

Orion gently took Timwanto's feet out of the water, carefully patted them dry with a soft cloth, and then placed a pair of fresh shoes on the mayor's feet, ensuring they fit comfortably.

As Timwanto stood, he smiled faintly, his expression one of quiet gratitude, though his hands shook slightly from the age and effort it took to rise. He looked at Orion, his voice cracking with emotion. "I can see," he whispered, his hands reaching up to touch his face, as if he were trying to confirm it was true.

Orion waved his hand once more, and with a subtle hum of power, the mayor's sight was fully restored. The transformation was simple, yet profound.

"Thank you so much, sir," Timwanto gasped, tears welling in his eyes. He placed his hand over his heart, overcome with the enormity of the gift.

Orion smiled softly, watching the mayor's reaction. "You've suffered enough. It's the least I could do for you."

The mayor took a moment, his eyes flicking back and forth as he absorbed the world around him, as if seeing it for the first time. His lips parted in awe, and for the briefest moment, it seemed as though time stood still.

"Words cannot express the gratitude I feel," Timwanto murmured, his voice raw with emotion. "I will do everything I can to serve you, Sire. You have my loyalty."

Orion nodded, his expression a mix of humility and determination. "You're welcome, but it's not just about loyalty. It's about rebuilding. We're all in this together, and I can't do it alone."

The old man, his face alight with gratitude, suddenly jumped up and wrapped his arms around Orion in a tight embrace. For a moment, Orion was caught off guard, but then a genuine smile spread across his face. This was the kind of leader he wanted to be, someone who brought comfort and hope to those who needed it most. He returned the hug briefly, the warmth of the gesture grounding him in the reality of his mission.

The mayor stepped back, tears still glistening in his eyes, and gave a deep, respectful bow. "I cannot thank you enough, Sire," he said, his voice thick with emotion.

Orion nodded, his smile lingering. "You've suffered enough. It's the least I could do."

The mayor hurriedly exited the room, his steps quick and unsteady, no doubt eager to share the news of his restored sight with the others. As the door closed behind him, Orion stood for a moment, letting the silence fill the space. His heart felt lighter, the burden of his leadership somehow more bearable. He had made a difference today, and it was a reminder of why he had come back, why he had chosen to fight for these people.

With renewed resolve, Orion walked to his wardrobe, his fingers brushing over the gleaming armour that awaited him. He dressed quickly, each piece a reminder of the responsibility he now carried. The armour fit perfectly, just as it had when he first donned it, but now, it felt like a second skin, an extension of his growing confidence.

He stepped out of his chambers, the heavy door creaking as it swung open. As soon as his boots hit the cold stone of the palace hallway, the stone guards, ever vigilant, fell into formation behind him. Their presence was reassuring, a symbol of the strength he had at his disposal, and they moved in perfect unison as they followed him into the main hall.

Upon entering the hall, Orion took his place at the centre of the grand room. He surveyed the intricate designs on the walls and the vast space before him, all of it a stark reminder of the legacy he was trying to rebuild. He felt the weight of it in his bones, but also the fire within him that urged him to press on.

Sitting down at the massive table that stretched before him, he scanned his schedule. The first task was to speak with the council, a necessary step in solidifying his leadership and planning the next phases of the rebuilding process. He leaned over to the guard stationed beside his throne, a tall figure who stood with perfect posture.

"Please, summon the council and my mother to the main hall," Orion requested, his voice steady but carrying the weight of authority.

The guard gave a sharp salute before turning on his heel and leaving the room, his boots echoing through the vast hall. As the door closed behind him, Orion allowed himself a moment of quiet reflection. The responsibilities were growing, but so was his understanding of his role.

"I think you were too nice to the old man," Eymd's voice echoed in Orion's mind as she materialized out of thin air, effortlessly spinning one of her swords in her hand.

Orion jumped at her sudden appearance, instinctively raising his hand to protect himself, causing a burst of energy to tear through the bathroom door. Eymd, ever quick, had stepped aside just in time to avoid the blast.

"God, can you not do that?" Orion exclaimed, still catching his breath.

Eymd tilted her head, a smirk playing on her lips. "You're not very Intenfli-like, are you?"

"I have a meeting in a minute, can you just behave?" Orion snapped, his patience fraying at the edges.

She raised an eyebrow. "Says the ruler who just blasted a door to smithereens. You need to focus, Orion."

Orion stood, taking a calming breath. With a swift snap of his fingers, the chairs and tables around him vanished, only to be replaced by a large, round table surrounded by high-backed chairs. He made his way to the table, taking a seat at the head, attempting to block out Eymd, who now continued her antics by tossing her sword into the air and catching it with fluid ease.

Moments later, the boy who had delivered Orion's breakfast walked into the hall, carrying a jug of water and a couple of glasses. He set the glass in front of Orion, who watched the boy with a curious eye.

"How old are you?" Orion asked, raising an eyebrow.

"The moon has gone around the planet four times since my birth," the boy replied, almost apologetically.

Orion thought for a moment, doing the quick math in his head. By Earth years, the boy was about nine. Orion frowned. *What was a child his age doing working?*

"How come you are already working?" he asked, his voice soft with concern.

The boy shifted uncomfortably, his eyes darting around before settling back on Orion. "My mother works in the kitchen, so I help her out occasionally."

Orion's heart tugged at the boy's answer. *A child forced into labour at such a young age...*

He pressed on, curiosity overcoming him. "So, why did you run off earlier? And what's your name?"

"I am Ryann, Sire," the boy answered, bowing deeply. "I ran off because the previous Lord and Lady bullied me whenever I brought them food, and I wasn't sure if you would do the same."

Orion's expression softened. "Don't worry, you have nothing to fear from me."

The boy gave a small, relieved smile and bowed again before leaving quickly, clearly eager to get back to his work.

"You're far too nice," Eymd commented from the shadows. "They'll take advantage of your kindness."

Orion shook his head, a slight smile tugging at his lips. "Maybe. But everyone deserves kindness. And you" he said, turning to face her, "you're no help at all."

Eymd gave an exaggerated sigh, her voice ringing through his mind as she replied gleefully, *I'd rather use my swords.*

Before Orion could respond, the large doors to the hall swung open. The members of the council began to file in, their footsteps echoing in the grand space. Eymd disappeared into the shadows with a swift motion as Aurorina, the last to enter, approached Orion. He beckoned her to sit beside him.

"Look at you, my son," Aurorina said softly, her voice filled with awe. "Your father would be so proud of you."

Orion, flushed with emotion, stood up quickly. He felt the weight of her words more deeply than he let on, but he quickly regained his composure.

"My Lords and Ladies, welcome," he said, his voice steady but full of purpose. "I have brought you here because for too long you have remained behind closed doors, blind to the suffering of the people you serve. I also wish to discuss the imminent war that is approaching and what plans we must put into motion to protect the citizens of this system."

As he spoke, a hologram of the star system appeared in the centre of the table, the positions of his uncle's fleet clearly marked.

"Pardon me for interrupting, Sire," Lady Valoria asked, her voice laced with scepticism. "But if you are truly this powerful god, why can't you simply end the war using your abilities?"

Orion's face hardened, but he remained calm. "I cannot intervene," he replied. "This war must happen; it was foretold, and it is set in stone."

Lady Valoria looked down, her face flushing with embarrassment. She seemed ready to apologize, but before she could, Lord Zanek stood.

"The people of the planet will be safe within the Vault, and we have drafted in more of the palace's reserve guard to protect them," he said, his voice strong and reassuring.

Zanek sat back down and turned to Orion. "Now, I need to know how many units we have left and how long it will take them to arrive. This is where we will make our stand."

Vando stood up next, his posture firm and commanding. "We have a mixture of five thousand artillery, infantry, and star magic soldiers on route to us. They should arrive in a few hours. Additionally, we have two hundred ships in orbit, small compared to your uncle's fleet, but still a formidable force."

The hologram shifted to show the position of Orion's fleet, which was just an hour away from the planet. It was smaller, but Orion wasn't worried. He had a few tricks up his sleeve.

"Vando," Orion said, his tone decisive, "You'll coordinate the fleet. Zanek, you'll coordinate the ground forces. The rest of the council will hold the line at the vault entrance."

Everyone nodded, but then Zanek hesitated. "Sire," he said, his voice hesitant, "Why can't you coordinate the fleet yourself?"

Orion's jaw tightened. "I have to leave. Have your fastest and smallest ship prepared for me."

A collective murmur passed through the room, and Zanek spoke up again, this time with a note of concern. "Who will accompany you, Sire?"

"No one," Orion replied, his voice resolute. "This is something I must do alone."

The room fell into uneasy silence. Aurorina, her face pale, buried her face in her hands, sobbing uncontrollably. "I cannot lose you again, my son," she cried, her voice ragged with emotion.

"Sire, you cannot go alone!" Vando exclaimed, his voice filled with concern. "You need protection."

Orion's patience snapped. He stood, slamming his fist down on the table. Sparks erupted from the impact, and everyone around him jumped back, startled by the intensity of his outburst.

Sanjen, ever calm, leaned forward and gently placed a hand on Orion's arm. "Remember the balance, Orion," he said softly, his voice steady and grounding.

Orion took a deep breath, his anger dissipating as he looked around the room at the concerned faces of his council. "I'm sorry for my outburst," he said, his voice softer now, though the resolve remained. "But I must do this alone. I cannot be a part of this war. I must prepare myself for what is to come."

As the council members rose, bowing in respect, Orion quickly excused himself. He left the hall, his footsteps heavy with the weight of his decision. He walked briskly toward his chambers, needing time to gather himself before the departure.

Inside his room, he found Eymd lying on his bed, playing lazily with Pragor. She glanced up at him, a wicked grin spreading across her face.

"Leave me, please," Orion said, his voice tired but firm.

"Sorry, no can do," Eymd replied bluntly, not even looking up from Pragor.

"I order you to leave."

Eymd rose from the bed with a fluid motion and glided across the room to him. Without warning, she slapped him lightly on the cheek, the gesture almost playful. "Now look who's bossy. What's got you all grumpy?"

"Please," Orion sighed, "just leave me be for a while."

Eymd's expression softened just slightly, and with a nod, she vanished into the shadows. Orion walked over to the golden balcony doors and opened them, stepping out into the cool air. He sat on the stone ledge, gazing out over the palace grounds and the ruined city beyond.

So much had been done in such a short time, guards now lined the streets outside the palace gates, and spikes of magical barbed wire stood firmly in place. Children played freely within the grounds, blissfully unaware of the horrors that were on the horizon.

Orion's thoughts were interrupted by voices outside his chamber.

"I'm sorry, Your Highness. He has asked not to be disturbed," a guard said.

"I'm his mother," a familiar voice replied, tinged with desperation. "Can you at least ask him?"

The door opened, and Aurorina entered, walking slowly toward him. Orion didn't say a word, only gestured for her to sit beside him.

"My son," she said softly, her voice trembling. "Please tell me you are not leaving so soon."

Orion sighed deeply. "I have no choice, as it is what has to happen."

Aurorina nodded, tears beginning to fall freely from her eyes as she wiped them away. "Will I get to see you again?"

Orion didn't respond, his gaze drifting toward the horizon. He wanted to tell her everything, but he couldn't. The weight of his secret felt too heavy to share.

"I would like for you to join me for dinner," he said, changing the subject. "I would like you to meet my family from Earth."

She smiled faintly, nodding. "As you wish, my son."

Aurorina kissed his forehead softly before standing. She left the room, leaving Orion to his thoughts.

15 The First Farewell

Orion sat at the head of a small, elegant table set up inside his chambers, awaiting the arrival of his family. The table was a sight to behold, adorned with shining gold plates, glasses made from the finest crystal, and gleaming silver cutlery. Each item was meticulously crafted, the royal crest engraved on them, symbolizing the grandeur of the monarchy. The room itself, bathed in warm golden light, exuded the quiet elegance of royalty. The air smelled faintly of fresh flowers, and the soft hum of anticipation seemed to fill the space as Orion patiently waited.

The door opened, and the Royal Announcer stepped forward, his voice carrying through the chamber with the practiced authority of one accustomed to grand occasions.

"Introducing Her Royal Highness, former Intenfna Lady Aurorina."

Orion's breath caught in his throat as Aurorina stepped into the room. She was a vision of regal grace and beauty. She wore a long, flowing red dress that shimmered in the light, its fabric elegant and understated, yet bold enough to draw attention. A white fur coat draped over her shoulders, its pristine edges adding to the refinement of her ensemble. A golden tiara adorned her long, golden hair, which cascaded down her back like a waterfall of light. As she moved toward the table, her presence seemed to fill the room. She was every bit the queen in the making, and for a moment, Orion couldn't tear his eyes away from her. When she reached the chair opposite him, a guard stepped forward to pull it out for her to sit, the gentle sound of the chair scraping against the floor a soft contrast to the grandeur of the moment.

"Introducing His Royal Highness, Prince Lawrence."

The announcement broke Orion's reverie. Lawrence entered the room next, exuding confidence and nobility. He was dressed to impress, in a white dinner jacket with golden buttons and the royal coat of arms embroidered in gold on his chest. A golden fur cloak draped across his shoulders, and a golden crown sat upon his curly black hair, completing the regal look. Lawrence moved with ease, his steps measured and deliberate as he walked to Orion's left and took his seat next to Aurorina. His gaze met Orion's for a brief moment, and though the bond between them was clear, there was a tension in the air, a subtle reminder of their shared history.

"Introducing Their Royal Highnesses, Prince Jake and Prince Anton."

The announcement made Orion look up again, and he was almost taken aback. His brothers entered the room, and for a moment, it was as if they were transformed. Jake was dressed in a golden breastplate, the royal crest proudly displayed at the centre. His silver crown rested atop his head, its intricate design matching the elegance of his attire, and a regal silver cloak trailed behind him, brushing against the floor as he walked. Anton stood beside him, equally majestic in his silver breastplate, with the golden royal crest at its centre. A matching silver and gold crown rested on his head, and his cloak shimmered as it followed behind him. Together, they radiated strength and authority, yet there was a warmth in their smiles as they took their seats to the right of Orion, completing the family at the table. Only one seat remained unfilled, and the anticipation in the room grew.

"Introducing Lady Auratium, the planet."

The announcement hung in the air, and just as Orion thought the moment could not become more profound, something extraordinary happened. The room seemed to shift in atmosphere, the very air thickening with energy. The ground trembled softly beneath their feet, and the temperature seemed to rise slightly, as though the essence of the planet itself was manifesting.

From the very centre of the room, the atmosphere seemed to warp and shimmer, and then, before their eyes, Auratium materialized. It was a sight beyond words. She was not just a physical being but a presence, a fusion of light, colour, and life. Her form flickered like the surface of a star, her skin shifting through a spectrum of brilliant hues, from the deep, dark blue of oceans to the green of lush forests, and the earthy browns of mountains and soil. She exuded the raw energy of creation itself, an embodiment of the planet that had given so much. Her eyes glowed like twin orbs of celestial fire, watching the room with a deep, ancient wisdom.

Her presence filled the room with an overwhelming sense of both awe and humility, reminding everyone of the profound connection they shared with the world they fought to protect. The shimmering figure hovered just above the ground, a being of both beauty and power, embodying the planet's very spirit. She glided forward, the air swirling gently around her, before she came to a stop near Orion's side.

Orion stared, his heart heavy with the realization that the planet, the very force that had sustained his people, was now here, standing in their presence. He could almost feel the pulse of the earth beneath his feet, as if the ground itself was alive with the power of the moment.

Orion stood up, his heart heavy as he prepared to greet his family one last time. The table before him was set with elegance befitting the occasion, gleaming gold plates and crystal glasses arranged meticulously. The royal crest was engraved on every piece of cutlery, signifying the weight of the moment. The soft glow of candlelight reflected off the polished silver, casting a warm, golden hue over the room.

The door opened, and the Royal Announcer's voice echoed through the chamber.

"Introducing Her Royal Highness, former Intenfna Lady Aurorina."

Orion's breath caught as Aurorina entered. She was a vision of grace and regal elegance. She wore a long, flowing red gown that shimmered softly, complementing her radiant golden hair, which cascaded over her shoulders. A white fur coat adorned her frame, its softness adding a touch of nobility, and a golden tiara rested atop her head. Every step she took exuded a calm, unshakable power. As she reached the table, the air in the room seemed to still in reverence. A guard pulled out the chair for her, and she seated herself opposite Orion, her eyes softening as they met his.

"Introducing His Royal Highness, Prince Lawrence."

Lawrence entered with the same commanding presence, dressed in a pristine white dinner jacket adorned with golden buttons, the royal coat of arms embroidered at the chest. A golden fur cloak draped from his shoulders, and a crown of gold rested atop his dark, curly hair. As he approached Orion's left, he nodded, a faint smile passing between them, before taking his seat next to Aurorina. The weight of his responsibility as the next in line to the throne was visible in the lines of his face, yet there was a warmth in his eyes that softened his strong demeanour.

"Introducing Their Royal Highnesses, Prince Jake and Prince Anton."

The doors opened once more, and the two younger princes walked in, causing a ripple of surprise in the room. Jake wore a golden breastplate with the royal crest at its centre, a silver cloak trailing behind him as he moved with assured steps. His crown, crafted from the finest silver and gold, rested atop his head, a symbol of the leadership he was now stepping into. Anton was equally imposing, wearing a silver breastplate with a golden royal crest, and his cloak shimmered in shades of gold and silver, adding to his regal appearance. Together, they made their way to the right of Orion and took their seats, a silent strength emanating from both of them.

"Introducing Lady Auratium, the planet."

The room fell silent, as if the very air held its breath. A palpable shift seemed to occur, and the space in front of them began to shimmer and warp. From the centre of the room, the figure of Lady Auratium appeared. She was not just a being but an embodiment of the planet itself, her form glowed with the colours of nature, from deep ocean blues to the vibrant greens of thriving forests. Her body flickered with hues of soil-brown, as if the land itself coursed through her veins. Her presence filled the room with an unspoken reverence, a connection to something much greater than any one individual.

Orion's heart skipped a beat at the sight of her. She was everything he had hoped for, a living manifestation of the planet's spirit. Her form seemed to pulse with life, and though she did not speak, her gaze held the wisdom of ages.

The family was finally assembled around the table. The air was thick with emotion as they all exchanged fleeting glances, aware that this night would be their last together before Orion's departure. He stood, his heart heavy with the weight of the moment.

"I welcome you all to what is to be our last meal together," he began, his voice steady but filled with sorrow. "I have taken the liberty of selecting a menu from Earth."

The room erupted in conversation, and for a moment, Orion allowed himself to smile, feeling the warmth of his family's love and support. But when the room quieted, he held up his hand to silence them.

"I will not be gone forever, but it must happen this way. I do have a request of you all before I leave."

The golden tears began to roll down Orion's face as he spoke. His heart ached, and he could feel the weight of his family's sorrow, each one of them struggling to hold back their own tears.

"I would like my mother, Aurorina, to run the system while I am gone. But you four," he gestured toward his family, "will be her personal council. Try to remember how I have ruled in my short time."

There was a solemn nod from the council members, and Jake, unable to contain his emotion, ran over to Orion and sobbed into his shoulder, leaving behind turquoise tear stains.

"Don't leave us, please," Jake begged, his voice trembling with the weight of the moment.

Orion took Jake's face in his hands, wiping away his tears before kissing his forehead.

"Oh, my brother, I will not be gone for too long," Orion replied softly, holding back his own tears.

Jake nodded, returning to his seat as Orion clapped his hands. At his signal, the Kalligah entered, bringing in the starters. They placed covered dishes before everyone. Once the lids were removed, prawn cocktails were revealed.

"What is this?" asked Aurorina, looking at her dish with curiosity.

Lawrence chuckled. "It's called a prawn cocktail. I think you'll enjoy it."

The family watched Orion, waiting for him to start. Orion picked up his fork and took a bite, savouring the familiar taste of Earth food. It felt like a small piece of home. He wondered how they had managed to bring Earth food to this place, but for now, he simply enjoyed the comfort it gave him.

Once he finished, he noticed everyone else had put down their forks, despite not finishing their dishes. The Kalligah quickly removed the prawn cocktails and replaced them with a roast pig, roast potatoes, macaroni cheese, and an assortment of vegetables. The scent of the food filled the air, and the Kalligah began carving the pig, placing generous portions on each plate. Orion made sure to eat more slowly this time, allowing everyone to finish at their own pace.

The food was delicious, and soon everyone was helping themselves to seconds. The laughter and chatter filled the room as they ate, forgetting for a moment the impending separation. Once the meal was finished, the table was cleared, and a jug of something golden was poured into their crystal wine glasses.

"What is this?" Orion asked, raising an eyebrow at the unfamiliar drink.

"It's called Sanrato," Aurorina explained. "Your father and I had it on our day of joining. Please, drink it slowly. The bubbles go to your head."

Orion took a sip. The liquid was sweet but potent, and as the taste lingered on his tongue, he felt a warmth spread through him.

As they drank, the Kalligah brought out the dessert, a massive trifle. Everyone dug in, with Aurorina smiling widely as she helped herself to a fourth bowl.

The mood was lighter now, filled with the joy of family. Conversations flowed easily as they ate, laughed, and forgot, for just a moment, that Orion would soon be leaving them.

Then, Vando stepped forward, whispering in Orion's ear before retreating. Orion stood up, his voice breaking through the chatter.

"It is time," Orion said, his tone filled with quiet resolve. "I thank you all for an enjoyable evening."

With a snap of his fingers, liquid from his forearm flowed, materializing into a sceptre, which he handed to Aurorina. He removed his crown, turned it in his hand, and melted it down into a tiara, which he also gave to her. She took the tiara, replacing her own, and stood.

She moved to embrace him tightly, her purple tears flowing freely now.

"My son, in the short time I've known you, you've done more than your father and I could have ever imagined. Please, return to us safe," she said, her voice breaking with emotion.

"Mother, look after everyone, please," Orion whispered, holding her close. "And know that I love you dearly."

He kissed her forehead, then turned to his father, embracing him with the same tenderness.

"Father, be happy, find love, and do not return to your old ways."

Lawrence nodded, his eyes glistening with unshed tears.

Orion's attention shifted to his brothers.

"My beautiful, wonderful brothers. Oh, how I wish I could stay to see the men you will become."

"We will make you proud, big brother," Anton sobbed.

"If you ever need me, just call, and I will come," Orion said, kissing both of them on the cheek.

As he reached the door, he paused and turned, offering a smile that was both sad and full of hope. He followed Vando to the awaiting ship.

In the hangar, Orion saw the smaller version of the ship he had used earlier, its sleek surface reflecting the dim lights. He brushed his hand across the top, and the ship purred to life, the hatch opening before him.

He saluted Vando, then turned and entered the ship, climbing up the ramp into the cockpit. Once inside, the ship came alive with the soft hum of its systems. He typed in the coordinates and pressed the ignition button. The ship lurched forward, rising slowly, then picked up speed once the hangar roof opened.

"I will protect them to my last breath," Yimmana said in his head.

"Thank you, Yimmana. There is one last thing I must do before I go."

He raised his hand, and small stars materialized in his palm. He blew on them gently, and they shot out of the window toward the planet below. When they settled, pillars of light erupted from the ground, and stone guards began to march out.

"Farewell, Yimmana. I will see you again one day."

As the song of the planet echoed in his mind, he closed his eyes, feeling the weight of what was to come. The ship lifted from the planet's atmosphere, and Orion looked out into the darkness.

"Preparing for star jump," the onboard computer crackled.

Orion felt the shift as the ship turned, and the stars stretched as the ship entered its jump. The universe blurred around him, and for a moment, everything felt infinite.

When the ship dropped out of star jump, the view outside was stark and devastating.

Auratium lay before him, a lifeless husk, surrounded by the wreckage of his uncle's fleet.

"Open hatch," Orion commanded.

"Caution, opening the hatch will depressurize the ship's interior and life support will cease," the computer warned.

"Just open it and stay in orbit," Orion insisted, ignoring the warnings.

With a hiss, the hatch opened, and alarms blared. Orion stepped out into the nothingness of space, a silent witness to the destruction that had been wrought.

16 A spark of hope

Orion coughed violently for a few moments as his lungs adapted to the cold, thin air of space. His body ached, the pressure of his descent pulling at him as he fell faster and faster towards the planet below. The air began to heat around him, and soon he was engulfed in flames, the heat searing through his skin, his body pushing against the gravitational pull as he plummeted toward the surface. The world spun in a dizzying blur until, with a deafening crash, he collided with the planet's surface, creating a massive crater.

He stood up slowly, dusting himself off, a grim determination etched across his face. His body felt heavy, like the weight of the world was pressing down on him. As he took two deliberate steps to his left, he paused, looking at the desolate, lifeless landscape around him. The planet felt dead, empty and void of life, as though all the light and hope had been drained from it. This, he decided, was as good a place as any to begin.

Orion began to spin in place, his body glowing faintly as he reached deep into the core of the planet. He bore down through the rock and stone, pushing himself further, sinking deeper. Time felt like it stretched and blurred, hours passing as he delved deeper into the planet's heart. Finally, after what felt like an eternity, his feet broke through the last layer of rock, and he drifted onto a ledge that seemed to be the very heart of the planet.

The sight before him, this dark, lifeless core, was haunting. He could feel the weight of it pressing down on him. Orion sank down to sit on the ledge, his legs pulled to his chest. The tears that had been burning his eyes finally spilled over, golden droplets falling into the emptiness around him. For the first time since the weight of his responsibilities had been thrust upon him, he allowed himself to cry.

He was alone here, no one watching, no need to hold back. His heart felt heavy, burdened with everything he had lost and everything he was now responsible for. Not long ago, he was just a boy, struggling with the typical problems of growing up, fighting bullies and worrying about his father. Now, the entire universe seemed to rest on his shoulders, and he had no idea what the future held.

As he wept, something vibrated in the pocket of his surcoat. He reached in, pulling out the metal disc that Sanjen had given him. The moment it left his hand, the disc floated in midair, glowing softly. Orion stared at it in confusion, wondering what it meant. Suddenly, with a bright flash, Rachel's hologram appeared before him, her form hovering in the air.

"This is... weird," Rachel said, turning around as she took in her surroundings.

"What are you doing here?" Orion asked, bewildered.

Rachel paced in mid-air, her eyes scanning the space around her. "Your dad called on this thing and said he was worried about you... And you, wow, you look... different. It's kind of scary."

"I may have to go away for a long time and I don't know if I will be the same once I come back." Orion looked at her and smiled through his tears, drying his golden tears on the back of his sleeve. "Even light-years away, you still worry about me."

Rachel's face softened, a deep concern in her eyes. "Why do you have to go? What's going on?"

"I can't say," Orion replied, his voice heavy, the weight of the secret pressing on him. "But remember me, and tell everyone that I will always protect them, no matter what happens."

Before Rachel could respond, Orion held up his hand, and a white fireball shot from his palm, melting the disc and vanishing the hologram of Rachel in an instant. He couldn't afford to be distracted anymore. Too much had to be done, and time was slipping away.

He stood, his body still trembling from the transformation that was beginning to take hold. His skin began to peel away, his body erupting with light as he gave himself fully to the powers he had yet to understand. His form grew, towering above the heart of the planet as his transformation reached its peak. When the light subsided, Orion stood twenty feet tall, no hair on his head, his eyes as dark as the void, and his body shimmering with radiant white energy. The transformation was complete.

He reached down, his massive hand sweeping toward the lifeless heart of the planet. He carefully plucked it from where it lay, holding it gently in his palm. He whispered to the heart, speaking the words he had kept hidden from everyone, all the fears and secrets he had been carrying with him. The planet's heart responded, pulsing faintly in his grasp as though it could hear him.

When he was done, Orion drew light from his arm, and with a soft gesture, he placed it onto the heart. It seeped into the stone, and as the light flowed through it, the heart began to beat slowly. The colour of the heart shifted, first fading to a dull grey, then shifting into vibrant red and gold. The once-dead heart was alive again, pulsing with energy.

With great care, he placed it back into the centre of the cavern, allowing it to settle. The cavern seemed to hum with life, and from the heart, golden and red tendrils shot out, slithering toward the planet's shell. The tendrils spread like veins, breathing life back into the planet's husk. Orion watched as the planet seemed to shift, to stir, the first signs of life returning to it after so long.

Satisfied with his work, he stood up, his body still massive. He made himself thin enough to fit through the hole he had created earlier, then shot upwards, breaking through the surface. As he rose higher into the atmosphere, he saw the devastation that had been wrought, craters and holes from bombs and spells that had scarred the surface. The planet was wounded, but there was hope now.

Orion shot up into space, rising until he was above the planet, the debris of war swirling below him. He continued to grow, stretching outward until he was large enough to hold the entire planet in his hand. His fingers gently closed around the sphere of the world, and he began to reshape it.

He pressed his fingers into the surface, moulding the landmasses, creating new continents, some large and sprawling, others small and remote. He formed oceans and rivers, sculpting the world as though it were clay. The final touch was when he placed a tear in his hand, allowing it to fall onto the planet. The tears transformed into golden oceans and rivers that shimmered like liquid light.

With the planet now whole again, Orion placed it back into its orbit and hovered there for a moment, looking down at the creation he had shaped. It was a symbol of rebirth, not just for the planet, but for himself. The future was uncertain, but at least there was hope again.

Floating above the planet, Orion watched in awe as silver grass began to sprout from the soil, its blades shimmering in the light. Trees of various shapes and sizes sprouted around him, some with red leaves, others with gold, and a few with dark purple hues. The planet was beginning to come alive, and a sense of peace filled his heart. A quiet smile spread across his face as he marvelled at the beauty of what he had created.

Slowly, he began to shrink, relinquishing the form he had taken. As he shrank back to his original size, he drifted back towards the surface. His feet finally touched the ground, and he sat down on the newly sprouted grass. His hands began to play with a small ball of light, tossing it back and forth, the soft glow illuminating the landscape around him.

It struck him then, there were no animals, no creatures to fill the land, no life to truly balance the planet. He paused and, with a thought, the ball of light turned orange. Out of it jumped an orange, sheep-like creature, followed by another, and another. As the ball changed colour once more, purple, cow-like creatures appeared, their horns golden and silver, their bodies built strong and sturdy. Orion laughed softly as he watched the creatures frolic across the newly created lands.

Not done, he split the ball of light into five smaller pieces and sent four of them zooming toward the sky. Each one spread out around the planet, filling the landmasses with life. He could feel the creatures being placed into the oceans and onto the land, filling every nook and cranny of the world. The final piece of light remained in his hand, and as he held it, he sent it towards the nearest mountain to inspect an area he had missed during his moulding of the planet.

Arriving at the mountain, Orion stepped toward the stone face, only to be met with an unexpected surprise. The rocks in front of him melted away, revealing a set of massive stone doors. Without hesitation, he stepped inside, the doors closing behind him, leaving the world outside in silence. Inside, darkness enveloped him, but the ground beneath his feet began to glow, revealing a winding path. He followed the path, walking for what seemed like an eternity, until he reached another stone wall. The wall melted before him, and to his amazement, he found himself standing once again in the heart of the planet, surrounded by its beating core.

Suddenly, a piece of rock broke away from the wall, turning into molten magma that slithered toward him. As the magma shifted, it began to take form, shaping itself into a human-like figure. When it reached Orion, it stopped, shining so brightly that he was forced to look away. The light faded, and standing before him was a replica of Orion, exact in every detail, only it radiated an otherworldly aura.

"Forgive me for startling you," the figure said, its voice crackling like lightning. "I merely picked a shape you would feel comfortable with."

Orion's heart raced as he gazed at the figure before him. "Who are you?" he asked, still in disbelief.

"I am the planet," the figure replied, bowing before him. "But I have no name, for you have not given me one yet."

A mixture of joy and sorrow filled Orion's chest. He had brought life to a lifeless world, and now the planet had a voice of its own. He smiled and wiped away a tear, overwhelmed with emotion.

"I... What would you like to be called?" he asked gently.

The figure sat down before him, its hands resting on its head. It beamed up at Orion before speaking, its voice calm but filled with meaning. "I would like to be called Promendium. It once meant 'new hope,' and I would like it too once again."

Orion's heart swelled with pride as he took a deep breath. He had created life, and now, he had given the planet a name. It was perfect.

"Promendium," he repeated, his voice filled with affection. "That is a perfect name."

With that, Orion extended his hand to help the planet's form rise. As Promendium stood, Orion pulled him into a tight hug. "I think that's perfect. You're different from the last planet I met; it couldn't take on a form."

"That's because you made me in a shape you could relate to," Promendium replied matter-of-factly, a small smile forming on his lips.

Together, they made their way back to the surface, and when they stepped out from the mountain, Orion gasped. The planet's surface was unrecognizable. A lush, vibrant forest stretched out before them, the trees towering above, their trunks twisted and gnarled in beautiful ways. The air smelled fresh, and the sounds of wildlife filled the atmosphere.

Promendium led Orion to a clearing in the heart of the forest. "I have a gift for you," he said. "A thank you for creating me."

Orion, still in awe of the transformation, shook his head. "You don't need to give me anything. This is all I wanted."

Promendium knelt down, his hands brushing the earth. Sand shot up from the ground, swirling around in a vortex that stretched into the sky. Orion felt a low rumble beneath his feet. Fireballs erupted from the ground, joining the swirling sand. In a blinding flash of light, Orion had to shield his eyes. When the light finally faded, he opened his eyes to find a magnificent glass manor standing before him.

The entrance was framed with arches of black, red, and white glass, with mist trapped between the panes, creating a hazy, ethereal effect. Orion could hardly believe his eyes.

Promendium, beaming with excitement, took Orion's hand and pulled him inside. "I designed it based on what you hold dear," Promendium explained. "Now your family can sit beside you."

The throne room within the manor was stunning. A varnished wooden throne stood at the centre, flanked by four high-backed chairs. Two marble fountains flanked the throne, their water flowing in perfect harmony, while a red carpet led up to the throne. Behind it, a massive portrait of Orion was etched into the glass, capturing his regal and powerful form.

"It's beautiful," Orion whispered, his heart swelling with gratitude.

Promendium smiled, watching Orion take in the sight. "I wanted to make this a place where you and your family could truly belong. This is for you."

As they explored further, Promendium led Orion down a series of corridors. Orion caught glimpses of rooms filled with furniture, each more magnificent than the last, though Promendium was moving too fast for him to properly see. When they stopped abruptly, Orion crashed into him, a small laugh escaping his lips as he steadied himself. Promendium opened a door to reveal a bedroom that took Orion's breath away. A hovering bed sat at the centre of the room, surrounded by oak drawers, a huge screen mounted on the opposite wall, and a sandalwood dressing table.

"Wow," Orion breathed, still trying to take it all in.

"I hope you like it," Promendium said. "It has bedrooms for you and your family, six guest rooms, each with its own en-suite, a ballroom, a large kitchen, a banquet hall, and a three-acre garden."

Orion nodded, feeling overwhelmed by the thoughtfulness of it all. "This is incredible. Thank you."

Promendium smiled warmly. "Where will you stay?" Orion asked, his mind racing with possibilities.

"I will return to the planet's core, if you no longer need me," Promendium replied solemnly.

Orion's brow furrowed, and he paced back and forth, wondering what to say. Finally, he stopped and turned to Promendium. "Wouldn't you like to stay up here with me?"

Promendium looked up at him, his face lighting up. "I suppose I could, if you'd want me to."

Orion smiled and placed his hand on Promendium's shoulder. "It would be nice to have you with me. You can stay with me and my family, or if you prefer, you can have your own space."

Promendium's eyes gleamed with excitement. "I would like that," he said, his voice cracking with emotion. He pulled Orion into a tight embrace. "As long as I can change my appearance."

Orion chuckled softly. "You control your own destiny, so you can change your appearance as you please."

With a shimmer of light, Promendium began to shift. His form grew dark, as deep and vast as the void of space, then brightened, shining as brilliantly as the sun. Light exploded from his eyes and mouth, and in an instant, the transformation was complete.

A teenage boy now stood before Orion, his hair made of purple leaves, his skin gleaming silver, and his eyes a striking shade of gold. When he spoke, his voice crackled like lightning.

"There we go, that's better," he said, his grin wide. "While I'm in this form, please call me Pro."

Orion looked at Pro, feeling a sense of hope bloom within him. This world, this new creation, was truly coming to life.

17 The Tale of Two Brothers

Two days had passed since Orion had created Promendium. Together, they had journeyed across the planet, shaping its surface, building homes, and cultivating farmlands for the future citizens. Orion found himself momentarily forgetting the weight of his responsibilities, immersed in the joy of creation and companionship. Promendium's childlike wonder and unyielding energy made it feel almost like a vacation. But reality struck as

Orion stared at the endless horizon of this new world, this was not the life he was destined to lead.

"This has been fun," Orion said with a bittersweet smile, "but I really must go now."

Promendium's expression shifted, the glimmer of joy in his golden eyes dimming. "Must you really?" he asked, his voice tinged with sadness.

Orion placed a reassuring hand on Promendium's shoulder. "You will not be alone for long," he said warmly. "I will send word to my family. They should arrive within the week. They'll take care of you and make this world flourish."

Promendium nodded reluctantly, a faint smile returning to his face. Orion gathered his belongings, pulling Promendium into a final hug before soaring into the skies. As he approached his ship, still orbiting the planet, he glanced back at Promendium standing among the silver grass and golden rivers. The sight filled him with pride and sorrow. With one last look, he entered the ship's open hatch.

Inside, he nearly tripped over an oxygen bottle. Frowning, he muttered, "Why is this here? I don't remember it being here when I left."

"Because I didn't want to die," Eymd's voice rang out, cutting through the silence. She emerged from the shadows, clutching an oxygen mask tightly to her mouth.

"What are you doing here?" Orion asked, his voice filled with exasperation.

"Does the term 'shadow warrior' or 'protector' mean anything to you?" she snapped back.

Orion sighed, pressing a button on the control panel. "Computer, close hatch and reinstate life support."

A hiss filled the cabin as the hatch sealed shut. The ship began to pressurize, and moments later, the life support system flooded the interior with oxygen.

"Finally," Eymd grumbled, removing the mask. "The computer wouldn't recognize my command code to override life support. It would've helped if you didn't leave me to suffocate."

"I didn't know you were here!" Orion snapped defensively.

"Right," she retorted coldly, crossing her arms. "The ship warned you about humanoid lifeforms perishing, and you didn't think to check?"

Orion opened his mouth to respond but quickly shut it as Eymd continued her rant.

"Don't bother answering; that was rhetorical. I mean, really, what have I done to make you want to kill me?" she asked, her voice dripping with sarcasm.

Orion sighed heavily. "I'm sorry," he muttered.

"'Sorry' wouldn't have helped if I hadn't found that oxygen canister, would it?" Eymd glared at him, her green, cat-like eyes glowing faintly in the dim cockpit.

"Maybe next time, let me know yourself instead of relying on the ship," Orion said, offering a hand to help her up.

Eymd slapped his hand away and climbed into the co-pilot's seat, glaring daggers at him. "So, where are we going?" she asked, her tone sharp.

"I'm not sure yet. Give me a minute," Orion replied, his tone equally curt. He pressed a button on the console. "Computer, call Aurorina."

A buzzing sound filled the cockpit before a polite male voice answered. "Good afternoon, temporary royal palace. How may I direct your call?"

"I wish to speak with Aurorina," Orion said.

"I'm sorry, sir, but I cannot just connect you to the Intenfna," the voice replied.

"This is Intenfli Orion," he barked, his patience thinning. "I wish to be connected to my mother. Now."

"Right away, sir. Connecting you now."

After a few seconds of eerie hold music, Aurorina's voice came through the speakers. "Orion? Is it really you?"

"Yes, it's me. Is everything okay there?" Orion asked, his tone softening.

"Everything is fine," Aurorina replied, though the sound of distant explosions and shouting betrayed her words. "We've had a few of your uncle's troops land earlier, but the stone guard has been holding them off."

Orion's shoulders relaxed slightly. "Good. I've just sent you some coordinates. If all fails, you are to evacuate there."

There was a brief silence before Aurorina's astonished voice replied, "That's where Auratium used to be."

"Yes. It's now Promendium," Orion explained. "He will protect you all."

"I see," Aurorina said, her voice heavy with emotion. "Be safe, my son. We love...."

Orion ended the call before she could finish, not trusting himself to keep his composure. He reached deep within his mind, past the cacophony of voices from the planets he had connected with, and focused on Yimmana's steady, calming presence.

"My friend," he began, "I have given you the power to teleport yourself and my people. You will join your new brother, Promendium."

"I understand, Intenfli," Yimmana replied serenely. "I will guard them as you have asked."

Disconnecting from Yimmana, Orion turned to the next task. He raised his hands, and dark tendrils shot out toward the planet below. The tendrils coiled together, forming a massive stone figure in the void of space. Within minutes, the figure replicated itself, creating two identical protectors. Orion broke the tendrils, and the two stone guards came to life.

"What are your orders?" they boomed, their voices deep and resonant, shaking the ship's hull.

"You will be protectors," Orion commanded. "Acknowledge."

"Confirmed," they replied in unison.

"You will guard all planets and citizens who seek refuge from my uncle's army. Is that understood?"

"As you wish, Creator," they boomed. One of the protectors moved to the far side of the planet, extending its massive arms. Lightning erupted from its fingertips, weaving a glowing barrier around the planet until it connected with the other protector. The planet shimmered and vanished from view.

Orion exhaled deeply, his final task in the system complete. "Set coordinates for the next damaged planet," he instructed.

"Affirmative, star-drive in five, four, three, two, one," the computer responded.

As the countdown hit one, the ship surged forward, throwing both Orion and Eymd back into their seats. The overwhelming sensation of acceleration pinned them briefly, but once the ship stabilized, Orion got up and stretched. He pressed a panel on his left, which dissolved to reveal a hidden alcove with two books nestled within. He reached for the top book, the one he had taken from the mansion's library, and settled back into his chair, opening it to a random page.

Before he could begin reading, Eymd's sharp voice broke the silence. *"Are you honestly just going to act like I'm not here, after you nearly killed me?"*

Orion sighed, placing the book down on his lap. *"I told you this journey needed to be taken alone. You decided to stow away."*

Eymd smirked as she shifted into a meditative posture on the cockpit floor. *"Fine, suit yourself. I've got meditating to do anyway."*

Shaking his head, Orion turned back to the book and began to read.

The Tale of Two Brothers

Long ago, two inseparable brothers were born to a powerful Intenfli, the guardian of a thriving star system. Each was promised a realm of their own to rule when their father passed. As they grew, their father, wise and just, taught them the values of compassion, love, and honour. The elder brother embraced these teachings, eager to inherit his father's mantle. The younger, however, scorned the lessons, finding them tedious and restrictive. Yet, despite his disdain, he followed his brother to every lesson, bound by an unspoken competition between them.

Years passed, and their father continued to impart his wisdom. But one day, the younger brother abandoned the palace, embarking on a pilgrimage to "find himself" among the galaxies. The elder remained, taking on his responsibilities and striving to uphold the ideals instilled in him.

Decades passed, and on the eve of the elder brother's hundredth birthday, the younger returned unexpectedly. His once-vibrant appearance was gone, his face gaunt, his eyes shadowed by sleepless nights, and his demeanour hardened. In his hands, he bore a gift: two jewel-encrusted swords, one for his brother and one for their father.

A week after his return, tragedy struck. The father fell gravely ill, his vibrant spirit diminished to a flicker. Despite healers arriving from across the universe, none could identify the cause of his ailment. The brothers were summoned to their father's chambers for a final farewell.

As they knelt beside the bed, the elder wept openly, grasping his father's frail hand. The younger brother remained stoic, a strange smirk tugging at his lips.

"My sons," their father rasped, "I have taught you all that I know. My kingdom will be divided equally between you. Remember what I've instilled in you, and honour the balance of creation."

He coughed violently, black blood staining the white handkerchief he used to cover his mouth. "My time has come to ascend to the next plane."

With one last, shuddering breath, the great Intenfli was gone.

The elder brother clung to his father's lifeless form, sobbing, while the younger sneered as he tore open the sealed letter left to him. His eyes narrowed as he read, then snapped to his brother. "Why does your kingdom thrive while mine crumbles?"

The elder sighed, folding his letter carefully. "Our father must have had his reasons, Rohanas. Trust in his wisdom."

Rohanas rose abruptly. "Trust? I trusted him to treat us equally. I see now I was a fool. There will be no alliance between us. I'll carve my destiny myself."

"What about Father's burial?" the elder asked, his voice heavy with sorrow.

"What about it?" Rohanas snapped, storming out of the room.

Years later, Auren, the elder brother, had lived up to their father's ideals. His system thrived, its citizens prosperous and content. He married his childhood sweetheart, Aurorina, and together they were blessed with a son, Orion. In contrast, Rohanas's realm fell into chaos, whispers of cruelty and corruption spreading like wildfire.

The two brothers' paths crossed again on the day of Orion's naming ceremony. The temple doors burst open, and Rohanas strode in, flanked by his elite guard. His presence was suffocating, his aura dark and malevolent. He marched directly to Auren, his piercing gaze settling on the infant Orion.

"So, this is your heir? This… mongrel?" Rohanas sneered.

"Brother," Auren began, stepping between Rohanas and his family.

"Silence!" Rohanas bellowed, his voice echoing through the sacred chamber. "I didn't come for pleasantries. Surrender your kingdom to me, or I'll raze it to the ground. You have twenty-four hours to decide."

Auren's heart sank. "What has become of you, Rohanas?"

Rohanas smirked cruelly. "I became what our father feared. I embraced what you were too weak to wield. I killed him, brother, and I'll do the same to you if you stand in my way."

Gasps echoed through the temple as Rohanas vanished in a plume of smoke, his elite guard trailing behind. The ceremony continued, though the joy had been overshadowed by the looming threat.

Once the naming was complete, Auren and Aurorina were escorted by the temple priestess to a hidden chamber deep within the temple's core. The air grew cooler as they descended, the walls glowing faintly with ancient runes.

They reached a ruby-encrusted door, which swung open to reveal a room bathed in golden light. Figures in silver robes stood in a semicircle, their faces hidden. One figure, clad in gold, stepped forward.

"You must send the child away," she declared. "He is the universe's only hope."

Aurorina clutched Orion tightly. "What do you mean? Why must we send him away?"

"You have forgotten the promise made when you met the Old Ones," the golden-robed figure said. "But we have not. He was created for a purpose greater than any of us."

Two robed figures approached, gently taking Orion from Aurorina's trembling arms. Aurorina collapsed to her knees, sobbing uncontrollably. The golden-robed woman lowered her hood, revealing a face identical to Aurorina's.

"Sister," she whispered softly. "He will be safe. You will see him again."

She kissed Aurorina's forehead before disappearing into the radiant light. Auren helped his wife to her feet, his own heart breaking as they left the chamber, their cries echoing in the silent halls.

Thus began the war that would rage for three centuries, tearing apart families, worlds, and the very fabric of the universe itself.

Orion closed the book, his golden tears falling freely. "So, Uncle wasn't always this way," he whispered to himself, his heart heavy with the weight of the truth.

18 Following the pilgrimage

Orion sat staring out of the cockpit window, watching the stars streak by in a mesmerizing blur. The weight of uncertainty bore heavily on him. How was he supposed to uncover the truth about his uncle? And what was he going to do about Eymd now that he had to continue the journey alone? Before he could dwell further, the ship's computer crackled to life, interrupting his thoughts.

"Approaching coordinates."

The ship dropped out of star-drive, shuddering slightly as it slowed. Before him lay a planet, vibrant and alive to the eye, its atmosphere swirling with rich colours. Yet as Orion guided the ship closer, he reached out with his mind. What he felt was dissonant, a cold, hollow thrum beneath its surface, like a dying heartbeat struggling to persist.

"Identify yourself," a commanding female voice echoed within his head, sharp and intrusive.

Startled, Orion responded, "I am Intenfli Orion, rightful heir to the Orion star system."

The planet did not reply directly. Instead, he sensed an ethereal murmur, as though it was whispering to itself.

"Did you hear what he called himself?" a voice said, mocking. "Rightful heir, indeed!" another chimed in, dripping with disdain. "Where has he been all these years?" a third voice sneered.

The cacophony of voices grew louder, causing Orion's head to throb. He gritted his teeth, trying to push back against the overwhelming noise. "I thought there was only one planet here!" he muttered.

Laughter rippled through his mind. "See? He's an imposter, doesn't even know there are three moons!" mocked one voice.

"Stop being rude," the original female voice cut in, more measured now. "I beg your pardon, sir. We've been alone for far too long."

"You are the main planet, I take it?" Orion asked, regaining his composure.

"I am," it replied, a tinge of sadness in its tone. "Moons do not usually speak. But I was lonely. After centuries of solitude, I fractured my consciousness and gifted pieces of it to my three moons. They are… imperfect reflections of me."

Orion reached deeper into the planet's consciousness, glimpsing fragments of its tragic past. Long ago, a vibrant civilization had thrived here. But as war ravaged the star system, its people fled, leaving the planet vulnerable. His uncle's forces arrived not long after, mercilessly scorching the surface and reducing it to ash. Left abandoned and bereft, the planet turned inward, splitting itself apart in a desperate attempt to stave off madness. The moons had been born of loneliness, a testament to the planet's fractured psyche.

"I'm sorry," Orion whispered. "Our maps marked you as destroyed. I was on my way to repair you."

"I am not beyond saving," the planet replied, its tone softening.

"You are no longer alone. Gather your moons and teleport to your brother's side. Stand together until the war ends."

There was a moment of silence before a loud *pop*. The planet and its moons vanished. Orion blinked at the now-empty space, lost in thought. The soft rustle of movement behind him jolted him back to reality. Spinning his chair, he found Eymd staring out of the viewport, her jaw slack in amazement.

"That was… awesome," she said, her usual sharpness tinged with awe. "Have you considered giving me some new powers, considering I'm your protector?"

Orion smirked. "I could grant you a power, I suppose. And for the record, you don't need protection from me."

"You say that like you didn't almost kill me," Eymd shot back, though there was no venom in her voice. "How about the power to breathe in any atmosphere, you know, just in case you leave the airlock open again?"

"That happened once," Orion sighed. "And I apologized."

"Fine," she muttered, folding her arms. "What about focusing on what happened to Rohanas instead?"

Orion turned back to the computer. "Do you have a record of the planets my uncle visited during his pilgrimage?"

"Please standby," the computer replied. *"Establishing a connection with palace archives."*

As the database loaded, Eymd chuckled softly. "You're thinking about ditching me, aren't you?"

"How do you always know?" Orion asked, genuinely puzzled.

"Telepathic, remember?" She tapped her temple. "Shield your thoughts better."

Before he could reply, the screen lit up with a list of four planets. Orion frowned. In fifty years, his uncle had only managed to visit four planets?

"Computer, display details on the planets," he ordered.

Danforndia: A water planet with a single landmass. The native Coffena species are aquatic, with embassies on the surface and in an underwater complex.

"Your uncle stayed here for a week," the computer reported.

Orion shook his head and scrolled to the next entry.

Spyron: A jungle planet where landmasses shift every few hours, inhabited by a primitive race.

"He was here for three months," the computer noted.

The third planet, however, was labelled **Borangus….Data Error.** Orion scowled. "Why is there no data?"

"All references to Borangus have been deleted," the computer replied.

"What about the fourth planet?"

Thalmorf…..Data Error.

"That's impossible," Eymd interjected, stepping forward. She began typing on the console, pulling up a shadowy interface labelled *Shadow Warrior Database*. Orion caught the faint glow of the words before she blocked his view.

"Even our systems have no record of these planets," she muttered, puzzled. "And that's… odd. Nothing can be deleted from our database."

Orion's unease deepened, though he kept his face neutral. "Computer, lay in a course for Borangus."

As the ship entered star-drive, both Orion and Eymd stared out at the stars, the silence between them heavy with unspoken fears. Eymd broke the stillness first. "I'm going to meditate and see if the other warriors know anything about these planets."

With a shimmer, she vanished. Orion sighed, letting the streaking stars lull him into a restless sleep.

Orion stared out of the cockpit window, his mind adrift. The stars zoomed past like streams of fireflies, their glow a soothing balm to his frayed nerves. The weight of his journey, the unanswered questions, and the looming threats seemed momentarily distant as the hypnotic streaks lulled him into a fitful sleep.

The piercing blare of alarms yanked him from his dreams. Disoriented, Orion sat up sharply, only to see Eymd leaning over him, her form battered and burned. Half her body was charred, and the soft blue glow that usually radiated from her was dim and flickering. Behind her, a jagged tear in the ship's hull revealed the void of space.

"What's happening?" Orion demanded, panic creeping into his voice.

Eymd's lips moved, and her voice came out high-pitched, strained, and unnatural. "Close… to death…" she gasped, the words barely audible. "Protect… yourself…"

Hearing her speak sent a chill through him. Eymd had always communicated telepathically, this was wrong. Her voice felt alien, fragile, and desperate. Orion's heart raced as he looked between her and the gaping wound in the ship, alarms screeching all around him. The chaos was suffocating, and he couldn't think. Couldn't act.

As Eymd's form slumped, her breath shallow and faltering, something in Orion snapped. A raw, primal energy surged through him, overriding the fear.

"STOP!" he bellowed.

The ship fell silent. The alarms froze mid-blare. Sparks from damaged consoles hung motionless in the air, and even the flicker of failing lights ceased. Time itself had ground to a halt.

Orion moved with grim purpose, his movements calm and precise as though guided by instinct. He laid Eymd gently on the floor, her body unnaturally still. Golden tears welled in his eyes as he reached into his chest, feeling the familiar, rhythmic pulse of his heart. With a trembling hand, he drew it out, a brilliant orb of radiant gold, alive and warm. It pulsed in his hand, filling the frozen space with an otherworldly hum.

Bracing himself, he tore off a fragment. Pain seared through his entire being, but he didn't falter. The piece of his heart glowed brightly, vibrating with life as he pressed it onto Eymd's chest. The fragment melted into her, its light spreading across her body like golden veins, knitting her wounds with celestial energy.

Replacing his heart, Orion turned to the gaping hole in the ship. He extended his hands, drawing threads of starlight from the void. Weaving them together, he formed a shimmering net, its glow vibrant and pure. He cast it over the tear, where it fused seamlessly with the ship's hull, restoring integrity.

Exhausted, Orion sank into his chair. As time resumed, the alarms blared again, though muted now. Eymd's body began to stir faintly, the golden glow of his heart fragment working to heal her.

"Engage defences and evasive manoeuvres," Orion ordered, his voice steady despite the turmoil.

The ship jerked forward, dodging a volley of light projectiles from an unseen foe. Orion gripped the controls, weaving through the storm of fire. The ship groaned as one shot struck its side, and another streak of light approached fast. Orion twisted the controls, narrowly evading the blast.

The communications panel crackled, and a stern female voice filled the cockpit. "Intenfli Orion, do you require assistance?"

Orion didn't reply. Instead, he stood, secured an oxygen mask onto Eymd, and depressurized the cockpit. With a burst of power, he leapt from the ship, his body expanding rapidly as he shape-shifted. In moments, he was towering above the ship, nearly as large as the planet itself.

The turrets turned their fire toward him, but the balls of energy dissolved harmlessly against his shimmering skin. Orion's massive hands reached out, gripping the nearest turret. With a roar, he hurled it into another, the collision detonating both in a fiery explosion. He clapped his hands together, sending a shockwave that obliterated the remaining defences.

The immediate threat neutralized, Orion shrank back to his normal size and returned to the cockpit. The ship was eerily silent now, the hum of its systems barely audible.

"Damage report," he said, his tone clipped.

"Star-drive offline, engines offline, life support failing, and weapons offline," the computer replied.

Before Orion could react, the ship lurched. It wasn't adrift, it was being pulled. Orion leaned forward, scanning the void, but there was nothing. Just empty space.

"Docking procedure initiated," the computer announced.

Out of nowhere, a massive floating palace shimmered into view above the ship. Its structure was breathtaking, an ethereal blend of glass-like walls and luminous arches, radiating an aura of power. The ship jolted to the left, connecting itself to a hatch.

Orion stood, ready to defend himself and Eymd. The airlock hissed as the doors slid open, revealing Vando, his head bowed in deference. Orion exhaled in relief, though his posture remained guarded. Beyond Vando, the corridor was lined with royal guards, their stances firm and disciplined.

"We need help. Eymd needs a healer," Orion said, his voice commanding.

"Is she…?" Vando began, concern flickering across his face.

"No. A piece of my heart is repairing her, but she needs rest."

Vando nodded sharply, snapping his fingers. Two guards stepped forward, conjuring a stretcher of star magic. They lifted Eymd with care and carried her away.

"I thought I told you to stay with the planet," Orion said sharply, his gratitude tempered by irritation.

Vando inclined his head, his expression apologetic. "Forgive me, Sire. The council insisted I find you."

"You shouldn't have left."

"Yimmana joined Promendium," Vando explained, his voice tinged with urgency. "He created this ship and told the council it was imperative to locate you."

"Why?" Orion asked, his voice softening slightly.

"He feared that if you went on this journey alone, you might… lose yourself."

Vando extended a hand, helping Orion out of the ship. The moment Orion's feet touched the palace floor, the guards snapped to attention. Their movements were synchronized, a testament to their discipline.

"Follow me, Sire. Eymd has been taken to the infirmary, but you are needed elsewhere," Vando said.

As they walked, Orion took in his surroundings. The palace bore the unmistakable mark of Promendium's craftsmanship, the same sweeping arches and intricate designs that adorned the royal palace. The walls pulsed faintly, as if the entire structure was alive.

They stopped before a door. Vando opened it and gestured for Orion to enter. The room beyond was serene, dominated by a large oval tub filled with steaming water. Orion stepped inside, hearing the door click shut behind him.

Approaching the tub, he sighed in relief. Stripping off his clothes, he slid into the water, the warmth enveloping his aching body. His muscles, sore from the strain of shape-shifting, finally relaxed. As he leaned back, letting the steam rise around him, Kalligah appeared at the door.

Orion raised a hand, signalling them to leave. "Not now," he murmured.

Kalligah bowed and retreated, leaving Orion alone. The silence was blissful, and for the first time in what felt like an eternity, he allowed himself to rest. The weight of his journey, his battles, and the sacrifices he'd made lingered in the back of his mind, but for now, he let it all fade into the soothing embrace of the water

Orion had just begun to drift off when a soft knock roused him from his fleeting tranquillity. Sinking deeper into the warm water, he ensured the bubbles concealed him completely before addressing the visitor.

"Come in," he said, his tone calm yet commanding.

The door opened, and Vando stepped inside, looking sheepish. His usual confidence was muted, his hands clasped nervously in front of him.

"Pardon the intrusion, Sire," he began, bowing slightly. "But Master Sanjen wishes to examine you, and the council has requested your presence at your earliest convenience."

Orion sighed, running a hand through his damp, golden locks. "Send Sanjen in. Tell the council I'll be there shortly."

Vando bowed again and exited, replaced moments later by Sanjen, the royal healer. Without preamble, the older man approached the tub, his sharp eyes scanning Orion with clinical precision. Ignoring any notion of propriety, he began gently pressing his hands against Orion's face and forehead.

"You've overextended yourself," Sanjen said bluntly, his brow furrowing. "Your powers are nearly depleted."

"I didn't have a choice," Orion replied, meeting the healer's gaze evenly.

Sanjen's expression softened as he nodded. "I know. I reviewed the ship's logs. You've done well, but you must tread carefully. Power is dangerous when untethered. Remember your humanity, Orion," he said, a faint smile tugging at his lips.

With that, Sanjen stepped back and left, leaving Orion to finish his bath in peace. Ten minutes later, feeling refreshed and steady once more, Orion climbed out of the water. He donned the armour and surcoat laid out for him, a masterful combination of functionality and elegance. The polished silver plates reflected the light, and the surcoat bore the insignia of the Orion Star System, a blazing sun cradled by celestial rings. As he adjusted the clasp on his chest, he caught his reflection in the mirror.

The face that stared back was no longer that of a carefree teenager. His golden locks, a new addition to his features, flickered faintly as if they were made of flame. His jaw was stronger, his eyes sharper, and his presence more commanding. He sighed and turned away from the mirror, leaving the room to find Vando waiting outside.

"We're running late, Sire," Vando said, a hint of urgency in his tone.

"They can wait," Orion replied, a playful grin spreading across his face.

Vando chuckled, his tension easing slightly. Instead of leading Orion through the ship, he mumbled into his sleeve, and silver flames erupted around them. In an instant, the flames subsided, and they stood before a set of magnificent golden doors.

Vando pushed them open, and the sound of trumpets echoed through the grand hall. Orion stepped inside, his presence immediately commanding attention. A small, green-skinned woman stepped forward, her voice resonating with surprising volume.

"All rise for Intenfli Orion I!" she bellowed.

The crowd rose as one, and as Orion made his way toward the central table, he caught familiar faces among them. Mayor Timwanto stood off to one side, waving enthusiastically. Orion smiled faintly in recognition but was nearly knocked off his feet as two figures barrelled into him.

His brothers, Jake and Anton, wrapped him in a tight embrace.

"Told you we'd see him again!" Anton said, his bright blue hair making him stand out as always.

Before Jake could reply, Lawrence approached, his expression stern. "You two, not now. Return to your seats."

Looking sheepish, the twins obeyed, hurrying back to the central table. Lawrence followed, his pace measured and deliberate. As Orion turned, his mother, Intenfna Aurorina, approached him with a curtsy.

"Honourable people of the Orion Star System," she began, her voice carrying an air of formality. "Our beloved Intenfli has returned and shall now resume his duties as our leader."

Orion's jaw tightened. He wasn't ready for this, wasn't ready to reclaim the throne. He glanced at his mother, silently pleading for more time, but her expression remained resolute.

"I, Intenfna Aurorina, now return to my son his crown and sceptres," she declared.

As she spoke, Orion felt the familiar warmth of the liquid sceptres flowing up his arm, settling once more on his forearms. Aurorina stepped forward, placing his crown upon him and kissing his hand before stepping back, pride radiating from her.

Turning to face the crowd, Orion mustered a smile. The hall erupted in applause, cheers echoing through the chamber. Music swelled as people rose from their seats to dance and celebrate.

Aurorina leaned close, her voice quiet. "I'm sorry, my son. The council left me no choice. They said it was not my place to rule."

"It's fine, Mother," Orion replied, his tone steady though his emotions churned beneath the surface. "I just wish I had more time."

As he took his seat at the central table, the festivities continued around him. He watched the dancers, the swirling lights of the chandeliers casting a golden glow over the revellers. The hall's beauty itself was breathtaking fifty gleaming glass tables surrounded a grand dance floor, and golden chandeliers hung like constellations above. Behind the throne stood a towering stone statue of Orion himself, holding a planet in his hand.

His brothers flanked him, their energy infectious despite the formal setting.

"So, you thought you wouldn't see me again?" Orion teased Jake, who sat beside him.

"It felt like goodbye forever when you left," Jake admitted, his voice tinged with vulnerability.

"I told you I'd always come back," Orion said, placing a reassuring hand on his shoulder. "Where's Dad?"

Jake gestured to the far end of the hall, where Orion's adoptive father danced with his birth mother. The two moved in perfect harmony, their smiles radiant.

"They seem happy, don't they?" Anton chimed in from Orion's other side.

"Yeah, they do," Orion replied. "Is there food? I'm starving."

As if on cue, a gong sounded, and Kalligah entered, carrying trays piled high with food. Plates were quickly filled, and Orion joined the others in the feast, his hunger matching the joy of the celebration.

From beneath one of the tables, Pragor, the ever-curious hound, sniffed around for scraps. A boy approached the central table, pouring blue liquid into glasses. Orion recognized him instantly.

"Ryann, why are you working?" he asked.

"All the kitchen staff have to work, Sire," Ryann replied.

"Not tonight," Orion said firmly. "Go back to the kitchen and tell everyone they're free to join the celebration."

"Really, Sire?" Ryann's eyes widened with excitement.

Orion nodded, and the boy darted off. Moments later, the kitchen staff hesitantly entered the hall, taking seats among the tables.

Aurorina leaned closer. "That was a kind gesture."

"It felt right," Orion replied simply.

Standing, he raised his glass. "Tonight, the walls of our society crumble. My uncle doesn't care if you're rich or poor, he'll destroy you all the same. So tonight, we celebrate. Tomorrow, the real work begins."

The hall erupted in cheers once more. Orion drank deeply, letting the moment wash over him. The party stretched into the early hours, but eventually, Orion retired to his chambers, leaving the celebration behind. Tomorrow awaited, and with it, the weight of a crown and a war yet to be won.

19 Entering Eymd's Dream

Orion awoke to the sound of someone calling his name. The voice was faint, almost a whisper, but it stirred him from his restless sleep. He opened his eyes to find himself in complete darkness. Summoning a small orb of light, he sent it floating upward, illuminating his surroundings.

He was in a cell.

The walls were bare and metallic, exuding cold indifference. In one corner stood a rusted toilet, while a thin, metal board with a tattered pillow served as a bed. On the floor, an untouched tray of food sat, its contents stale and unappetizing.

"I knew you would come," rasped a hoarse voice from the shadows.

Orion turned sharply toward the sound. Chains jingled as a figure stepped into the light, a woman, frail and broken, but unmistakably familiar.

"Lillithan," he gasped, his chest tightening.

She looked ill, her once-vibrant skin now pallid and grey. Her long, flowing hair had been shaved to stubble, and she wore a black jumpsuit that clung loosely to her gaunt frame. Star-magic-infused chains coiled tightly around her body, glowing faintly with a sinister energy.

"I have been trying to call to you since they captured me," she said, her voice wavering.

"Where are we?" Orion asked, his voice low and urgent.

"I don't know," she replied, her eyes darting around the cell as if the shadows themselves were listening. "But one of your uncle's generals keeps interrogating me."

Orion stepped closer and knelt beside her, his heart heavy with guilt. "Let me try to help."

He extended his hand and murmured an incantation, sending a healing spell toward her. The chains immediately reacted, glowing fiercely and absorbing the magic before it could reach her. He tried again, this time attempting to melt the chains as he had once done for his mother. Again, the chains absorbed the spell, their glow intensifying until the magic fizzled out.

"There's no point," Lillithan said with a tired sigh. "I've tried everything I know. These chains are unlike anything I've ever seen."

"I'm so sorry I couldn't save you," Orion whispered, his voice thick with emotion. "But I swear, we'll find you. I won't rest until you're free."

A faint smile tugged at her lips, and she leaned her head against his shoulder. "You truly are like your parents."

"Speaking of parents," Orion began, his tone softening, "we found my real mother. She's alive, she never died."

Lillithan's eyes widened, and a spark of joy momentarily brightened her weary face. She stumbled to her feet and, with what little energy she had, spun around the cell in a clumsy dance.

"By the gods, she's alive!" she exclaimed before collapsing back down beside him, breathless but smiling.

Orion chuckled softly, but his expression grew serious again. "Do you know which of my uncle's generals is here?"

"I don't," Lillithan admitted, her smile fading. "She wears a mask every time she comes for me."

Orion opened his mouth to respond, but Lillithan continued, her voice dropping to a whisper. "There were explosions a little while ago. Everyone rushed off in a panic."

Before Orion could process her words, the faint sound of jingling chains echoed in the distance. A key turned in the lock, and the light vanished abruptly, plunging the cell into darkness.

Orion jolted awake, his chest heaving. He was back in his bed, the vision lingering in his mind like a phantom. Swinging his legs over the side, he quickly donned his dressing gown and rushed out of his chambers, straight into a guard. The collision sent the man flying into the opposite wall.

"I'm so sorry!" Orion exclaimed, hurrying to help him up. "Are you alright?"

"Thank you, Sire," the guard said, dusting himself off. "No harm done."

"Is Vando around?" Orion asked.

"I'll summon him for you, Sire. Please return to your chambers."

Orion nodded and retreated to his room. He sat on the edge of his bed, stroking Pragor, who was snoring softly at his feet. His thoughts raced, replaying Lillithan's words about the explosions and the sense of urgency they carried. A knock at the door snapped him out of his reverie. Vando entered, his hair dishevelled and his dressing gown only half-secured.

"Sir, you called? Is everything alright?" Vando asked, slightly out of breath.

"I had another vision of Lillithan," Orion said, his tone resolute. "I think she's on the planet below."

"What makes you think that, Sire?"

Orion beckoned Vando to sit beside him and recounted the vision in detail, emphasizing the explosions and the hurried departure of the guards.

Vando frowned, pacing the room. "It's possible. Our scans of the planet didn't reveal anything, but… perhaps they're using some kind of advanced shield to mask their presence."

"She felt close, Vando," Orion insisted. "Too close to ignore."

Vando nodded. "I'll assemble a strike team to investigate."

"I'm coming too," Orion said firmly.

"Sir, with all due respect,"

"I'm coming," Orion repeated, his tone leaving no room for argument.

Vando sighed in defeat. "Very well, but please promise me you won't take unnecessary risks."

"Is Eymd awake yet?" Orion asked, changing the subject.

Vando shook his head. "Not yet, Sire. The healers… they're not sure she ever will."

Orion ran a hand through his hair, the weight of the news settling heavily on him. "I hope she does. She deserves to wake up."

"She will," Vando said, his voice filled with quiet conviction. "When she does, she may not show it, but she'll be grateful for what you've done."

Orion looked at him curiously. "How do you know Eymd?"

"That, my Lord, is a story for another time. For now, you need to rest," Vando replied with a small smile before leaving.

Orion lay back down, his exhaustion pulling him into sleep almost immediately.

He was in a vast, endless field. The tall grass swayed in the breeze, scattered with uprooted trees as though a great force had ripped them from the earth. The sky was locked in an eerie twilight, neither day nor night, and an oppressive silence hung in the air.

Behind him, the grass rustled. Spinning around, Orion saw a small figure emerge, a girl. He gasped. It was a young Eymd.

"Quick, get down," she hissed, grabbing his arm.

"Eymd, you're……"

"Shh!" she pressed a finger to his lips, her expression serious. "If it hears you, it'll find us."

Before he could respond, the grass ahead rustled violently. A massive boar emerged, sniffing the air. Orion's stomach dropped as he saw its face, it was grotesquely human, its twisted features eerily childlike.

"Come out, dear child," the creature said, its voice dripping with malice. "I know you're here. I can smell you."

Eymd darted forward, swords materializing in her hands. She lunged at the creature, her movements swift and precise, but the boar leaped into the air, evading her strike.

"Did you really think it would be that easy?" the creature mocked, spitting a glob of corrosive liquid toward her. The spit hit the ground, sizzling as it dissolved the earth.

Eymd rolled to the side and broke into a sprint, the beast in hot pursuit. It swooped low, its gaping mouth opening wide, and in one swift motion, it swallowed her whole.

Orion screamed.

Orion sprang to his feet and tried to summon a fireball, but nothing happened. His powers, the strength he so often relied on, were absent. Panic crept in, but before he could dwell on it, the beast turned toward him. Its childlike face twisted in mock curiosity, but it didn't seem to notice him. Instead, it floated past him, indifferent to his presence.

Confused but determined, Orion followed it. Spotting a still-standing tree nearby, he climbed swiftly, the rough bark scraping against his hands. Perching on a sturdy branch, he waited for the beast to pass below. When it did, he leapt onto its broad, furry back, clutching tightly. The beast didn't react; it simply continued its slow, deliberate flight, as though he weren't there.

The beast carried him toward a towering mountain, entering a dark, yawning hole at its base. Inside, the air grew damp and musty, the tunnel twisting and turning as they descended into the depths. Orion flattened himself against the beast's back, his heart racing as he ducked to avoid low-hanging rocks. He counted the turns, one, two, three, until he reached thirty. At last, a faint light appeared ahead, growing brighter with each beat of the beast's wings.

The tunnel opened into a massive cavern, alive with an eerie glow. Phosphorescent slime dripped from the walls, illuminating the space in shades of green and blue. Bioluminescent trees and mushrooms sprouted throughout the clearing, their faint light casting strange shadows across the cavern floor.

"Master, I am home from the hunt," the beast announced, its voice a mix of childlike innocence and monstrous guttural tones.

A voice from behind the glowing trees responded, thick with mockery. "Catch anything good?"

"One of those little shadow children," the beast replied proudly, lowering itself onto a patch of glowing grass.

"Oh, goodie. I can make a roast."

From the trees emerged a grotesque figure, tall and hunched, with skin like tree bark and hair the colour of deep moss. His face was pockmarked with odd, dark holes, and his tattered grey robe dragged behind him as he walked. The sight of him sent a shiver through Orion.

The beast opened its mouth, and Eymd spilled out, her body tumbling onto the ground. Before the grotesque man could react, she disappeared into the shadows. His face twisted in rage.

"You stupid beast! That's not a normal child, it's a shadow warrior! You've done this on purpose!" he bellowed.

Frustration overtook him, and with a deep breath, he exhaled a freezing wind. Frost coated the cavern in seconds, and the glowing mushrooms dimmed as a frozen figure emerged from the shadows, Eymd, encased in a layer of ice.

The man stomped toward her, his heavy steps echoing through the cavern. He picked her up effortlessly and carried her to a tree, pressing her frozen form against the trunk. Vines slithered out like serpents, wrapping around her tightly.

Satisfied, he slapped the beast across its grotesque face. "Fetch some firewood," he snapped.

The beast whimpered, tears welling in its strange, humanlike eyes. It shuffled off, its wings drooping. Orion, still perched silently on its back, reached out and stroked its fur gently. The beast shivered at the touch but continued its task, gathering firewood in its mouth.

As the beast returned to the clearing, Orion slid off its back and crouched low, watching from the shadows. The beast dropped the firewood, curled up on the ground, and shook with quiet sobs.

"Ah, I see you've thawed, my dear," the man said, his voice dripping with cruel amusement as he glanced at Eymd, now awake and struggling against the vines.

"When will your people learn that sending trainees after me is pointless?" he sneered, crouching to ignite the pile of wood.

"Jammeron," Eymd spat, her voice defiant despite her restraints. "Your reign of terror is over."

Jammeron chuckled darkly, tossing glowing mushrooms into a pot of water he'd set to boil. "Brave words for a girl in your position. But I must admit, you'll make an excellent stew."

Orion crept closer to the tree where Eymd was bound, tugging at the vines with all his strength. They wouldn't budge, their grip as unyielding as iron. Eymd glanced down at him, her expression stern.

"Don't," she hissed. "Save your strength."

Jammeron continued humming as he added glowing vegetables to the pot. The cavern filled with a sweet, enticing aroma that made Orion's stomach growl despite himself. Jammeron, satisfied with his bubbling concoction, approached Eymd.

"Let's see how well you season," he said, yanking her free from the tree. The vines remained coiled tightly around her as he carried her to the pot.

Orion's heart pounded as he tried to summon his powers, but nothing came. He was helpless.

Jammeron threw Eymd into the pot. The boiling water hissed, and Eymd screamed, a sound of pure agony. Orion fell to his knees, his own body wracked with unbearable pain, as though he were the one in the pot. He clutched his chest, tears streaming down his face as he cried out.

Jammeron leaned over the pot, a twisted smile on his face. "Not so defiant now, are you?"

Eymd's scream faded, replaced by a chilling silence. Orion, still trembling on the ground, forced himself to look up. Just as Jammeron turned away, Eymd erupted from the pot. Her shadowy form blurred with fury, twin blades of darkness materializing in her hands.

With a single, swift motion, she slashed across Jammeron's throat. His eyes widened, his bark-like skin cracking as he let out a hollow chuckle. His body crumpled backward with a resounding *thud*, dark sap oozing from the wound.

Eymd landed gracefully, her shadowy swords dissipating. She looked down at Orion, her expression unreadable. He staggered to his feet, the pain slowly fading, and met her gaze

"I, Eymd of the Shadow Academy, have passed my final trial and claim a piece of you as my trophy," she declared, her voice steady despite the weariness in her frame.

She walked to Jammeron's lifeless body, bending over it for several moments. When she rose, she held one of the creature's gnarled fingers in one hand and a key in the other. Turning toward the beast, still cowering on the ground, she reached under its neck and unlocked the thick collar around it.

"Great spirit Jammeron is dead, and I free you," Eymd said, dropping to her knees and bowing deeply.

The beast stirred, its human-like face twisting into an expression of gratitude. "Young shadow warrior, thank you," it said, its voice trembling with emotion. "I have tried for centuries to break his binding, but this collar was forged by the gods themselves, long before your time."

The beast's body began to glow, growing brighter and brighter until the light burned Orion's eyes. He shielded his face with his arm but couldn't look away as the creature began to change. Its fur melted away, replaced by shimmering scales of black, white, and silver. Its body stretched and elongated, becoming serpentine and graceful. Arms and legs sprouted, and wings of midnight black and radiant white unfurled from its back.

When the transformation was complete, the light faded, and the great spirit stood tall, its form towering over the trees. It flexed its claws, crushing a nearby boulder with ease, before lowering its massive head to Eymd. With one of its colossal fingers, it gently tapped the ground before her.

"Child, gaze upon me," the spirit said, its voice resonant and commanding.

Eymd lifted her head wearily, her dark eyes glinting with reverence. She avoided meeting the spirit's gaze directly, bowing again as she spoke. "Great spirit, I am honoured."

The spirit smiled, a strange warmth in its fierce expression. It opened the hand that had crushed the boulder, revealing two sleek black swords that sparkled with stardust, along with a belt adorned with throwing knives, each one black as obsidian.

"A gift for you, my saviour," the spirit said, placing the items on the grass before her. "But I must ask one last thing of you."

"Anything, great spirit," Eymd replied, sitting upright and gazing up at the towering figure.

"Please, call me by the name your people once gave me, Salmanta," the spirit said, bowing its head slightly. "When you leave this place, you must devote your life to the service of the Shadow Warriors, but there is only one you are destined to serve."

Eymd frowned. "What do you mean, only one? We are nomads, we serve no one."

Salmanta waved its clawed hand, and a shimmering vision materialized in the air before them. Orion saw himself in the image, frantic and terrified, placing a piece of his heart into a broken and lifeless Eymd.

"Your humanity saved her," Salmanta said, looking directly at Orion, though he thought himself invisible. "This act will bond you both for all eternity. You will be his chaos to his calm, his dark to his light."

Eymd stared at the vision, her lips pressed into a thin line. "Shadow High Command will never permit this. The task is too important."

Salmanta plucked a handful of strange grey flowers from the ground, their petals glinting like moonlight. Tossing them into the air, the flowers dissolved into starlight, the particles flowing toward Eymd. They touched her skin, forming intricate star-like patterns that climbed to her neck and shaped themselves into a brilliant silver chain with a crown at its centre.

"This will show them you speak the truth," Salmanta said, its deep voice carrying the weight of destiny. The spirit heaved itself off the ground, towering even higher. "It is vital that you show him this memory when the time comes."

"Why?" Eymd asked, her voice tinged with uncertainty.

Salmanta turned and locked eyes with Orion, who had remained silent throughout the exchange. Orion gasped, stumbling back in surprise.

"You… you can see me?" he stuttered.

Salmanta's grin widened. "Yes, child. I am the one who silenced your magic here."

"How?" Orion asked, stepping forward hesitantly.

"I am like the Old Ones," Salmanta said, its tone grave. "I can reach across time, but only in this way. You must not descend to Borangus. The enemy allowed Lillithan to communicate with you, but it is a trap."

"But I have to save her," Orion protested, his fists clenching.

Salmanta sighed, the weight of its own words visible in its glowing eyes. "Yes, but those who pull your uncle's strings have created a weapon, a weapon designed to kill a god."

Orion froze. "But I was told I couldn't die."

Salmanta looked away, a flicker of guilt passing across its face. "My future self helped them create it. You must understand, I had no choice."

Orion stumbled back, his chest tightening. He turned away, walking to the nearest tree and resting his head against it. Tears streamed down his face, and he struggled to compose himself. After a moment, he wiped his eyes and returned to Salmanta, his expression resolute.

"I understand," he said, his voice steady. "But… how do you know me?"

Salmanta's gaze softened. "A day will come when you rescue the future me, and we fight together to protect all that is, all that was, and all that can be. I am sorry we had to meet like this, old friend, but my message is delivered. Now, you must wake."

Orion opened his mouth to respond, but a distant voice called his name, pulling him from the dream. His vision blurred, and he felt an overwhelming fatigue. His eyes grew heavy despite his resistance, and he fell into darkness once more

20 Rescuing Lillithan

Orion sat up in bed, rubbing the sleep from his eyes, and saw Maximus standing at the foot of the bed, holding a tray of food. With a respectful nod, Maximus placed the tray across Orion's lap and silently stepped back. As Orion adjusted the covers and lifted the tray lid, Maximus bowed deeply and exited the room without a word, leaving Orion to eat in peace.

The aroma of freshly baked bread and spiced fruit wafted upward, mingling with the scent of rich, Savory meats. Orion ate absently, his thoughts tangled with the vivid images of Eymd's dream. The weight of her warning, and the presence of the enigmatic Salmanta, pressed heavily on his mind. Should he abandon the mission to heed the spirit's advice, or was this rescue operation too important to delay?

He was still wrestling with the decision when a knock came at the door.

"Come in," he called, setting the tray aside.

The door opened, and a figure clad in sleek, black battle armour entered, the polished surface catching the morning light. The figure strode confidently toward Orion's bed, and with a subtle press to the side of its carbon-fibre helmet, a faint hiss sounded. The helmet collapsed into the breastplate, revealing Aurorina's face.

"Morning," she said warmly, brushing crumbs from his chin with maternal affection. "The council has been briefed on the rescue operation, and the units are waiting for you in the hangar."

"Mum," Orion said, his brow furrowing, "why are you dressed like that?"

"I'm coming with you," she replied matter-of-factly.

"No," he said firmly, setting his jaw. "I'm not going to lose you again."

Her expression softened, but her resolve was unshaken. "Orion, she's my best friend. I need to be there. I have to make sure she's safe."

Orion sighed, recognizing the determination in her eyes. "Fine," he said at last. "But you're staying close to me. Now, can you help me put on my armour?"

Aurorina's face brightened with approval as Orion climbed out of bed. She moved swiftly, attaching thin metal strips to his legs and arms. The pieces, lightweight but sturdy, clicked seamlessly into place. Next, she pressed a golden royal crest onto his chest. The insignia glowed faintly, and a second later, a carbon-fibre-like material began to unfurl from the crest and the metal strips. It wrapped around Orion, encasing him in jet-black armour. The helmet formed last, sliding over his head and sealing with a soft hiss.

As the visor dropped down over his face, a display flickered to life before his eyes. It showed a clear view of his room, overlaid with a message: **Initializing Systems**.

"Good afternoon, Intenfli Orion," said a calm male voice inside the helmet. "I am your Personal Intelligent Life Support System, or P.I.L.S.S. for short."

Orion blinked, startled. "Uh… hi?"

"Designating call sign as 'Phoenix One,'" P.I.L.S.S. continued. "Upgrading armour skin to include custom insignias and uploading command functions."

Orion glanced at his mother, unsure how to respond to the disembodied voice. "You seem to do a lot more than just life support."

"Affirmative," P.I.L.S.S. replied. "My species once had physical forms like yours, but we outgrew our biological skins and uploaded our consciousness into the systemwide database."

"That's… a little unsettling," Orion admitted.

"It's no stranger than your parents sending you to Earth as an infant, young master," P.I.L.S.S. said with a tone that almost sounded mocking.

Orion rolled his eyes. "Alright, fine. Who designed your personality?"

"Technically, my creators did. Though, I must say, humour is an underrated survival tool," P.I.L.S.S. replied smoothly. "Now, designate your second and third in command for this mission."

"Vando will be my second, and my mother will be third," Orion said.

The display updated, showing Vando's and Aurorina's names, along with their designated positions. Additional readouts appeared, highlighting integrated weapon systems, thruster status, and power reserves.

"I am receiving new schematics for your suit from an unknown source," P.I.L.S.S. informed him. "Should I initiate the upgrade?"

Orion frowned. "Unknown source? Where did it come from?"

"It contains the Elite Shadow Warrior encryption key," P.I.L.S.S. explained. "The package is labelled 'God Destroyer Armor.'"

"God Destroyer?" Orion echoed, the words sending a chill through him. "Let me talk to my mum first, then I'll decide. Lower my helmet."

The visor hissed as it retracted into the helmet, which collapsed neatly into the breastplate. Orion's face was grim as he turned to Aurorina.

The helmet hissed softly as it retracted into Orion's breastplate. He turned to see his mother sitting at the end of his bed, her gaze distant, lost in thought.

"Do you know anything about this armour upgrade?" he asked, breaking the silence.

Aurorina shook her head. "No, I've never heard of it. P.I.L.S.S., can you request confirmation of the transmission's origin from the Shadow Council?"

"Requesting verification. Please standby," P.I.L.S.S. replied, its voice emanating from Aurorina's suit.

Aurorina's expression softened as she glanced at Orion. "These suits are extraordinary. I could never have dreamed of such technology when your father was alive."

Orion paused, struck by the wistfulness in her voice. "What was he like?" he asked gently.

A warm smile spread across her face, though her eyes glistened. "He was kind. Always helping others, even when it wasn't convenient. He hated staying in the palace, always looking for ways to make himself useful. You remind me of him, especially when you opened the palace to refugees. It brought back memories of the early days of the war when he helped evacuate people to the bunkers beneath the palace."

Orion smiled and moved to embrace her. Though his parents had been absent for most of his life, he felt an undeniable closeness to her, as if the bond had always been there, waiting to be rediscovered. Warm tears streamed down his cheeks as they hugged, and he felt the quiet tremble of her own sobs.

When he finally pulled back, he wiped her tears and kissed her cheek. "Thank you, Mum," he said softly.

Their moment was interrupted by P.I.L.S.S.'s voice cutting through the air. "Pardon me, ma'am. I have the information you requested."

Aurorina straightened. "Who sent the schematics?"

"It's... peculiar," P.I.L.S.S. said, its tone laced with curiosity. "There is no point of origin, but I can confirm when the file was uploaded."

"When was that?" Orion asked, frowning.

"Approximately 700 years ago, during the Shadow Empire's early technological era. However, the schematics are far more advanced than anything we possess even today."

Orion exchanged a concerned glance with Aurorina. "Hold off on the upgrade for now," he said decisively.

Aurorina nodded and rose to her feet. "Right. The troops are waiting in the hangar. We shouldn't keep them waiting."

As she pressed a button beside the door to signal for the hall to clear, P.I.L.S.S. spoke again. "One more thing before departure, Sire. You must set an authorization code. Would you also like to establish a neural link with me?"

"Yes, to the neural link," Orion said after a moment's hesitation. "Set the authorization code to Omega-pi 6974."

"Voice print confirmed. Authorization code set. Establishing neural link," P.I.L.S.S. said.

Thin wires shot out from the suit, connecting seamlessly to Orion's temples. There was a brief, tingling sensation as the neural link activated, followed by P.I.L.S.S.'s voice inside his head.

"Neural link established. Welcome, Sire."

Orion followed his mother out of the room, stepping into a swirling vortex of stars. The shimmering portal tugged at him, and moments later, the vortex dissolved to reveal the ship's hangar.

Orion stepped onto the solid floor and stopped to take in the scene. Fifty troops stood at attention, their armour gleaming. Some carried advanced rifles slung across their backs, while others seemed unarmed but radiated an air of precision and lethality.

Vando approached, bowing slightly as he handed Orion the sword hilt and the bow and quiver, he had recovered from the box of the Old Ones.

"Good morning, Sire," Vando said. "The troops await your orders."

"Is Eymd awake yet?" Orion asked, taking the weaponry and strapping it to his suit.

"I'm afraid not, Sire."

Orion nodded grimly, then turned to face the troops. Taking a steadying breath, he raised his voice. "Good morning. Unknown forces are holding Lillithan on the planet below, and it is our mission to rescue her. I know some of you may fear the dangers we may face, but we must stand strong. Together, we will bring her back. Let's move out."

The troops saluted in unison before splitting into two lines, marching toward the glass manta-shaped shuttles waiting nearby. Vando bowed again and joined one of the lines, leaving Orion with his mother.

"Come on," Aurorina said, taking his arm and leading him to the same shuttle Vando had entered.

The shuttle's door closed behind them with a hiss, and the craft began to move toward the open hangar doors and the empty void beyond. Orion looked around, marvelling at the sleek interior of the vessel.

"Engage ship defences systems and prepare for star-shield activation," Vando said to the pilot.

"What's star-shield?" Orion asked, glancing at his mother.

"It's a cloaking system that renders the ship and its occupants invisible to all sensors," Aurorina explained.

As the shuttle descended toward the planet, a cool, liquid sensation washed over Orion. He looked down at his arm and gasped, it was gone. No, not gone, but invisible. The ship and everyone inside had vanished, leaving him feeling as though he were floating in empty space. Just as he began to adjust to the eerie sensation, the ship reappeared, solid and visible once more.

"That was the star-shield engaging," Vando said as he approached. Noticing Orion's unsettled expression, he added, "Don't worry. You'll get used to it."

The shuttles descended and Vando gestured toward the spot on a holographic display.

"This is where we'll start. It's as if the area doesn't exist, which makes it the perfect hiding place," he said. His gaze flicked to Orion, noticing the tension in his face. "You, okay?"

Orion nodded, though his mind churned. The dream of Salmanta, the warning, and now this, he couldn't shake the feeling that they were walking into something far more dangerous than they anticipated.

"What do you mean it shows nothing there?" Orion asked, his tone sharp with disbelief.

"Exactly that, Sire," Vando replied. "On a planet teeming with life, there's a dead zone, no energy signatures, no life signs. It's as if that area simply doesn't exist."

Orion nodded, his expression thoughtful, and moved to stand by the shuttle's window. Below, the planet's surface began to come into view as they pierced through the thick atmosphere. His breath caught as a colossal worm soared past the ship, its segmented body rippling like liquid metal. The shuttle rocked slightly from the force of its passage. Moments later, a four-headed flaming bird streaked after the worm, its cries echoing even through the hull.

Beyond the chaos, a seemingly endless desert stretched below, golden dunes shimmering in the light. The stark beauty of the scene was interrupted by a loud bang. Orion turned just in time to see the shuttle ahead of them spiral downward, smoke trailing behind it.

"EVASIVE MANEUVERS!" Vando bellowed. "How did they spot us?!"

Before anyone could respond, a massive fireball hurtled toward their own shuttle. The pilot swerved sharply, but it was too late. The fireball slammed into the rear of the craft, tearing a gaping hole in its hull. Alarms blared, and the shuttle lurched violently, losing altitude.

"Brace yourselves!" Vando shouted as the shuttle began to spin.

Orion acted instinctively, pressing his hand against the wall. **Slow down. Make us undetectable,** he thought, willing his power into the ship. A blinding flash of light filled the interior, and suddenly the shuttle slowed to a crawl, steadying itself in midair.

Orion peered through the jagged hole in the hull. Below, he saw a plume of smoke rising where the first shuttle had crashed. He pointed toward it, and the shuttle turned smoothly in response.

"Sir, I've lost control of the ship!" the pilot cried out, his voice trembling.

"It's fine," Orion said, his voice calm. "I've got it. We're heading to the crash site."

The shuttle drifted downward, gliding toward the smoking wreckage. Orion scanned the horizon, searching for their attackers, but nothing appeared, not a single hint of movement. The desert seemed unnervingly still. As the shuttle landed, the troops poured out, weapons ready. Vando and the soldiers made their way toward the ruined shuttle, moving swiftly through the swirling sand.

"P.I.L.S.S., helmet up," Orion commanded as he stepped toward the breach. "Show survivors of the crash on screen."

The helmet slid over his head, sealing with a soft hiss. The display inside flickered to life, overlaying his vision with thermal and biometric readings. Multiple figures were visible beneath the wreckage, their life signs faint but stable.

Orion moved to the nearest survivor, a soldier pinned beneath a large piece of debris. Scanning the figure, his helmet confirmed the individual was uninjured. He gripped the debris and heaved it aside, then extended a hand to the soldier.

"Thank you, Sire," the young man said shakily as Orion helped him to his feet. "What happened?"

"We were attacked from somewhere, but the source is still unknown," Vando replied, joining them. "My readings show only one casualty from your shuttle."

The soldier nodded grimly. "It must have been Quillena, the High Star Mage. She cast a protective spell over us, weaving it from the outside." His voice faltered, and his eyes darkened with sorrow. "She sacrificed herself to save us."

Orion placed a reassuring hand on the soldier's shoulder. "Her sacrifice won't be forgotten. We'll mourn her loss later, but for now, we must stay focused. We need to find Lillithan."

The soldier saluted and hurried to join the other troops as they worked to secure the crash site.

"Pardon me, Orion," P.I.L.S.S. said, its voice cutting through his thoughts. "Might I have a word with you on a secure channel?"

"Go ahead," Orion replied, stepping away from the group.

"I've uncovered the authorization code used to upload the schematics for the armour upgrade into the Shadow Empire's systems."

Orion's curiosity piqued. "Whose code, was it?"

"It was yours, Sire."

Orion's breath caught. "Mine? That doesn't make any sense. How could…?"

"There's more," P.I.L.S.S. interrupted. "I've also found an encrypted recording embedded deep within the file. Would you like me to play it?"

"Yes, please," Orion said, his heart racing. "What's the unlock code?"

"Authorization code required," P.I.L.S.S. replied.

Orion hesitated for a moment before speaking. "Omega-pi 6974."

The display in his helmet shifted as a faint hum filled his ears. The encrypted recording began to play, the voice unmistakably his own, though older, graver, and laced with exhaustion

The screen in Orion's helmet flickered, and a recording of himself appeared. The figure on the screen was almost unrecognizable, his helmet was shattered, his armour in tatters, and his skin burned so severely that Orion winced at the sight. His eyes were glazed and milky, as if he had gone blind, and his voice was ragged with exhaustion.

"Don't go in there without the armour upgrade," the recorded version of himself said, his voice trembling. "It was a trap. The god destroyer was far worse than any of us could have imagined. It wiped everyone out in one hit."

The recording paused as the figure took a shuddering breath. "I've gone back in time for what will now be the twenty-second attempt. I hope this version of the armour works. If not…" His voice faltered briefly before continuing. "I've embedded a failsafe into the schematics that will automatically jump you back in time to refine the design. I wish you luck, and goodbye."

The recording ended, and Orion's helmet retracted into his breastplate. His hands trembled slightly as he processed what he had just seen. Around him, the troops and Vando had gathered, concern evident in their eyes.

"P.I.L.S.S., initiate the armour upgrade for all units," Orion ordered, his voice steady despite the storm brewing inside him. "Authorization Omega-pi 6974."

"Affirmative. All units, please stand by for the upgrade. The process will take approximately one hour. May I suggest that we remain here while the upgrades are applied?" P.I.L.S.S. responded.

The armour buzzed as the carbon fibre began retracting into its casings. In its place, a white mesh-like material started to weave itself around Orion, forming a new, sleeker configuration. He watched as the other soldiers' armour underwent the same transformation, their exteriors shifting into the same luminous, advanced design.

Vando approached, his curiosity piqued. "That's one impressive modification," he said, reaching out to touch Orion's armour. The moment his fingers made contact, the suit glowed red and sent him sprawling backward.

Vando stood and dusted himself off with a sheepish grin. "That's new."

Orion smirked faintly. "You, okay?"

"Fine, fine," Vando said, stepping back into formation. He turned to the troops and bellowed, "Fall in! The blank zone is just beyond that dune."

The soldiers assembled quickly, forming a square around Orion, Aurorina, and Vando. They began their march toward the towering sand dune, their boots sinking slightly into the shifting ground with each step. The wind carried an eerie stillness, as though the planet itself was holding its breath.

Halfway up the dune, a searing pain shot through Orion's head, dropping him to his knees. He clutched at his temples as a bone-chilling voice echoed inside his mind.

"You are not welcome on my surface. Leave now, before it is too late."

"Emergency protocol Alpha One engaged," P.I.L.S.S. announced, slamming Orion's helmet shut. The pain subsided immediately as the protective systems activated.

"The planet knows we're here," Orion muttered, rising unsteadily to his feet. "Expect resistance at the top of the dune."

The troops pressed on, reaching the summit with cautious determination. As they did, the ground beneath them gave way. The sand vanished, and the group plunged into darkness below. Orion's thrusters activated too late, and he hit the ground hard, the impact knocking the breath from his lungs. He lay there for a moment, trying to steady his breathing, before a faint glow illuminated the space around him.

"Orion, are you alright?" Vando's voice came from nearby.

Orion turned his head and saw Vando offering him a hand. Grasping it, he hauled himself up. "I'm fine. What just happened?"

Vando surveyed their surroundings. "It looks like we've fallen into a tunnel. I can't tell if the planet is trying to help us, or lead us into a trap. Either way, I think we should see where it leads."

Orion nodded, and after ensuring everyone was accounted for, the group began cautiously navigating the tunnel. The star mages kept their hands sparking with defensive magic, while the riflemen scanned the area with their weapons raised. Orion drew his sword hilt, and with a crackling surge, a blade of lightning and fire erupted from it.

The tunnel twisted and turned before ending abruptly at a large metal door. Vando stepped forward, peering through a small viewport before carefully opening it. Inside, a dimly lit cell revealed a frail figure huddled in the corner, her sobs echoing softly.

"Lillithan," Orion whispered, pushing past Vando and kneeling beside her. "We're here for you, my friend."

She lifted her head slowly, her tear-streaked face filled with anguish. "You shouldn't have come," she murmured. "They have a weapon…"

The star mages moved quickly, combining their powers to destroy the chains that bound her. But before they could succeed, the floor trembled violently. The entire tunnel began to rise, the walls shifting and groaning as it emerged from beneath the sand. Sunlight flooded the space, blinding them momentarily, and when the vibrations stopped, the walls had vanished, revealing a massive circular arena.

Orion squinted, barely able to make out the crowd cheering wildly in the stands. His troops formed a protective circle around him as the realization of their situation set in.

"I think we're in trouble," he said grimly.

"Quiet down," a deep, commanding voice echoed around the arena. The crowd instantly fell silent, all eyes turning toward a figure in silver armour seated high in the stands. The man rose slowly, his presence radiating authority. "It seems our gracious leader has decided to trespass. And we all know what happens to trespassers, don't we?"

The crowd erupted into wild cheers, the cacophony reverberating through the air. The masked man leapt gracefully from his perch, landing on the arena floor with a resounding thud. He straightened, his movements slow and deliberate, as if to show he had no fear of Orion or his troops.

Vando's voice rang out over the din. "Take him down before he reaches the Intenfli!"

Twenty soldiers stepped forward, forming a tight line. They unleashed a barrage of orange laser blasts from their rifles and roaring fireballs from their hands. The masked man, however, didn't even flinch. The attacks fizzled out before reaching him, vanishing into harmless sparks.

A low chuckle rumbled from behind the mask. "Is that the best you've got?" he taunted. Reaching into his pocket, he pulled out a small pad and pressed a button. The ground trembled as a hidden door opened in the sand before him. From the opening, a turret began to rise, its transparent shell filled with a dark, sparkling liquid that shimmered ominously in the sunlight.

The masked man sauntered over to the turret, taking a seat in a chair positioned beside it. With a smirk, he pulled a lever, causing the liquid within to churn violently.

"Are you sure you're ready to face me, little boy?" he mocked, his voice dripping with derision. "Let me show you the power of the God Destroyer."

With a dramatic press of a button, the turret fired. A torrent of dark liquid surged forward, striking the line of soldiers. Screams of agony filled the air as the liquid consumed them, leaving them crumpled and lifeless on the ground.

Orion's fists clenched, his heart pounding with fury. He moved to charge, but Vando grabbed his arm, holding him back.

"We're not ready for this!" Vando hissed. "P.I.L.S.S says the armour upgrades aren't complete yet!"

The masked man clapped his hands, and more soldiers began pouring from hidden passages in the arena walls, surrounding Orion and the remaining troops. Their weapons gleamed in the sunlight, and their movements were precise and coordinated.

"You see, boy," the masked man sneered, "I knew you'd come for her. Now, let's end this."

He pressed the button again, and two more turrets emerged from the sand, flanking Orion's group. They began firing the same dark liquid, each blast searing through the air. Aurorina stepped forward, her face set with determination. Raising her hands, she began weaving intricate gestures. Streams of light erupted from her body, forming a barrier around the group. With a final flourish, she slammed her hand into the ground, and the barrier hardened into shimmering silver, blocking out the relentless assault.

"I don't know how long I can hold this," she said through gritted teeth. Her voice trembled with exertion. "We need to find a way out!"

"I can take him," Orion said, his voice laced with frustration. "Just let me get close."

"No!" Vando snapped. "You're too important to risk. Aurorina, can you move the barrier closer to the main turret?"

"I can try," Aurorina replied, though her face was pale and sweat dripped from her brow.

Vando motioned for the troops to close ranks as they began their slow advance. Each step forward strained Aurorina further, and by the halfway point, she was leaning heavily on Vando for support.

"I don't think she can take much more of this," Vando said urgently, glancing at Orion.

Before Orion could respond, P.I.L.S.S. spoke directly into his mind. **"Sir, your armour is now 85% upgraded. If you tap into your latent powers, you could survive. I can create a small breach in the shield for you to step through."**

Orion hesitated, his breath shallow. The thought of giving in to his powers frightened him, but he couldn't stand by any longer. "Do it," he said, his voice low.

The barrier shimmered as P.I.L.S.S. adjusted the frequency, creating an opening just wide enough for Orion to slip through. He stepped out, and the shield sealed shut behind him.

The masked man's soldiers immediately turned their attention to Orion, firing bullets and spells in unison. But as the projectiles reached him, they fizzled into nothingness against the energy radiating from his partially upgraded armour. The air around him seemed to ripple with suppressed power.

The soldiers moved to surround him, closing in like a tightening noose. As the first wave charged, Orion raised his hand, and they froze mid-stride, their weapons falling from their hands. It was as if an invisible force held them in place.

But Orion's focus wavered. A searing pain erupted in his shoulder as a dark liquid projectile from the turret struck him. The liquid burned through his armour and into his skin, sending fire coursing through his veins. He collapsed to his knees, screaming in agony, as the pain threatened to consume him.

The soldiers surrounding Orion began to close in as he lay crumpled on the ground. His breath came in ragged gasps, the searing pain from the god destroyer's shot consuming his body. He closed his eyes, bracing himself for the end.

But instead of the final blow, he heard screams, agonized cries that cut through the battlefield like a blade.

Orion's eyes shot open. All around him, enemy troops lay lifeless, their bodies twisted and motionless. Standing before him was a dark figure, her blonde hair shimmering like molten gold in the arena's light. She wore a blue gown, torn and flowing, the open back exposing faint glowing lines that pulsed like lightning. The figure turned toward him, her face fierce but familiar.

She reached down, grabbing his arm. A surge of energy, powerful and electric, coursed through him as her touch sent a healing spell rippling through his battered body. Orion felt his pain fade, his strength returning as she pulled him to his feet.

"I'm not even allowed to recover in peace," Eymd said, her voice resonating with power, crackling like a summer storm.

Orion stared at her, stunned. "Eymd… you're talking. And you… you look different."

Eymd's piercing gaze softened for a moment. "We'll talk about it later," she said firmly. "Right now, we need to help them." She pointed toward the protective dome shielding Vando, Aurorina, and the remaining troops. The shimmering barrier was flickering, cracks of light splitting across its surface.

Orion nodded, and they moved in unison toward the main turret. As they weaved through the volley of dark liquid and enemy fire, Orion became acutely aware of Eymd's presence, not just beside him but within him. It was as if their minds were linked, their movements synchronized without the need for words. Every step, every shift in position felt natural, their bond directing them with flawless precision.

As they reached the turret, they leapt into the air simultaneously, their hands clasping together. A surge of energy erupted between them, forming a massive sphere of lightning that crackled and pulsed with raw power. The sphere grew brighter and brighter until it became blinding, then shot downward, slamming into the turret with a deafening impact.

The turret shuddered violently as the masked man dove from his seat, barely avoiding the explosion. The structure imploded with a sharp *pop*, the force of the blast sending shockwaves through the sand. Lightning tendrils split from the epicentre, racing toward the other two turrets. In seconds, they too imploded, crumpling into themselves like collapsing stars.

Orion and Eymd descended, their feet touching the ground almost in unison. Without hesitation, Orion summoned a bolt of lightning and hurled it at the masked man. The strike hit him square in the chest, sending him sprawling to the ground. His body twitched as residual energy coursed through him.

The pair approached cautiously, their senses heightened. Orion's sword hummed with latent energy, and Eymd's hands crackled with shadowed lightning. As they reached the fallen figure, Eymd nudged him with her foot, flipping him onto his back. She knelt and slowly removed his mask.

Both of them gasped.

The face beneath was a grotesque patchwork of different features. The top right quadrant was the face of an aged man, sagging and grey. The top left was that of a child, pale and cherubic. The lower portion of the face bore the soft, feminine mouth and chin of a woman. Each segment was crudely stitched together with glowing purple threads that pulsed faintly.

"You may have destroyed these god destroyers," the man rasped, his voice barely audible. "But we have others. This will not be the last time we meet."

With one final, shuddering breath, a black mist escaped his body, swirling upward and dissipating into the sky. All that remained was a deflated husk, the skin suit crumpling into itself like discarded fabric.

"What just happened?" Orion asked, his voice tinged with disbelief.

"I don't know," Eymd replied, examining the empty skin suit. "That was... far from normal." She glanced toward the failing shield. "Look, the dome!"

As if on cue, the silver barrier shattered, dissolving into particles of light. The scene it revealed was grim: Vando cradled an unconscious Aurorina in his arms, his face lined with worry. The remaining troops, battered but resolute, had formed a defensive perimeter around them. As the masked man's soldiers fled in disarray, the troops relaxed their stances, lowering their weapons and making their way toward Orion.

Vando's voice crackled through the comms system. "Her body couldn't handle it. She'll recover, but she'll need time to rest."

"She'll be okay, though?" Orion asked, his voice heavy with concern.

"Yes," Vando replied, and a faint smile touched his lips. "She'll be fine. Who's that with you?"

"It's Eymd," Orion said, glancing at her. "She… well, she's blonde now."

"She's not gonna like that," Vando said with a chuckle, shaking his head.

Before the conversation could continue, a deep rumble echoed from above. The arena fell silent as a shadow loomed over them. Orion looked up to see the palace ship descending, its massive form blotting out the sun. A plume of sand erupted as it touched down beside the arena, the ground trembling from its weight.

With a mechanical hum, a ramp extended, lowering to the sand below. The troops instinctively turned toward the ship, their postures stiffening.

Orion took a deep breath, turning back to Vando. "Get her on board," he said, nodding toward Aurorina. "We need to regroup and figure out what the hell just happened."

Eymd stepped closer, her energy still crackling faintly. "Whatever's coming, this isn't the end. It's only the beginning."

Orion nodded, his jaw tightening as he looked at the palace ship. The battle had been won, but a darker storm loomed on the horizon.

21 The Bond

Orion turned and began making his way toward the ramp leading up to the palace ship. His steps were heavy, his thoughts swirling with the events that had just unfolded. Before he could reach the ramp, the ship's main doors opened with a hiss. The council members, flanked by star healers, rushed out to meet the returning troops. Relief was evident on their faces as they saw Orion unharmed.

The healers immediately attended to Aurorina and Lillithan, carefully guiding their unconscious forms back toward the ship to provide care. Orion watched for a moment, a pang of guilt and concern tightening in his chest. He took a step forward to follow, but a firm hand gripped his arm, stopping him in his tracks.

"We need to talk," Eymd said, her tone low and insistent.

Without waiting for his reply, she pulled him away from the others. They walked in silence for several minutes, the sound of the desert wind their only companion. Finally, Eymd sat down on the ground and motioned for Orion to sit opposite her. He obliged, though the tension in the air made him uneasy. She opened her mouth as if to speak, but each time she hesitated, shutting it again.

"Um… why's your hair blonde?" Orion asked, attempting to break the silence.

"Because you and your precious humanity wouldn't let me die a shadow warrior's death," she snapped, though her tone lacked venom.

"I couldn't lose anyone else," Orion said softly. "I'm sorry."

Eymd's expression softened slightly, though her frustration lingered. "I don't mind the hair, I can change it at will. I just wanted to mess with you." Her lips twitched into a faint smirk before fading again. "It's these eyes I can't stand." She leaned forward, her face close to his, revealing her now-brilliant silver irises. They glowed faintly, almost unnaturally, catching the light.

"Do you want me to check the Book of the Old Ones?" Orion offered.

"Yes," she said quickly. "Maybe it will explain what I've become."

Orion nodded and held out his hand. Concentrating, he summoned the ancient book from the Old Ones' chest. With a soft pop, it appeared in his grasp, its weathered cover gleaming faintly.

"Think of your question and open to any page," he instructed, handing her the book.

Eymd closed her eyes for a moment, her fingers trembling slightly as they hovered over the cover. She flipped it open to a random page and began to read. Her eyes darted across the text, and her face slowly twisted into fury.

"I'm tethered to you," she said, her voice rising. She thrust the book at Orion. "Because we share one heart! Look!"

Orion took the book from her, his brow furrowed. A fleeting thought crossed his mind: *It would be easier if I could absorb this knowledge directly.* Before he could dismiss it, the words on the page began to shift. They snaked up his arms in glowing tendrils, disappearing into his skin. He gasped as a torrent of information flooded his mind, though it came jumbled and fragmented.

"What are you doing?" Eymd demanded, her voice sharp with alarm.

"I'm reading the entire book," Orion replied, his voice distant as he processed the flood of data. "Almost finished."

They both sat in stunned silence, watching as the last of the writing disappeared into Orion's arm. The book crumbled to dust in his hands, disintegrating into the breeze.

"Great," Eymd muttered, crossing her arms. "How am I supposed to read about what you've done to me now?"

"Wait for it," Orion said with a small smile, his eyes glinting.

"What do you mean, oh." Eymd's voice trailed off, her eyes glazing over. "It's all in my head."

"I think we share knowledge now," Orion said thoughtfully. "It's part of the bond."

"Great," she said with mock enthusiasm. "Now I'm a freak. What am I supposed to tell the council when I report in?"

"Don't," Orion said quickly. "We can't let them know about this, not yet. Mask your eyes. No one will suspect a thing."

Eymd huffed but nodded reluctantly. Orion stood and began pacing, his thoughts racing. Who was the masked man? What was his purpose? The stitched-together face and the ominous warning haunted him.

A hand tapped his shoulder, snapping him from his thoughts. He turned to see Lord Sanjen standing there, his expression a mixture of concern and curiosity.

"I heard what happened," Sanjen said, his deep voice steady. "Are you both alright?"

"I'm fine," Eymd said quickly, cutting off Orion before he could speak. She narrowed her eyes at him. "Wait, you were going to say that! You've messed with my head. You should've let me die."

Sanjen raised a bushy eyebrow, his fingers stroking his long beard. He looked between the two of them, confusion etched on his face. Before he could ask what was happening, Orion placed a hand on his temple and transferred the memories of the battle and the events following Eymd's near-death.

Sanjen's eyes widened briefly as he processed the information. "Ah," he said slowly, his voice heavy with understanding. "So now the two of you are bonded... more than before." He paused, his tone turning stern. "You shouldn't have done this, Orion. A connection like this, especially with a shadow warrior, makes you vulnerable."

"Why can't any of you understand?" Orion snapped, his voice cracking with emotion. "I couldn't let another person die because of me."

Eymd stood, brushing the sand from her gown. Her expression softened as she looked at Orion. "I'm sorry," she said quietly. "I... I'm grateful you saved me. It's just... hard for me to say it."

Orion met her gaze, his frustration easing slightly. "It's okay."

"I did ask for new powers," Eymd said, her lips quirking into a faint smile. "Guess I got more than I bargained for."

Sanjen studied them both for a moment before sighing. "The council's going to demand answers, you know."

"They'll get them when the time's right," Orion said firmly, his confidence returning. "But not a moment before."

Eymd nodded, and Sanjen reluctantly relented. The three of them turned toward the distant palace ship, its ramp still extended as troops and healers bustled inside. Despite the tension between them, an unspoken understanding passed among the trio.

Orion couldn't help but admire Promendium's craftsmanship as they approached the palace ship. Where the sun struck the glass panels, intricate etchings of Orion's crest shimmered, giving the structure an almost celestial quality. The smoke trapped between the glass shifted continuously, changing colours in mesmerizing patterns.

"Pro really did outdo himself, didn't he?" Orion remarked, unable to hide his awe.

"Yes," Vando replied, his brow furrowed in thought. "He's a remarkable being, though I'm still unsure whether to call him a planet or a young man."

Orion chuckled. "Young man, I think. But I should ask him next time I see him. After all, he *is* the first of his kind."

Vando nodded thoughtfully, but their conversation was interrupted by Sanjen. "Lillithan has asked if you could visit her in her chambers when you get the chance."

Orion nodded and made his way to the nearest lift, with Eymd silently trailing behind him. As they stepped into the lift, Orion hesitated, realizing he didn't know where Lillithan's chambers were.

Poking his head out of the lift, he called, "Sanjen, where exactly are her quarters?"

"Deck four, section D, room 605," Sanjen shouted back.

"Thanks," Orion replied, stepping back into the lift. "Computer, deck four, section D."

The lift doors closed with a hiss, and it began to ascend slowly. The silence between Orion and Eymd was heavy, neither quite knowing what to say. Finally, Orion broke the tension.

"I'm sorry I didn't let you have a warrior's death."

"It's okay," Eymd replied after a pause. "It was foretold that you would save me. You saw the dream. Besides..." She hesitated, glancing at her reflection in the lift's mirrored surface. "I suppose it makes me a better warrior, having all these new powers."

"Yeah," Orion said softly. "I guess it does."

The silence returned, but thankfully, the lift soon came to a stop. The doors slid open to reveal two soldiers standing at attention and Maximus waiting just beyond them.

"I'll escort you to Lillithan's chambers," Maximus said, falling into step beside Orion. "By the way, the council has requested your presence again."

"Of course, I'll see them after I visit Lillithan," Orion replied.

They turned a corner, and Maximus stopped outside a plain door. Orion knocked gently, and it slid open almost immediately. Aurorina stood inside, her expression weary but composed. She stepped aside to let Orion enter.

The room was dimly lit, the curtains drawn tightly. The air was heavy, the atmosphere subdued. Basic furnishings filled the space, but Orion's attention was drawn to the bed where Lillithan lay. Her face was pale and drawn, her breathing shallow. The chains that had once bound her had left deep cuts in her skin, now covered in a glowing, translucent liquid that seemed to speed the healing process.

"Mum, you're supposed to be resting," Orion said as he conjured a chair and sat by the bed.

Aurorina smiled faintly but didn't move. "I can rest later. The healers gave me a tonic to help me recover faster. I need to be here for her."

"How is she?" Orion asked, his gaze fixed on Lillithan's still form.

"She's been through a terrible ordeal," Aurorina said, her voice tinged with sorrow. "But she stayed strong and gave them no information." She placed a comforting hand on his shoulder.

"I wish I could heal her, but I've already interfered too much," Orion said, his voice heavy with guilt.

"You've done all you can," Aurorina replied gently. "Go see the council. I'll stay with her and send word as soon as she wakes."

Reluctantly, Orion nodded and left the room. Outside, Maximus was deep in conversation with Eymd, who looked utterly disinterested, her gaze fixed somewhere in the distance. When she noticed Orion, relief washed over her face.

"Please stop leaving me with the natives," she said in his mind, her voice tinged with irritation.

"Why don't you try talking to them?" Orion replied telepathically, a grin tugging at his lips.

"I have no desire to talk to *them*. You, I tolerate. Them? Absolutely not."

Orion laughed aloud, drawing a confused look from Maximus. "Sorry," he said quickly. "Right, where's the council?"

"They're in the conference room on this floor," Maximus replied, glancing at his tablet.

As they walked, Orion and Eymd continued their silent telepathic exchange.

"You know," he teased, "you should probably wear something more appropriate before we meet the council."

"I'm supposed to be recovering, remember? And I like the way this gown lets the air in," she replied, a sly smile crossing her face.

"Just put on something decent," Orion insisted. "You need to at least look professional."

Eymd stopped, rolling her eyes dramatically. Her gown shimmered, and black flames spread across her body. When they subsided, she was clad in a sleek, skin-tight black breastplate, chainmail leggings, spiked boots, and her usual array of weapons.

"Better?" she asked, adjusting the breastplate.

"Almost." Orion reached out, touching the breastplate. A phoenix emblem accompanied by two crossed swords appeared on her chest, etched in glowing silver. "There. Now it's perfect."

"You're so extra," she muttered, though a smirk tugged at her lips. "Let's go before Maximus implodes."

They caught up with Maximus, who was waiting impatiently outside a white door. He shot them a pointed look, tapping his foot. As they approached, he opened the door, and the corridor was immediately filled with the sound of heated voices.

The council was in session, and clearly, they had much to say.

When Orion walked into the council chamber, the room fell silent. The council members, who had been engaged in a heated argument, now stood stiffly, their eyes following him as he made his way to the head of the table. Orion avoided meeting their gazes, his expression calm but guarded. He took his seat, the weight of leadership pressing heavily on his shoulders.

"It's good to see you unharmed, my Lord," Lord Sanjen said with a slight bow as he took his seat.

Orion glanced at him briefly. "Could this meeting not have waited?"

"No, it could not," Lord Jandavinr snapped, his tone sharp and biting. "The war rages on, and you, like the inexperienced child you are, continue to 'swan around,' dragging more trouble into our laps." He slammed his fist on the table, sparks of his magic flickering as his frustration boiled over.

Before Orion could respond, Eymd vanished into a wisp of black smoke. She reappeared behind Jandavinr, her blade pressed firmly against his throat. The council gasped collectively, and Jandavinr froze, his eyes darting nervously.

"Eymd, stand down," Orion commanded, rising from his seat.

She hesitated, her expression a mixture of disappointment and defiance, before slowly lowering her blade. She remained standing behind Jandavinr, her presence looming as a silent reminder of her readiness to act. Jandavinr gulped audibly, sweat glistening on his brow as he glanced nervously between her and Orion.

"Lord Jandavinr," Orion began, his voice steady but firm. "It is true that I am but a child in many ways. But the knowledge I carry from the Old Ones and my bloodline could fill an entire planet. Imagine living a life of normalcy, only to be thrust into the depths of war and responsibility overnight. If I falter, speak to me. Help me. But under no circumstances will you disrespect me in this council chamber again."

The colour drained from Jandavinr's face. "I… I am deeply sorry, my Lord," he stammered. "My anger got the better of me."

Orion inclined his head slightly. "Apology accepted. I won't pretend this role is easy, and I will admit to struggling. But that is why I have this council, to advise me. Let us not waste our energy on discord when the war demands our unity."

He returned to his seat, and the tension in the room eased slightly.

"There is an urgent matter to address, Sire," Lord Zanek said, standing and activating a holographic map that projected above the table. "Your uncle's fleet is only two days behind us. We must decide where to make our stand."

Zanek gestured to the glowing map. "As you can see, they are advancing quickly. Vando has sent word to our fleet, but they will not arrive until four hours after your uncle's forces do."

Orion studied the map for a moment. "I will command the fleet from the main battleship. This ship and my mother must be taken to safety."

"This ship isn't fast enough to outrun your uncle's fleet, Sire," Zanek countered.

"It won't need to. I've already opened a vortex large enough for our fleet to arrive in orbit momentarily. The first ships should be arriving soon," Orion explained. "Once I've transferred to the command ship, I'll open a similar vortex for this vessel."

Lady Valoria stood, her face etched with concern. "My Lord, I must insist the council accompanies you to safety."

Orion shook his head. "That cannot happen. If something happens to me, the council must remain to guide my family and my people. Your presence here is essential."

Valoria opened her mouth to protest, but Orion raised a hand to silence her. "No arguments. This is how it must be. If we're all in agreement, please instruct the pilot to take off immediately."

With that, Orion stood and exited the chamber before anyone could object further. Once outside, he took a deep breath, the weight of his decisions catching up with him. For the first time, he realized how difficult it was to assert himself, and how exhilarating it was to stand his ground.

"I think you handled that quite well," Eymd said, stepping up beside him. "Though, you should have let me take Jandavinr out. It would've saved you some trouble."

"Not everything requires killing someone," Orion replied, shooting her a look.

"If you say so. Where to now?"

"I need to see my family," Orion said with a tired smile. "Then bed."

"Fair enough. I'll meditate," Eymd replied. She paused, then added, "Oh, before I go, I'll contact the Shadow Council and request reinforcements."

"Thank you," Orion said. Eymd disappeared in a puff of smoke, leaving him alone.

Orion thought of his brothers and took a step forward. The ship blurred and spun around him, and when his foot touched the floor again, he stood between Anton and Jake.

"Boo," he said with a grin.

Anton yelped, jumping nearly a foot in the air. "Where did you come from?!"

"A portal," Orion replied with a chuckle. "What are you two up to?"

"Trying to learn spells from this book, but they keep fizzling out," Jake said, holding up a tattered tome.

Orion peered at the page, then watched their attempts. Their gestures were clumsy, their movements lacking precision. "Here," he said, stepping in front of them. "Follow me."

He swayed gracefully from side to side, his hands tracing delicate arcs in the air. Within moments, a glowing orb of lightning formed before him, crackling softly. He turned to see that Anton and Jake had managed to create smaller, dimmer orbs.

"You make it look so easy," Jake muttered, his eyes wide with awe.

"Show off," Anton added with a grin.

"I could make staffs for you," Orion offered. "They'll help you harness your magic."

"There aren't any books on using star magic like that," Anton said, his voice tinged with disappointment.

"There were, long ago," Orion replied. "But the knowledge was lost. The spells had to be spoken aloud."

He held out his hand, and an ancient book materialized, its cover thick with dust. Blowing it clean, he handed it to Jake. "This is from that time. Use it wisely."

Before they could respond, Orion raised his hand again. Two silver staffs began to materialize before them. As the twins reached out, the staffs transformed. Anton's became a wand with a dragon engraved along its length, while Jake's turned into a pair of silver gauntlets, the letter "J" engraved in gold.

The twins stared at their new tools, speechless.

"There we go," Orion said, stepping back to admire the newly formed weapons in his brothers' hands. A smile tugged at his lips. "Where's Dad, by the way?"

"He's with Aurorina in Lillithan's room," Jake replied, his voice quieter as he turned the gauntlets over in his hands, marvelling at their craftsmanship.

"Ah, okay," Orion said, nodding. "Well, I think I'm going to grab some sleep. I'm shattered. I'll catch you guys later."

Both twins looked up, their smiles fading slightly. Without a word, they stepped forward and wrapped their arms around Orion in a tight hug. The gesture caught him off guard, but he quickly returned it, his own exhaustion momentarily forgotten.

"You'd better rest properly," Anton said, his voice muffled against Orion's shoulder. "No running off in the middle of the night without telling us."

Jake pulled back just enough to look up at Orion, his expression serious. "And remember, we're here if you need anything. You don't have to do this alone."

Orion smiled, ruffling Jake's hair affectionately. "I know. You two take care of each other, and keep practicing with those. You've got potential."

The twins nodded, releasing him reluctantly. With a final wave, Orion stepped forward into a shimmering portal, its edges flickering like starlight. The ship seemed to blur and twist around him, and in an instant, he materialized in his quarters. The familiar hum of the palace ship greeted him, a soft reminder of its protective embrace.

His room was dimly lit, the warm light from the overhead panels casting a soothing glow. Orion didn't bother changing out of his armour. Instead, he simply let it retract into its casings with a faint hiss, leaving him in a simple undersuit. He kicked off his boots, crossed the room, and sank onto the bed.

The fatigue hit him like a wave, the events of the day crashing down all at once. The battle, the council meeting, the revelations with Eymd, it all swirled in his mind. Yet, as his head hit the pillow, those thoughts faded, replaced by the deep, dreamless pull of much-needed sleep.

For the first time in what felt like an eternity, Orion allowed himself to let go.

22 Preparing for War

Orion woke feeling refreshed, the first genuine rest he'd had since the whirlwind of events had begun. For once, his mind was clear, unburdened by the constant weight of responsibility and uncertainty. He stretched, his muscles relaxing as the tension of the previous days ebbed away. After a quick shower, he dressed in the simple clothing that had been laid out for him, a welcome relief from the heavy armour he had grown accustomed to.

Before leaving his room, he paused to look at himself in the mirror. His reflection seemed almost foreign. His once-familiar features now bore subtle yet profound changes: the faint glow in his eyes, the golden strands of his hair, the calm yet unnerving aura that clung to him like a second skin. He could barely recall the life he'd left behind, where the biggest concerns were a few bruises and school bullies. Now, the fate of entire worlds rested on his shoulders.

As he gazed into the mirror, a pang of guilt struck him. The last time he had spoken to Rachel, he'd destroyed the calling disc. She must have been worried sick. He couldn't leave things like that, not without letting her know he was alright. Thinking of her, he reached out with his mind and opened a shimmering vortex. The edges of the portal rippled like liquid starlight as he stepped through. Unlike his usual instantaneous crossings, this one required a long walk. He trudged through the ethereal corridor for nearly ten minutes before spotting the exit.

When he emerged, he was in the mansion's familiar living room. The room was dimly lit, the soft glow of moonlight filtering through the curtains. It was the middle of the night. Rachel was curled up on the sofa, fast asleep, her face streaked with dried tears. Her red, puffy eyes told a story of sleepless nights and relentless worry.

"Rach," Orion said softly, leaning closer to her.

She stirred, her eyes fluttering open. At first, she looked disoriented, but as she rubbed her eyes and sat up, recognition dawned on her. "Orion? Is that you?"

"Yeah," he replied gently.

"You sound… different." She fumbled in the darkness for the lamp switch. "Let me just turn on the light."

"Wait, before you do, I need to warn you. I don't look the same anymore."

"What do you…." she began as she flipped the switch. The soft light flooded the room, and she gasped as her eyes met Orion's transformed appearance. "Oh. You really *do* look different. And… you're not see-through."

"That's because I'm actually here," he said with a small smile.

Her brow furrowed as she processed his words. When the realization hit, she shot off the sofa and wrapped her arms tightly around him. "You're really here," she whispered, her voice cracking. She pulled back, her eyes scanning his face. "But… there's a reason you've come, isn't there? And it's not a good one."

Orion sighed heavily and sank onto the sofa. He motioned for her to sit beside him, the weight of the moment making his throat tighten. Why was this goodbye so much harder than the last?

"Rach," he began, his voice trembling slightly, "you know I care about you. You've been my best friend for as long as I can remember. But… there's something I need to tell you."

Her brows knitted together in concern. "What is it?"

Orion hesitated, looking down at his hands. "There's a point in my near future, a moment where I can't see anything. Nothing. It's like… everything ends."

"What do you mean?" Rachel asked, her voice quivering. "I don't understand."

"I can see everything," Orion said quietly, his gaze distant. "Everything that was, everything that is, and everything that could be. But after the battle that's coming… there's nothing. I don't know what happens to me."

Rachel grabbed his hands, her grip firm. "Stop it. You're being overly dramatic. You'll survive this, because you have to. You always find a way."

Before Orion could respond, a voice cut through the room. "Oh, how poetic. 'Everything that was and is.' You sound like a bad prophecy," Eymd quipped as she stepped out of the shadows, her arms crossed, a smirk on her face.

Orion sighed. "I should've known you'd follow me."

"I had a feeling you'd be all sentimental before this battle," Eymd replied, her tone teasing. Her gaze shifted to Rachel. "So, this is your human pet?"

"Eymd," Orion snapped, his voice sharp, "apologize. Now."

Eymd rolled her eyes. "Fine. I'm sorry. But let's not pretend she can even begin to understand what you're capable of."

"Wait for me in the hall," Orion commanded, his tone brooking no argument.

Eymd huffed but complied, vanishing in a puff of smoke as she made a show of leaping at Rachel, who barely flinched.

"She's a bit rude," Rachel muttered, watching the smoke dissipate. "But I'm sure you'll be okay."

"I don't think so," Orion admitted. "I couldn't leave without saying goodbye and making sure you'd be alright."

Rachel's face crumpled, and she hugged him tightly, her tears wetting his shoulder. "Egg, you can't just disappear. I won't let this be goodbye."

Orion closed his eyes, his heart aching. "I don't have a choice," he said softly. "What must be, must be. I can't change it."

"No," Rachel said fiercely, pulling away to look him in the eyes. "We've been friends for too long for you to just *die*. I won't accept that."

Orion placed a hand on her shoulder, his voice calm but tinged with sadness. "Sleep," he said, his words laced with a powerful sleeping spell.

Rachel's eyes fluttered shut, and she slumped back onto the sofa, breathing deeply. Orion stood and carefully tucked a blanket around her. Before he turned to leave, he reached into the air and pulled out a book. It materialized in his hand, ancient and worn. Flipping it open to a random page, he placed a cotton bookmark bearing his crest inside and set it gently on the table beside her.

"May you only remember me as a character from the book I've given you," he whispered, pressing a soft kiss to her forehead.

As he stepped into the portal to leave, he cast one final glance at her sleeping form. A single tear rolled down his cheek before the portal closed behind him, sealing him off from the life he had once known.

Orion walked toward the front room door, pausing for a moment. With a deep breath, he raised his hand, and a faint glow gathered at his fingertips. He released a memory modification spell, a delicate ball of light splitting into three. Two of the fragments drifted upward, passing through the ceiling in search of Sharon and Bell. The last fragment entered Rachel's temple, merging seamlessly into her consciousness.

"Goodbye, old friend," he whispered, his voice tinged with regret. "I'm sorry."

He closed the door softly behind him.

"You made her forget," Eymd said from the shadows, her voice uncharacteristically gentle. Her silvery eyes glistened with black tears, which she wiped away quickly, as if embarrassed to show emotion.

Orion nodded, avoiding her gaze. "It was kinder this way."

Without another word, he opened a vortex back to the palace ship. Both he and Eymd stepped through in silence. When they emerged in Orion's quarters, Eymd sat heavily on the edge of his bed, her expression clouded with unfamiliar vulnerability.

"I don't like this bond between us," she said, finally breaking the silence.

"Why?" Orion asked, genuinely curious.

"That pain you're feeling right now, I feel it too," she admitted, her voice wavering slightly. "My heart actually aches. How do you people cope with this?"

Orion offered her a small, sad smile. "One day at a time. I just… needed to say goodbye."

Eymd sighed, running a hand through her hair. "I need to see Lillithan. Are you coming?"

"Yeah," Orion replied, straightening. "By the way, the High Matriarch of the Shadow Council is on her way. She wants to meet about the reinforcements I requested."

"Oh, goodie," Eymd said dryly. "We'll discuss it after we've seen Lillithan."

Orion nodded and opened another vortex. Moments later, they stepped out into the hallway outside Lillithan's quarters. One of the guards stationed by the door saluted before opening it for them.

Inside, Aurorina sat in a chair by Lillithan's bed, fast asleep, her head resting against the wall. Lillithan, however, was wide awake, propped up against several pillows and engrossed in a book. When Orion entered, she looked up and smiled warmly.

"Young master, it's good to see you," she said, her voice soft but steady.

Aurorina stirred, startled awake. She blinked a few times before sitting upright. "Oh, Orion. I didn't hear you come in."

"It's good to see you doing better," Orion said as he approached the bed. Lillithan shifted over, patting the space beside her, and Orion sat at the foot of the bed.

Eymd leaned down and whispered something to Aurorina, who nodded and stood.

"If you'll excuse us," Aurorina said, addressing Lillithan and Orion. "Eymd and I need to discuss something outside."

The two women left, leaving Orion and Lillithan alone in silence. Lillithan watched him for a moment before speaking.

"You risked yourself to save me, young master," she said, her tone heavy with guilt. "I'm not that important."

"You're important to my mother," Orion replied, smiling softly. "And to me. You've helped me so much in such a short time."

"But, Sire…" Lillithan hesitated. "If you hadn't been wearing the new armour, you wouldn't have survived."

Orion stood and began pacing the room, her words cutting deeper than he cared to admit. He didn't know how to respond. Before he could collect his thoughts, the door opened, and Aurorina and Eymd returned.

"Eymd told me about what you did for Rachel," Aurorina said, walking up to Orion and embracing him. "That was very brave of you."

"I couldn't let her feel the pain," Orion said, his voice heavy. "If this all goes wrong…"

"Maybe something is blocking you from seeing what's to come," Aurorina said thoughtfully. "I've spoken with our seers and the Shadow Council's seers. They're all struggling to see past the end of this week."

"Pardon me, Your Highnesses," Lillithan interrupted. "I overheard one of my guards talking about the god destroyer turrets. They said they were only prototypes."

Aurorina's face paled. "I dread to think how much worse the real ones will be."

"We'll deal with it," Orion said firmly. He moved toward the door, steeling himself. "I need to go to the council chambers and meet the Shadow Matriarch."

As he glanced back, he noticed both Aurorina and Lillithan looking pale, their expressions uneasy. He filed it away for later, stepping into the hall.

When Orion emerged in the council chamber through another vortex, he found Eymd lounging at the table, her legs propped up, casually picking her teeth with a dagger.

"I think having the Shadow Matriarch here is a bad idea," she said without preamble, sliding the dagger back into its sheath.

"Why?" Orion asked, arching an eyebrow. "What's the worst that could happen?"

"I know I'm the only Shadow Warrior you've met, but my race isn't exactly as sociable, or cuddly, as I am," she said, her tone laced with sarcasm.

Orion stifled a laugh. "They honestly can't be that bad."

Eymd gave him a look that could only be described as pity. "You have no idea," she muttered.

"It's not like they can hurt me," Orion replied confidently.

"Maybe not physically," Eymd said, standing and beginning to pace. "But just because you're invincible doesn't mean your mind is. We're very, very good at breaking people, Orion."

"I've never seen you like this before," Orion said, frowning.

"They'd never ask me to hurt you, we're too close. But the Matriarch?" Eymd paused, looking troubled. "She's another story entirely."

Their conversation was interrupted by P.I.L.S.S., whose calm voice filled the chamber. "The Shadow Matriarch has arrived."

"Quick, mask your eyes," Orion said, remembering Eymd's altered silver irises.

Eymd nodded and changed her eyes back to their normal state just as the doors opened. The air in the chamber grew heavy as the Shadow Matriarch entered.

She was tall and commanding, her charcoal-black skin seeming to absorb the light around her. She wore a gold and black suit of intricate armour, her movements smooth and deliberate. Her eyes, one blood red, the other emerald green, seemed to pierce through everything in the room. A long black cloak trailed behind her, brushing against the polished floor, and a dark crown adorned her silver-grey curls. Twenty guards followed her, clad in matching armour with helmets and silver swords gleaming at their sides.

As the Matriarch approached, Eymd dropped to one knee, bowing her head low in deference. Orion stood his ground, meeting the Matriarch's gaze as her lips curled into a faint, inscrutable smile.

"So," the Matriarch said, her voice smooth and commanding, "this is the young Intenfli."

"He isn't planning on killing you," Eymd said quietly, her head bowed low. Her voice was calm, but Orion could feel her discomfort through their bond.

Orion attempted to reach her through their telepathic link, but his thoughts fizzled out like static and were replaced by a single word: **No.**

"There's something different about you," the Shadow Matriarch hissed at Eymd, her voice serpentine, dripping with menace. Her blood-red and emerald-green eyes narrowed as she leaned forward, scrutinizing her subject.

Eymd didn't flinch. "I was human for a while," she admitted. "I'm still waiting for the effects to wear off. May I rise?"

"No, you may not," the Matriarch replied with a cruel smirk. "I rather like seeing you in your rightful place."

Orion stepped forward, his presence commanding. Though he still felt unsure about his authority over the Shadow Empire, he decided to take a gamble based on the fragments of knowledge he had absorbed from the Old Ones. He straightened his back and let his voice carry the weight of his station.

"Eymd is under my command on this ship, and if she wishes to rise, she may."

Eymd's sharp intake of breath was barely audible. *"Are you trying to get us killed?"* she whispered through their bond, though her head remained low.

"She is only on loan to you, boy," the Matriarch sneered, her words sharp enough to cut. "And if you don't watch your tone, I'll cut it out myself."

"Matriarch," Orion said firmly, his gaze locked on hers, "are we really going to play this game? We both know your warriors are no match for the Stone Guard. Now, please, take a seat, so we may begin."

The Shadow Matriarch's laughter was soft at first, a low rumble that grew louder and more unsettling. Finally, she leaned back and gestured dismissively with her hand. "Very well. Now we all know where we stand." She waved toward Eymd. "You may rise."

Eymd stood, her movements graceful but restrained. Orion could feel her simmering irritation through their bond, though she said nothing.

"Before we begin," Orion said, his tone measured, "I must ask your guards to leave. This discussion is not for them."

The Matriarch raised her hand lazily, and her guards saluted in unison before filing out of the room without a word. Orion couldn't help glancing at Eymd, and through their bond, he felt the sharp twinge of smugness radiating from her.

"It would be fascinating to cut you open," the Matriarch said suddenly, her voice slicing through the silence like a blade. Her head tilted slightly, and her eyes gleamed with macabre curiosity. "I've always wondered what a god looks like on the inside."

Orion swore he saw a thin, pointed tongue dart out from between her lips as she spoke.

"That would trigger a war neither of us could win," he replied evenly, his tone unwavering. "And you know it. You took an oath to protect our people. Are you really willing to jeopardize that just to satisfy your curiosity?"

Before the Matriarch could answer, Eymd's voice rang out, sharp and defiant. "Apparently, she's forgotten her place, and it falls to me to remind her."

The Matriarch's face contorted with fury. Shadows erupted from the corners of the room, snaking toward Eymd. In a flash, they pinned her against the wall, immobilizing her. The Matriarch rose from her seat, her expression cold as she spat, "Know your place, child."

"Apparently, it's reminding you of yours," Eymd shot back, her voice laced with venom.

One of the shadows detached from the wall and morphed into a blade, slicing cleanly across Eymd's cheek. A thin line of blood appeared, and a small droplet hit her lips.

"Well, that's mature," Eymd said with a laugh, licking the blood off her lip.

Before the situation could escalate further, Orion raised his hand and cast a shimmering force field between them. The shadows dissipated instantly, freeing Eymd.

The Matriarch eyed Orion with a mix of disdain and begrudging respect. "I see the Shadow Seers were right about you. You would indeed make a worthy adversary." She sat back down slowly, her lips curling into a smile that was anything but warm. "But for now, let us talk about this war."

Orion cautiously lowered the force field but kept his senses heightened, ready to act if necessary. He glanced at Eymd, who had returned to her seat, dabbing the cut on her cheek with the edge of her sleeve.

"What should I call you during this meeting?" Orion asked, steering the conversation back on track. "Matriarch feels far too formal."

"You may call me Elskar," she said, her tone suddenly sweet. She turned her sharp gaze to Eymd. "And you, little shadow warrior, must never speak that name."

Eymd burst into laughter, loud and unrestrained. Orion couldn't fathom what had amused her so much, but he made a mental note to ask her about it later.

Elskar's composure cracked briefly as her lips thinned in irritation. "It's fortunate the Great Shadow Spirit assigned you here, Eymd. Otherwise, you would have been discarded with the rest of the trash."

"Charming," Eymd replied in a mocking tone, her grin unfaltering.

"Enough!" Orion snapped, slamming his fist on the table. The sound echoed through the chamber, silencing them both. "We have far more important matters to discuss. Eymd, hold your tongue."

"She started it," Eymd muttered under her breath as she sat back in her chair, arms crossed.

"Elskar," Orion said, his tone firm, "we need 250 ships and at least 100 boarding troops."

The Matriarch examined her nails, feigning disinterest. "The Shadow Empire cannot spare that many," she said casually.

Eymd stood and strode toward Elskar, her movements deliberate. Orion tensed, preparing to raise another force field, but Eymd stopped just short of the Matriarch and smiled.

"This meeting won't work if you keep lying to him," Eymd said, her voice dripping with false sweetness.

"What do you mean?" Orion asked, confused.

"At last count," Eymd began, turning to Orion, "the Shadow Empire had 2,500 ships, each equipped with 50 troops. That doesn't include our ground forces, shadow archers, or mages. She could give you half the army and still have enough to fight another war and defend the empire."

Elskar's eyes widened, her composure faltering for the first time. "There really *is* something different about you," she said, her tone both intrigued and wary. "I think I like it."

"There are only seven people on our entire planet who know you better than I do," Eymd continued, her voice calm but cutting. "You wouldn't have come here if you weren't willing to send reinforcements. You know this war needs to end, and Orion is our best hope. So, stop playing games and get to the point."

Eymd sat back in her chair, her smile smug. Orion stared at her, his mouth slightly open in astonishment.

"Well," Elskar said after a moment, her lips curling into a sly smile. "It seems you've found your voice, little shadow warrior."

"Little one," Elskar said, her piercing eyes fixed on Eymd, "that is the most you have spoken since your final trials. You must be serious."

"See, your Earth has Lady Godiva," Eymd replied with a sly grin, "and the Shadow Empire has me. But under no circumstances am I doing *that* horse ride."

Orion raised an eyebrow, amused and slightly puzzled by the exchange, but it was Elskar who spoke next. "Who is this, Lady Godiva?" she asked, tilting her head in confusion.

"She's important in Earth's history," Eymd said with a casual shrug. "I'll lend you some Earth literature next time I see you."

Orion's brow furrowed as he studied Eymd and Elskar. The ease of their banter hinted at a history he wasn't aware of. He opened his mouth to ask how they knew each other but decided against it. He knew Eymd would dodge the question, and now wasn't the time to press for details.

"Thank you, little warrior," Elskar said to Eymd, her tone almost warm. Then, turning to Orion, she added, "Orion, you may have all the ships and troops you require. My personal guard, stationed on the closest moon, is at your disposal. Use them wisely." She stood gracefully, her cloak swirling around her as she began to leave.

Just before disappearing, Elskar turned back to Eymd, her red and green eyes glinting with a rare softness. "Verjast and Snjallt send their regards and hope you'll visit them during your next return."

Eymd opened her mouth to respond, but Elskar vanished in a puff of black smoke before she could utter a word. For a moment, the chamber was silent.

Then Eymd burst into laughter, so intense that she clutched her sides and collapsed onto the floor. Her laughter echoed off the chamber walls, tears forming in the corners of her silver eyes.

"Why are you laughing?" Orion asked, bewildered. "What's so funny?"

"Her name!" Eymd managed to say between fits of laughter. "How did you not laugh?"

"What's so funny about her name?" Orion crossed his arms, genuinely confused.

"Well," Eymd began, wiping a tear from her eye as her laughter subsided, "you know how all Shadow Warriors' names have meanings, right?"

Orion frowned. "Not really. There isn't much documented history on your people."

Eymd smirked, clearly relishing the opportunity to enlighten him. "In our culture, names reflect who we are, our strengths, our character, our destiny. For example, names like Strength, Destroyer, or Ruler are common. Even silly ones like Bullseye. They're all significant. But hers?" Eymd chuckled again. "Elskar means *love*. It's just so un-Shadow Warrior-like."

Orion blinked, the irony hitting him. A ruler of one of the fiercest, most feared factions in the galaxy had a name that meant love. A small smile tugged at his lips. "Alright, I admit, that's unexpected."

"Unexpected? It's hilarious!" Eymd exclaimed, shaking her head. "She's terrifying, commanding, and… her name is love. You couldn't make this up."

Orion chuckled softly, but his curiosity lingered. "Alright then, what does *your* name mean?"

Eymd paused, her expression shifting to something more reserved. "My mother had a twisted sense of humour," she said finally, her tone dry. "My name means *misery*."

"Sounds about right," Orion quipped with a grin.

Eymd smirked, pretending to be offended. "Careful, Intenfli. Misery is my specialty."

Orion decided not to press further, though another question lingered. "And those names Elskar mentioned, Verjast and Snjallt, who are they?"

Eymd's smirk softened into a cryptic smile. "That's a story for another time. For now, you're needed on the command ship."

Orion opened his mouth to ask how she knew that, but before the words could leave his lips, Eymd disappeared in a swirl of shadow and smoke, leaving him alone in the council chamber.

He stood there for a moment, letting the silence settle around him. The bizarre meeting with Elskar replayed in his mind. The weight of responsibility pressed down on him, but a flicker of amusement lingered from Eymd's antics.

23 The Eve of War

Orion sat alone, lost in thought, his mind swirling with the weight of the upcoming battle and the sting of using the memory modification spell on Rachel. He stared at the empty council chamber table, his hands clasped tightly together as if trying to anchor himself in the moment. The heavy silence was broken by the faint creak of the door behind him. He didn't hear it at first, too wrapped up in his inner turmoil, but the sound of someone clearing their throat snapped him back to reality.

He turned sharply, startled, to see his entire family standing in the doorway. They entered quietly, their faces solemn, and took seats around the table. Each of them carried an expression that mirrored the sadness Orion felt in his own heart.

"Why are you all here?" he asked, his voice hoarse.

"You lost a friend today," Lawrence said gently, his tone brimming with understanding. "We wanted you to know we're here for you."

Aurorina clapped her hands softly, and Kalligah entered, carrying trays of food. As they laid the dishes on the table, Orion's eyes widened. Spread before him was an array of familiar foods from Earth, jerk chicken, curry goat, coleslaw, roast potatoes, vegetables, and macaroni and cheese. The sight of the meal brought an ache to his chest, a bittersweet reminder of simpler times.

"I used the last of the supplies we brought from Earth to make this for us, and for everyone on the ship," Lawrence said with a smile, clearly pleased by Orion's stunned expression. "I thought it might bring a little comfort."

As everyone tucked into the meal, the door opened again. Auroratium, Vando, Alexi, and Zanek entered, taking the remaining seats around the table. They helped themselves to the food with no hesitation, their curiosity about the Earth dishes apparent.

"How did I never taste this on Earth?" Zanek said through a mouthful of curry goat. "It's simply divine."

"I've had nothing quite like it," Auroratium added, eagerly helping herself to more macaroni and cheese.

"You didn't have to do this," Orion said softly, his voice breaking slightly as he looked at his family and friends. He could feel the weight of their love and care, and it nearly overwhelmed him.

"This might be the last meal we all have together," Eymd said suddenly, appearing in a puff of smoke. She grabbed a piece of jerk chicken from the nearest tray. "Why didn't we have food like this in the mansion? Instead of that tasteless, bland stuff we were served?"

The table erupted in laughter, the tension momentarily lifted by Eymd's blunt humour. Orion chuckled along with them, appreciating the moment of levity in the midst of so much uncertainty. For the first time in days, he allowed himself to relax and enjoy the company of the people he held dear.

When the main course was finished, Kalligah returned, this time carrying trays of jelly and ice cream. The simple dessert brought a surprising wave of nostalgia for Orion. Leaning back in his chair, he let the sounds of laughter and conversation wash over him, savouring the warmth of this shared moment. Though the shadows of war loomed ahead, he knew he would carry this memory as a light to guide him through the darkness.

The door opened again, and the council entered, Lord Sanjen leading, followed by the other members. They conjured chairs and joined the table.

"Did we miss the main course?" Sanjen asked, looking genuinely dismayed as he took his seat. "I could smell it being cooked as I passed the kitchens."

"The Kalligah have plates made up for you," Zanek said with a smirk. "They should be here any moment. What took you so long?"

"That can be discussed after dinner," Sanjen replied, dismissing the question. "For now, let's eat."

Kalligah reappeared, serving the council members heaping plates of food. Orion watched as the council devoured their meals with gusto, their voices rising in praise for the dishes. Lady Valoria even licked her plate clean before eagerly helping herself to some jelly and ice cream.

Half an hour later, the room fell quiet as the last plates were cleared away. The cheerful atmosphere began to shift, and Orion could feel tension creeping back into the space. Sanjen rose from his seat, his expression serious.

"There is another reason we all came to this meal, Sire," he began. "The council has decided that I will accompany you to the command ship. The rest of the council will remain aboard this vessel."

"I assume I have no say in this?" Orion asked, his tone resigned.

Sanjen nodded solemnly. "It has been decided."

Aurorina stood, her face etched with determination. "Lawrence and I have also discussed it," she said, her voice firm. "We, along with your brothers, will be joining you on the command ship."

Orion shot out of his seat, his chair scraping loudly against the floor. His heart sank at her words, a mixture of fear and frustration welling up inside him. "No," he said, his voice cracking. "They can't come. They're too young, and I couldn't live with myself if anything happened to you."

"They will not stay, Orion," Aurorina said softly. "We tried to make them see reason, but…"

"We're a family," Anton interrupted. "And you've always protected us."

"Now it's our turn to protect you," Jake finished, their voices blending seamlessly.

Orion stared at them, his emotions in turmoil. He wanted to argue, to force them to stay behind where it was safe, but their determination was unshakable. With a deep sigh, he sank back into his chair, defeated.

"I won't argue tonight," he said quietly. He waved his hand, and long-stemmed black glasses appeared on the table alongside a large bottle of Sanrato. He poured the sparkling amber liquid into each glass and raised his own.

"It has been an honour sharing this meal with all of you," he said, his voice steady. "May we have many more after this day. Cheers."

"Cheers," everyone echoed, raising their glasses in unison.

Orion took a sip of his drink, glancing around the room. Despite the uncertainty of what lay ahead, the sight of his family and friends brought him a rare moment of peace.

As the meal concluded, Orion stood once more, his movements slow and deliberate. He took a deep breath, steadying himself before addressing those gathered. "My Lords and Ladies," he began, his voice calm but tinged with gravity, "it has been an honour serving as your leader. Lady Valoria, I entrust you with temporary reign over my kingdom until such a time that my mother or I return. Please, look after it."

Lady Valoria rose gracefully from her seat, her expression a mix of pride and sorrow. "I will, cousin," she said, her voice steady though her eyes glistened. She leaned in and kissed his cheek. "Please, be safe."

Orion reached up and removed his crown. For a moment, he stared at it, turning it over in his hands. As he did, the golden circlet shimmered and transformed into a delicate tiara. With a quiet resolve, he placed it into Valoria's hands. Holding out his other hand, he summoned the rainbow-colored sceptre, its glow reflecting the weight of the moment. He offered this to her as well.

Turning to his family, he asked, "Are we ready to go, then?"

Those accompanying him to the command ship nodded and rose from their seats. They gathered near him, expressions of quiet determination etched onto their faces. Orion opened a swirling vortex, its edges shimmering with light, and stepped through, followed closely by his family and closest allies.

When Orion emerged on the other side, he was struck by the familiar yet distinctly altered surroundings of the command ship's bridge. At first glance, it bore a resemblance to the ship where his journey had begun, but the changes were undeniable. The once-empty screens lining the walls now hummed with activity, manned by a full crew. In the centre of the bridge stood the command chair, now flanked by a large tactical display and four additional chairs, two on either side.

"Sire," Vando said as he stepped through the vortex behind Orion, "you'll need to name the ship and address the fleet."

Orion turned toward the command chair, his gaze contemplative. "The ship shall be named *Rachel I*," he said firmly. "I will address the fleet once all ships have arrived."

He turned to see his family standing near the four chairs, unsure of where to situate themselves. Orion smiled faintly. He decided it would be best to let them choose their own roles tomorrow. For now, rest was what they all needed.

"We have long days ahead," he said, his tone soft but resolute. "I suggest we all get some sleep. Vando, where are the quarters?"

"Your room is the first door on the left, sire," Vando replied, pointing toward the hallway. "The twins' room is next to yours, and the others are across the corridor."

Orion nodded, stifling a yawn. "Alright. I'll see you all in a few hours."

He made his way to his quarters and pushed the door open. The room was stark in its simplicity, a double bed in the left corner, a desk with a tablet on the right, and a closed door opposite that likely led to the bathroom. He laid down on the bed, his armour dissipating as he exhaled, and quickly drifted into a restless sleep.

Orion awoke to someone gently shaking him. He groaned and opened his eyes to see Vando standing beside him, holding a steaming glass of amber liquid.

"What is it?" Orion asked, his voice heavy with sleep.

"The fleet has fully arrived, sire," Vando said. "Also, we found a stowaway wandering the halls."

Orion sat up, taking the glass from Vando's hands. "Who was it?"

"It was Pragor," Vando said, a faint smirk on his face. "I think he was looking for you. As soon as I opened your door, he ran under your bed."

Setting his drink on the desk, Orion crouched to peer under the bed. Sure enough, Pragor had transformed into a kitten and was swatting playfully at the silver bed sheets. Orion chuckled, reaching out to scratch Pragor's head.

As soon as he made contact, Pragor shifted into a Labrador and bounded out, wagging his tail enthusiastically.

"Alright, boy," Orion said, scratching Pragor's ears. "I suppose it's time to address the fleet."

He stood and clipped the crests of his armour into place. The familiar weave of black and silver began wrapping around him, forming his battle-ready suit. With Pragor at his side, Orion stepped out of the room and made his way to the bridge.

When Orion entered the bridge, he was surprised to find his family already there. Aurorina and Lawrence stood on one side of the four chairs, with Anton and Jake on the other. Sanjen stood nearby, observing with a quiet intensity.

Orion walked to the command chair at the centre of the room and sat down. As he did, the neural interface activated, and the room dissolved around him. Suddenly, he was seeing through the ship itself, gazing out into the vastness of space. The ship moved as he leaned, banking left, then right, before he corrected its heading.

"P.I.L.S.S., disconnect external view, please," Orion instructed.

"Yes, sire. Disconnecting," P.I.L.S.S. responded. "Would you like me to open fleet-wide communications?"

"Yes, please."

The room returned to normal as Orion's vision reverted to the ship's interior. He stood and moved to the central screen as P.I.L.S.S. counted down. "Broadcasting in three, two, one…"

A live stream of Orion appeared on the screen, and his voice carried through every ship in the fleet.

"On this eve of war, some may call you soldiers. Others may call you troops. But I stand before you as a friend and an equal," Orion began, his voice calm but growing stronger with each word. "Today, we go into battle not for ourselves, but for the innocent and the fallen. To honour their memory. To protect those who still live."

He paused, letting his words settle, then continued in a tone that resonated with confidence and power. "Unlike my uncle, we fight in a place where no innocents can be harmed. Today, my brothers and sisters, we stand united. Today, we win!"

Orion raised his fist into the air, and a deafening chant of his name erupted across the fleet. He didn't need the communications system to hear it, his name echoed beyond the ships, a roar of unity and resolve.

P.I.L.S.S. disconnected the broadcast, and Orion returned to his seat. He opened a vortex for the palace ship to escape. As the final glimmers of the palace ship vanished through the portal, the first of his uncle's ships dropped out of star drive.

The enemy vessels loomed large and menacing black, tank-like behemoths bristling with turrets and wicked, sword-like protrusions mounted at the front. They were engines of war, designed to intimidate and destroy.

Orion's grip tightened on the arms of his chair as he steeled himself for the fight ahead. "Prepare for battle," he said firmly. "Today, we protect the future."

"Battle stations!" Vando's voice boomed through the ship's communication system, sharp and commanding. The urgency in his tone sent a ripple of energy through the crew, each member scrambling to their assigned posts.

Orion connected to the external view of the ship, immersing himself in the vastness of the battlefield. Through the neural interface, the bridge disappeared, replaced by the endless expanse of space. His breath caught at the sight of the imposing enemy fleet before them, an ominous armada of sleek, black ships, their turrets bristling like a predator poised to strike.

He felt a gentle hand on his, warm and reassuring. The connection thrummed with a pulse of love and strength. Without needing to look, he knew it was one of his family members, an anchor amidst the chaos.

"P.I.L.S.S.," Orion commanded, his voice calm but firm. "Send drone ships one through sixty into defensive position alpha."

"Confirmed," P.I.L.S.S. responded.

Orion watched as sleek, manta-shaped drones detached from the underside of his fleet. The metallic ships glinted faintly in the distant starlight as they streaked toward the enemy, forming a shimmering wall between his fleet and his uncle's. The drones opened fire, their precision strikes targeting the enemy's weaponry. One by one, turrets and cannons were disabled, forcing some enemy ships to retreat to repair.

But the reprieve was brief. Larger, more menacing ships emerged from star drive, their hulls black as the void and weapons systems glowing with a malevolent red. They wasted no time, firing relentlessly. The drones put up a valiant defence, their coordinated attacks managing to take out a few of the new arrivals, but they were no match for the sheer power of the larger ships. One by one, the drones were obliterated, bursts of light marking their destruction.

"P.I.L.S.S., deploy all remaining drone ships and alert all ships to converge on my position," Orion ordered hastily, his fists tightening.

"Confirmed. Deploying all remaining drones and broadcasting convergence orders," P.I.L.S.S. replied.

The remaining two hundred drone ships detached themselves and shot forward like a swarm of starlight, engaging the enemy ships with unyielding ferocity. Orion focused his attention on one of the closest enemy vessels, his mental commands channelling through the neural link. Fifty drones converged on the ship, hammering its shields with a relentless barrage of energy. The enemy ship's shields faltered, flickering before collapsing entirely.

"Disable," Orion commanded, his tone resolute. The drones obeyed, systematically dismantling the ship's weaponry until the turrets lay silent and smoking.

"P.I.L.S.S., broadcast to all units: Move to board and secure enemy ships. Use non-lethal methods where possible."

"Message sent," P.I.L.S.S. confirmed.

From his vantage point, Orion watched as some of his ships, alongside reinforcements from the Shadow Empire, broke formation and approached the now-disabled enemy vessels. Docking ports extended like metallic arms, connecting with the enemy ships. One by one, the boarding parties entered.

"Commander, the ship is empty," came a female voice over the COMM system.

"Other teams, report," Orion said, a note of unease creeping into his voice.

"Negative on hostiles here, sir."

"Same," echoed the other teams.

Orion frowned, his mind racing. The empty ships made no sense. Why would his uncle send unmanned vessels into battle? The answer eluded him, but a gnawing unease settled in his chest.

"All teams, undock and return to formation," Orion commanded.

But there was no reply, only static and faint crackling filled the COMM channel.

"Team One, report!" he repeated, his voice rising slightly. "Team Two, Three, four….respond!"

Silence.

Then, a low, ominous hum resonated through the external interface. Orion's breath hitched as he recognized the distinct sound of star drives powering up. On the display, he watched in horror as the enemy ships, now reactivated, engaged their star drives. In a flash of light, they disappeared into the void, taking his boarding party ships with them.

The neural interface disconnected abruptly, and the bridge's interior swam back into view. Orion stumbled, his vision blurring as nausea churned in his stomach. He barely managed to steady himself before turning toward Vando.

"What just happened, Vando?" Orion asked, trying to keep his voice steady despite the dread tightening his chest.

"Someone's trying to hack into the ship's systems," Vando replied, his brow furrowed. "That shot that hit us earlier, it wasn't normal. It carried a virus."

"What kind of virus?" Orion demanded.

"A signal, we think," Eymd cut in, her voice sharp. "The Shadow Empire ships are working to trace it now."

Before Orion could respond, a sudden, searing pain lanced through his skull. His knees buckled, and he collapsed to the floor, clutching his head as agony rippled through him.

The world around him dimmed, the lights of the bridge fading until all that remained was a suffocating blackness. He gasped for breath, but the pain was relentless, his mind overwhelmed by a chaotic storm of fragmented images and dissonant whispers.

"Orion!" He barely registered the voices calling out to him, Vando, Eymd, his mother, but their words seemed distant, muffled as if coming from underwater.

The darkness deepened, swallowing him whole, and for the first time in his life, Orion felt truly powerless.

24 The Final Battle

Orion could hear the sound of footsteps echoing in the darkness. He turned his head sharply, straining to see who was there, but the figure remained just out of sight. Scrambling to his feet, he cautiously moved toward the sound, the shadows around him pressing in like a living force. As the figure came into view, Orion gasped.

Standing before him in shining chains was Rohanas, his uncle. But he was almost unrecognizable, his hair was matted and so long it trailed the ground, his sunken skin clung to sharp bones, and a wild grey beard wrapped around his neck like a scarf. His eyes, once sharp and cunning, were clouded with age and torment.

"There isn't much time," Rohanas rasped, his voice hoarse and strained. "I've only just managed to break their bonds."

"What kind of game are you playing?" Orion demanded, his voice sharp and sceptical as he eyed the man warily.

"No game," Rohanas replied, his cracked lips curling into a bitter smile. "Just a warning. I am not the enemy you face."

Orion narrowed his eyes. "But I saw you on Yimmana, you threatened me, swore you would destroy everything I hold dear."

Rohanas' brittle laughter echoed, filling the void around them. "That wasn't me. I've been trapped here for so long I'm not even sure you're real."

Orion stepped back instinctively as Rohanas lunged toward him, the chains binding him glowing with a searing light. The man recoiled with a shriek of pain and crumpled to the ground.

"If it wasn't you, then who am I facing?" Orion asked, his tone edged with suspicion.

Rohanas lifted his weary head. "I don't know. My memory fades after the last planet I visited on my pilgrimage. I remember landing there, entering a temple… and then nothing. Whoever took my place has been there ever since."

Orion studied his uncle closely, trying to determine if he was lying, but the sorrow in Rohanas' face was too raw to fake. As if sensing Orion's doubt, the man's chains began to glow brighter, and his anguished screams pierced the air.

"Quick, go! He comes for me!" Rohanas shrieked.

The world around Orion imploded into darkness, and he felt himself being pulled away. When his senses returned, he was on the bridge of the command ship, sprawled on the floor. Faces loomed over him, worry etched into every one of them. He sat up, rubbing the back of his head where a dull ache throbbed.

"What happened?" his mother, Aurorina, asked, kneeling beside him.

"I... I saw Rohanas. He looked... old, broken. He said he's been imprisoned and that someone else has taken his place."

"He could be trying to deceive you," Aurorina said, her voice cautious but laced with concern.

Before Orion could respond, P.I.L.S.S interrupted. "Pardon me, Sire, we have an incoming transmission from one of the Shadow Empire ships. Shall I display it on the main view screen?"

"Yes," Orion replied, steadying himself as he rose to his feet.

The screen flickered to life, revealing one of his soldiers. The man's face was battered, his armour scorched and dented. Behind him, a shadowy figure loomed just out of view.

The soldier stepped forward and spoke in a strained voice. "I have a message from Intenfli Rohanas III. He says: 'Let's end this like men. Meet me on the planet below at sundown if you wish to save your captured troops.'"

"How do I know he'll release you if I show up?" Orion asked, his voice firm but tinged with doubt.

The soldier hesitated, glancing back nervously. A low whisper echoed behind him, audible only to Orion. "You have his word as the one true Intenfli. Come alone, and he will release us."

Orion clenched his fists. "Fine. I'll meet him at sundown in the arena below." He disconnected the transmission, the weight of his decision pressing on him like a boulder.

The bridge erupted into chaos. Voices overlapped as his crew and family protested, pleading with him to reconsider.

"Enough!" Orion shouted, his voice cutting through the noise. He let out a sharp whistle that silenced the room, everyone wincing as they covered their ears. "I need my family, Vando, Eymd, and Sanjen in my chambers. Now."

Without another word, Orion turned and strode toward his quarters, his shoulders tense and his mind racing. Once inside, the room filled with the people he trusted most, but the atmosphere was heavy with tension.

"I have to do this," he began, his voice steady but resolute.

Eymd stepped forward, her eyes blazing. "Stop being so human. You know this is a trap!"

"I can't lose you again. I just can't," Aurorina pleaded, her voice breaking.

"If I get into trouble, you can come for me. But not before," Orion said, his tone leaving no room for argument.

Eymd's jaw tightened. "It is my duty to protect you. I will not allow you to jeopardize my honour or your life."

"I am the Intenfli," Orion said sharply. "You will obey my orders. Vando, Sanjen, Eymd go. I need to speak to my family alone."

Eymd glared at him, fury written across her face, but she saluted stiffly and stomped out, followed by Vando and Sanjen.

Once they were gone, Orion turned to his family, his face softening. "The time has come for me to say goodbye."

Aurorina's hand flew to her mouth, and tears filled her eyes. "No, Orion. Please, no."

He knelt before his brothers, kissing each of their foreheads. "Anton, Jake…"

Anton shook his head furiously. "No! No, you're not leaving us!"

Jake's voice was calmer but filled with sorrow. "You knew this was coming, didn't you?"

Orion nodded, his throat tightening. "I thought I could change it."

Jake's lips trembled, but he managed a faint smile. "It's okay. I think I knew, too. There was this old book in the library. It said a great leader would sacrifice himself to save his people. I think I knew it was you."

Orion turned back to his parents, taking a moment to steady himself. His heart ached at the sight of them, standing together with love and worry etched on their faces.

"Dad, Mum," he began softly, "I've seen the way you are with each other. Don't be afraid of the love you both share. You deserve happiness."

He stepped forward and hugged them tightly, drawing strength from their embrace. As he pulled back, his eyes lingered on their faces, memorizing every detail. "I love you both. Thank you for everything."

He turned quickly, not wanting them to see the tears that threatened to fall, and walked out of his quarters toward the bridge. Each step felt heavier than the last, but his resolve carried him forward.

"P.I.L.S.S.," he said as he entered the command deck, "open fleet-wide communications, please."

"Yes, Sir. You're live in three… two… one."

Orion stood tall, his voice firm but filled with emotion as he addressed his fleet. "My brothers and sisters, it has been my greatest honour to serve as your leader. But now, I must say goodbye. Cherish the moments you have with your friends and families. Rebuild a better, more compassionate kingdom. And never forget the destruction that jealousy and hatred have wrought upon us.

"Let us honour the contributions of all, those with star magic, those who labour through science and technology, and those who give in ways unseen. These are my last words to you."

As he finished, the screen went dark. Orion took a deep breath, turned to his family one last time, and gave them a bittersweet smile before stepping into the vortex he had created. The swirling light closed behind him, and the room felt emptier in his absence.

Orion emerged in the centre of the arena, the air heavy with foreboding. His eyes immediately locked onto Rohanas, or at least the figure pretending to be him, seated cross-legged in the sand. The dim light from above cast eerie shadows across his sharp features.

"Rohanas, let my people go," Orion demanded, his voice echoing through the silent arena.

The figure stood, a smirk curling on his lips. "Come now, Orion. Let's not pretend your dear uncle didn't contact you." His tone was mocking, his words dripping with false sweetness. "You must admit, it was a rather clever ruse. Even you were fooled, until he broke his bonds."

Orion's eyes narrowed. "Who are you?"

The figure's smirk widened as he began to stretch unnaturally, his form distorting. "I was awoken by my master long ago. Over the years, I have worn many names. But you may call me *Strixium*."

Before Orion could react, Strixium melted into the ground like ink spilling into water. Moments later, he reemerged in his true form, a towering shadow wreathed in crimson and black, his eyes blazing with purple fire. He yawned exaggeratedly, taking a casual step toward Orion.

"That's better," Strixium said, his voice echoing unnaturally. "Your troops have been returned to your ship. Now, bow before me."

Orion's neural link buzzed to life as he silently queried P.I.L.S.S. "Are they safe?"

"Affirmative, Sir. All troops have been accounted for."

"Deploy the god armour," Orion ordered. "Then disconnect and return to the command ship."

"Yes, Sir. Activating now."

The crest on Orion's chest glowed as the armour began to weave itself around his body, transforming him into a being of celestial energy. A sharp pain lanced through his head as P.I.L.S.S severed their connection, leaving Orion completely alone.

"Now," Orion said, his voice amplified by the armour, "it's just the two of us."

Strixium's smirk widened, his shadowy form rippling with dark energy. "About that... I might have lied."

Before Orion could react, troops and turrets materialized around Strixium, their weapons humming with lethal power.

"Did you really think I would come here alone?" Strixium sneered. "You're even more foolish than I thought."

The enemy soldiers surged forward, but Orion no longer held back. He let his godly essence consume him, white fire igniting across his armour as he grew to towering proportions. His vision shifted, no longer seeing physical forms but the life forces and star magic of those around him. Tendrils of energy shot from his body, snaking through the air and binding the powers of Strixium's star mages.

Their screams filled the air as Orion ripped their magic away, leaving them powerless. The remaining soldiers, terrified, began to flee. Strixium, however, stood unfazed.

"That's an impressive trick," Strixium said, his voice laced with mockery. "But my magic is far older than theirs. You'll find it far less easy to take away."

He lunged, his sword, a jagged blade forged from the void itself, cutting through the air. Orion leaped back, flames trailing from his feet as he landed with a resounding crash. The ground beneath him cracked as his power surged.

"Now," Orion said, his voice reverberating with celestial energy, "it's just me and you."

He sent a bolt of lightning hurtling toward Strixium, but the shadowy figure absorbed it effortlessly, redirecting it back toward Orion. The bolt struck his shoulder, and he cried out in pain, his armour dimming as his energy began to wane. Strixium's laughter echoed through the arena.

"You're not the only one who can bind powers, boy," Strixium hissed. "But let's not end this too quickly. I do enjoy watching you squirm."

Weakened but defiant, Orion drew his sword and charged. Their blades clashed with a thunderous crash, sending shockwaves rippling through the air. The impact jolted Orion's injured arm, and he fell to one knee, gasping in agony. Strixium loomed over him, raising his blade for the killing blow.

As the sword descended, a surge of energy flooded back into Orion. In a desperate act, he created a protective barrier, deflecting the strike and sending Strixium hurtling backward. The shadowy figure rose, dusting himself off, his expression darkening.

"Impressive," Strixium said as a strange beeping sound emanated from his wrist. He glanced at it, a sinister smile spreading across his face, as a vortex opened next to him. "Ah, it seems my reinforcements have arrived."

From the vortex, three figures emerged, each clad in black, horned armour that shimmered as if alive. They moved with a predatory grace, their presence amplifying the oppressive energy that filled the air. They took positions beside Strixium, standing like sentinels of destruction.

The first figure stepped forward, removing her horned helmet. Her hair ignited into black flames that licked the air, casting a flickering light across her molten-gold eyes. She scanned Orion from head to toe, her expression cold and dismissive, as if judging a disappointing prey. Without a word, she stepped back into line.

The second figure approached next, his movements deliberate, his smile unnervingly wide. As his helmet was removed, Orion's heart skipped a beat. The man's face bore a striking resemblance to the masked adversary he had fought earlier. The same mismatched features stitched together with dark magic. His menacing grin widened as he locked eyes with Orion, then he, too, stepped back.

Finally, the third figure came forward, his towering frame making the others seem almost diminutive. When his helmet was removed, Orion took an involuntary step back. The man's skin was green and scaly, his eyes glazed over as though blind, and a twisted purple beard curled beneath his chin like coiled serpents. His voice, deep and resonant, seemed to vibrate in Orion's very bones.

"Why is he not dead yet, brother?" the green-scaled figure asked, tilting his head as if sniffing the air.

"I was toying with him," Strixium replied lazily, as though Orion were nothing more than a child's plaything. "It's quite fun, seeing how pathetic he is."

Orion straightened himself and drew his sword, its blade crackling with celestial energy. "Who are you people?" he demanded, his voice steady despite the dread pooling in his stomach.

The woman stepped forward again, her flaming hair casting a halo of flickering shadows around her. "We, child, are the *Great Four*. When our master escaped the old ones' bonds, she awoke us from our slumber."

She gestured to the others. "I am Enaquia, the flame of vengeance. The brother you faced before, with his stitched-together vanity, is Lucandr. And our reptilian brother, who hungers for chaos, is Josnan."

Orion's mind raced. He reached into the vast reservoir of knowledge he had absorbed from the *Book of the Old Ones*, but no mention of the Great Four or their master surfaced. How could this be? The book contained knowledge from across the universe. Were they so ancient, so hidden, that not even the Old Ones had known of them?

"Your time is over," Orion said, infusing his voice with the commanding power of his lineage. "Surrender now, and face trial for your crimes."

Enaquia laughed, her voice a melodious mockery. "Poor child. You bark like a cub, thinking you're a lion. You should have trained harder if you hoped to stand against us."

Before Orion could reply, Josnan snarled, his deep voice reverberating like thunder. "Enough talk."

He raised a clawed hand, and a swirling shadow ball materialized in his palm. With a flick of his wrist, he hurled it at Orion.

Orion ducked, the shadow ball tearing through the air above him and exploding against the arena wall, leaving a crater of blackened stone. He retaliated instinctively, sending a fireball at Josnan. The fireball struck true, sending the scaled giant hurtling into the wall with a deafening crash.

As the dust settled, Josnan rose, his green scales scorched but intact. He growled low, a sound like grinding stone, and lunged forward with impossible speed. Orion barely had time to raise his sword before Josnan crashed into him, the impact like a freight train. They tumbled across the arena floor, Orion's armour sparking and groaning under the assault.

Josnan roared, ripping at Orion's celestial armour with clawed hands. The enchanted material resisted but began to weaken under the relentless assault. Pieces of it splintered and fell away, exposing Orion's vulnerable flesh beneath.

The other three surrounded them, forming a circle of malevolent power. Lucandr's stitched face twisted into a cruel smile as he conjured dark chains from the ground, sending them snaking toward Orion. Enaquia ignited her hands with black flames, ready to strike the moment an opening appeared.

Orion struggled beneath Josnan's crushing weight, his thoughts racing. He reached deep within himself, summoning every ounce of power he could find. Tendrils of white lightning crackled around him, forcing Josnan to release his grip momentarily.

"Enough!" Orion shouted, his voice resonating with godly authority. The lightning surged outward in a brilliant explosion, throwing Josnan off him and forcing the others to take a step back.

Panting, Orion rose to his feet, his armour battered but still functional. "You think I'm just a child," he said, his voice steady. "You think I'm weak. But I've faced worse than you, and I will not fall here."

Strixium stepped forward, his void-like form shifting with anticipation. "Bold words for a boy who has already lost so much."

The Great Four began to close in, their combined power suffocating the air around Orion. But instead of retreating, he planted his feet firmly in the ground, gripping his sword tightly.

"If you want me," Orion said, his eyes glowing with unyielding determination, "then come and take me."

And with that, the battle began in earnest.

25 Waking up

Enaquia conjured a massive battle axe, its blade dripping with dark fire, and ran at Orion swinging with brutal force. Suddenly a white arrow whistled through the air, striking Enaquia's axe and knocking it from her grasp. Another arrow followed, embedding itself deep into her leg.

"Do not touch my son!" Aurorina's voice rang out, sharp and commanding.

Orion turned to see his mother standing with her bow drawn, her expression fierce. Beside her were his father, Lawrence, his brothers Anton and Jake, and his closest allies, Vando, Sanjen, and Eymd, all advancing toward him.

"I told you not to come!" Orion shouted, his voice tinged with a mix of frustration and relief.

"We are a family," Aurorina said, nocking another arrow and firing at Enaquia. "We stand together."

"I told them I'd handle it myself," Eymd muttered, throwing a dagger that lodged itself in Josnan's shoulder. "But no one ever listens. Don't expect me to babysit."

"The twins don't even know how to use their powers!" Orion yelled, barely dodging a massive punch from Lucandr, whose stitched face twisted into a grotesque sneer.

But to Orion's surprise, his brothers were already summoning warriors of lightning, each strike of their conjured forces crackling against Josnan, who roared in fury.

"You underestimate us," Jake said, his hands sparking with electric energy.

"We learned from the best," Anton added, hurling a shadow bolt that exploded against Josnan's armour.

Orion watched, momentarily stunned. His brothers, so young, so inexperienced, were standing their ground. His mother and father worked in perfect synchronization, Aurorina loosing precise, glowing arrows while

Lawrence sent bolts of searing lightning at Enaquia. Eymd, ever unpredictable, became a blur of black smoke, reappearing behind Lucandr and slicing at him with ruthless efficiency.

Vando came to stand beside Orion, his blazing sword drawn, the weapon humming with stored energy. "Your mother shared her knowledge with them before we came," he said, catching the astonishment on Orion's face.

Orion tightened his grip on his sword. "Let's end this."

The two of them surged forward, charging at Strixium. Their swords danced through the air, seeking purchase against the shadowy figure. But each time their blades swung, Strixium shifted, his form warping like smoke, leaving them striking at nothing. Orion gritted his teeth in frustration.

Enough of this. Orion dropped his sword and summoned a towering wall of fire and lightning, encircling Strixium. The flames roared, crackling with unbridled fury, forcing Strixium to pause.

"You won't escape this," Orion said, stepping closer. Turning to Vando, he added, "Go help the twins. I've summoned the Stone Guard; they'll be here soon."

Vando hesitated. "Are you sure…."

"Go!" Orion commanded, his voice brooking no argument.

Vando nodded and ran to assist Anton and Jake, leaving Orion to face Strixium alone. He focused on maintaining the prison of fire and lightning, its ferocity growing with each passing moment.

With a thunderous crash, two massive figures descended from the sky, landing beside Orion. The Stone Guard, beings of ancient power carved from the very earth, loomed over the arena, their glowing eyes fixed on Strixium.

"Cuff him and hold him," Orion ordered.

The Stone Guards plunged their colossal hands into the flames, their stone skin impervious to the searing heat. They emerged moments later, each holding one of Strixium's arms in an unbreakable grip. Strixium thrashed and writhed, but the more he struggled, the tighter their hold became.

Orion approached, his gaze cold and unyielding. "You enjoyed pretending to be my uncle," he said, his voice low and dangerous. "Perhaps you should live as him."

"No!" Strixium's voice cracked with desperation, the arrogance drained from his tone. "You can't! Anything but that!"

A dark smile flickered across Orion's face. He raised his hand, channelling an intricate spell. Power surged down his arm, manifesting as a glowing sigil at his fingertips. Strixium's shadowy form shuddered violently as the spell began to take hold turning him more solid.

"Tell your forces to surrender," Orion commanded, his voice now an otherworldly echo.

Strixium's glowing eyes widened in fear. "If I do, will you spare me?"

"Perhaps," Orion said with cruel deliberation. "But you'll have to take that chance."

Strixium hesitated for a moment, then closed his eyes. His body pulsed with dark energy as he muttered a guttural incantation. Across the battlefield, his siblings froze. Enaquia lowered her fiery axe; Lucandr's mismatched features twisted into a scowl as he dropped his blade; and Josnan hissed, his scaly hands unclenching as he reluctantly tossed his weapon aside.

They raised their hands, signalling their surrender, and began walking toward Orion.

"Stop where you are!" Orion barked, his tone cutting through the air like a whip.

Orion had already summoned more stone guards to take the Great Four into custody. As the guards emerged from the shadows, their footsteps heavy and unyielding, he watched with cold satisfaction as they cuffed the remaining three. Slowly, he released his grip on Strixium's forehead, his hand trembling with restrained fury. Turning to face the others, he stopped a few paces away, his expression twisting into one of disgust.

His body began to glow, an ominous red light emanating from within. The air around him grew thick with tension, crackling with raw energy as he allowed his hatred and anger to consume him. His form began to swell, muscles expanding and veins glowing like molten lava beneath his skin. He felt the power of a destructive spell building within him, ready to unleash devastation upon the Great Four.

Just as the energy reached its peak, a hand rested gently on his leg.

"Orion," came the soft yet firm voice of his mother, Aurorina. He looked down, startled, to see her gazing up at him with calm yet pleading eyes. "This is not who you are. Make them pay, yes, but not like this."

His voice, a deep and booming thunder, shook the ground as he replied, "How can you say that? They killed your husband, my father, and countless others!" His words caused the arena walls to crack and crumble, raining debris around them.

Aurorina's voice remained steady. "Your father wouldn't want you to lose yourself because of them. Remember your compassion, my son. You are greater than your rage."

Her words cut through his fury, like a lighthouse piercing a violent storm. Slowly, the fiery glow receded, and his form began to shrink. The oppressive heat dissipated, leaving him standing there, his shoulders heaving as he fought for control. Once more in his normal form, he reached for his mother, embracing her tightly. She held him with a warmth that only a mother could provide, a reminder of his humanity.

Stepping back, Orion turned to the guards. "Bring me Strixium, so they may witness the fate that awaits them all."

The guards marched forward, dragging the shadowy figure of Strixium, whose once defiant demeanour had dimmed. Orion studied him coldly, his gaze a blade that cut deeper than words.

"You are accused of genocide and the murder of a royal family member. How do you plead?" Orion demanded, his voice sharp and unyielding.

Strixium's laughter echoed, manic and defiant. "Foolish boy. My master will come for me."

Orion's lips curled into a smirk. "Your master? Do you truly believe she will rescue a failure? Think, Strixium. You've served her poorly."

The realization hit Strixium like a blow. His eyes widened as his confidence wavered. "I…I acted in her name! Please… show mercy."

"Mercy?" Orion's tone was laced with venom. "I find you guilty of all charges. For your crimes, I sentence you to live the rest of your days encased in stone. And I strip away your powers."

Before Strixium could protest, dark tendrils erupted from Orion's hands, striking the condemned man. Strixium screamed as his magic was forcibly ripped from his body, leaving him a trembling husk. Orion stepped forward and placed a hand on his forehead, sending a spell coursing through him. Strixium's form began to harden, his shadowy figure transforming into solid stone. A flash of light marked the spell's completion, and when it faded, a statue stood before them, a twisted image of Strixium's last scream frozen in time.

"You monster!" Enaquia shouted, stepping forward with defiance in her eyes. "Killing him would've been kinder."

Orion turned to her, unfazed. "Enaquia, Lucandr, and Josnan, you stand accused of the same crimes. How do you plead?"

Before they could answer, a sudden blast melted the stone guards holding Enaquia. Blackened liquid hissed against the ground, forcing Orion to step back as Enaquia laughed triumphantly.

"You forgot about the god-destroyer turrets," she sneered. "Now, tell your soldiers to release my brothers!"

Reluctantly, Orion clicked his fingers. The remaining guards released Lucandr and Josnan, retreating a few steps. Enaquia smirked as Lucandr grabbed Lawrence and Aurorina, dragging them forward.

"Which of these wretches do you care for the most?" Lucandr taunted.

Eymd lunged in shadow form, but Enaquia caught her mid-air, slamming her into the ground with brutal force. A sickening crack echoed, and Eymd re-materialized, crawling back toward Orion's family. Vando rushed to help her up, casting a protective glare toward the enemies.

"Any more resistance, and I will kill them all!" Enaquia snapped.

Orion clenched his fists, his voice cracking with desperation. "Please, stop. I'll do whatever you want, just don't hurt anyone else."

Enaquia grinned, pointing to the ground before her. "Kneel, boy. Take your rightful place."

Helplessly, Orion turned to his family. Their faces were etched with despair, the twins clinging to each other in tears. Swallowing his pride, he stepped forward and knelt before Enaquia and Josnan.

"Now," Enaquia hissed, "tell me who you care about the most."

"I won't," Orion said firmly.

"Then I'll kill them all!" she spat. "Lucandr, bring them to me."

Orion watched in horror as Aurorina and Lawrence were dragged to the ground in front of him. Enaquia grabbed Aurorina by the hair, pulling her to her feet.

"Let's see how long she can last," she mocked, her hand glowing with dark magic. Aurorina screamed in agony as the spell seared into her.

"Stop! Please!" Orion begged, his voice breaking. "Take me instead!"

With a cruel laugh, Enaquia tossed Aurorina aside and seized Orion. "Let's see how *you* like your powers being taken." Dark tendrils shot from her and her brothers, striking Orion in the chest. The pain was indescribable, like his very soul was being set ablaze. He screamed as tears streamed down his face, his body trembling under the onslaught.

When it was over, Orion collapsed, powerless and broken. Enaquia stood over him, her grin triumphant.

The arena was silent, save for the sound of Orion's laboured breaths and the muffled sobs of his family.

Lying on the cold, cracked ground, Orion felt a strange numbness overtaking him. The world around him seemed muted, as if someone had turned the volume of existence down to a faint whisper. He couldn't hear the battle cries or the chaos echoing through the arena, but he could feel his body betraying him. The fiery strength that once coursed through his veins was gone. His form flickered uncontrollably, shifting between his divine and human states as if his body couldn't decide what it was anymore. Convulsions wracked him, leaving him gasping for air.

Desperate, Orion reached inward, searching for the magic that had always been a part of him. He tried to summon it, just as he had done when Strixium had bound his powers, but there was nothing, no spark, no ember. Only an empty void where his connection to the arcane once thrived.

Through the haze of his disorientation, sound began to creep back into his awareness. Shouting. Clashing weapons. The roar of chaos. His eyes fluttered open, and he saw blurred figures moving frantically in the distance. His family. They were fighting the Great Four, holding their ground against impossible odds. His heart twisted at the sight. Despite their bravery, they were outmatched.

Gritting his teeth, Orion pushed himself onto his hands and knees. Every muscle in his body screamed in protest, but he forced himself to rise. His eyes fell on his sword, lying just a few feet away. With staggering steps, he stumbled toward it, his legs barely holding him upright. His fingers brushed the hilt, gripping it tightly.

"You won't be interfering again," came Enaquia's cold, mocking voice.

Before Orion could react, she appeared behind him like a phantom, her presence suffocating. With a sharp tug, she yanked the sword from his grasp and flung it far across the arena. The sound of it clattering against the ground echoed like a death knell.

Enaquia's hand seized Orion by the front of his armour, lifting him effortlessly into the air. Her eyes burned with cruel delight as she held him suspended, his feet dangling above the ground. Time seemed to freeze as the battlefield blurred around them.

"Goodbye, Orion," she said, her voice a venomous whisper. She drew back her glowing fist, her power radiating like the heat of a thousand suns.

The punch landed with devastating force, sending Orion hurtling through the air. Pain exploded across his body, every nerve alight with agony. He tumbled like a broken doll, the world spinning uncontrollably around him, he felt the tug of a vortex opening up behind him.

As he entered it, his fading consciousness clung to one final image: Anton, his brother, struck down by a roaring fireball. The searing flames engulfing him, and Orion watched, helpless, as he crumpled to the ground, lifeless.

Then, everything went black.

In the void of darkness, Orion could hear a faint, rhythmic beeping. It pulsed steadily, cutting through the nothingness like a distant signal calling him back to the surface. The sound was both comforting and alien, anchoring him to reality as he floated in the haze between consciousness and oblivion.

He strained to remember, his mind fumbling through fractured memories. What had just happened? The arena. The fight. The Great Four. Images flickered in his mind like shards of broken glass, his family in peril, the clash of magic and steel, and then... the fireball.

Anton.

The memory struck him like a physical blow. He saw it clearly now, the fireball hurtling through the air, its searing heat, the way it engulfed Anton, and the lifeless collapse that followed.

The realization sent a jolt through his entire body, snapping his other senses back into place. His limbs felt heavy, like they were made of lead, but adrenaline coursed through his veins, forcing him to move. Gasping, he sat bolt upright, the motion sharp and frantic.

"ANTON!" he yelled, his voice raw and trembling. The name tore from his throat like a plea, filled with equal parts desperation and anguish.